Praise for Roslund and He

"Well written and powerful." —*The Times*

"Gripping, intelligent." —*Guardian*

"Journalist Roslund and ex-criminal Hellström are among Sweden's most popular thriller writers with a reputation for down-and-dirty detail and an eye for political intrigue and police corruption . . . extraordinarily compelling." —*Daily Mail*

"This is crime writing at its most ambitious and morally complex." —*Financial Times*

"[In Ewert Grens] the authors have created an eccentric, alienated, socially inept hero worthy of comparison with Swedish mystery master Henning Mankell's Inspector Kurt Wallander." —*Wall Street Journal*

"The Swedish team of Roslund and Hellström is writing explosive crime novels as good, if not better, than those of Stieg Larsson." —*USA Today*

"Roslund/Hellström are among the very best crime novelists around. They write with courage and intensity about the important issues of our time." —Maj Sjöwall

Also by Roslund and Hellström

Box 21
Three Seconds
Cell 8
Two Soldiers
Three Minutes

ROSLUND & HELLSTRÖM

PEN 33

Translated from the Swedish by

Elizabeth Clark Wessel

Quercus

New York • London

Quercus

New York • London

© 2004 by Roslund and Hellström
English translation copyright © 2016 by Elizabeth Clark Wessel
First published in the United States by Quercus in 2017
First paperback 2018

ISBN 978-1-68144-057-6

Library of Congress Control Number: 2017953456

Distributed in the United States and Canada by
Hachette Book Group
1290 Avenue of the Americas
New York, NY 10104

Manufactured in the United States

10 9 8 7 6 5 4 3 2 1

www.quercus.com

probably four
years earlier

HE SHOULDN'T HAVE.

They're coming from over there. They're coming now. Over the hill, past the jungle gym.

Twenty meters away, maybe thirty. Near the red flowers, like the ones outside Säter Psychiatric Institution, which he used to believe were roses.

He shouldn't have.

It wasn't going to feel the same now, because he had. Lesser, somehow. Almost numbed.

There are two of them. They're walking side by side, talking—friends. Friends talk to each other in a certain way, with their hands. The dark-haired one seems to be doing most of the talking. She's eager, wants to say everything, all at once. The blond one mostly listens. As if she's tired. Or as if she's the type who doesn't speak, who doesn't need to take up space all the time to show she's alive. Maybe that's the way it is: one dominates and one is dominated. Isn't that how it always is?

He shouldn't have jerked off.

But that was this morning. Twelve hours ago. Maybe it didn't matter. Maybe it didn't make much of a difference.

He knew this morning, as soon as he woke up. Tonight was going to be a good night for it. Today is a Thursday, just like last time. The day is sunny and clear, just like last time.

They're wearing similar jackets. Thin, white, some kind of nylon with a hood on the back; he'd seen quite a few of them since Monday. Two small backpacks slung over their shoulders. All those backpacks, everything in a pile in one large compartment, he can't understand it, will never understand it. They are close, closer, he hears their conversation, their laughter again, they're laughing at the same time, the blond one more carefully, not afraid, just taking up less space.

His choice of outfit was deliberate. Jeans, T-shirt, a cap on backward, just like he'd been seeing in the park since Monday; they wear them that way nowadays, backward.

"Hi there."

They jump, stop. Then silence. The kind of silence that happens when an ambient sound suddenly stops, forcing the ear to listen. Maybe he should have adopted a southern accent? He's good at that, and some pay more attention, because it sounds important somehow. He's been collecting voices for three days. No southern accent. No northern accent either. This is a city that speaks what might be called proper Swedish. No diphthongs, and not much slang. Boring, actually. He fingers his cap, rotates it one turn, pressing it a little harder against his neck, still backward.

"Hi, girls. What are you doing out so late?"

They look at him, at each other. They attempt to leave. He tries to appear relaxed, leaning slightly against the backrest of the bench. Which animal? Squirrel? Rabbit? A car? Candy? He shouldn't have masturbated. He should have prepared better.

"We're on our way home. We're allowed to be out this late."

———

She knows that she's not supposed to talk to him.

She's not supposed to talk to adults she doesn't know. She knows that.

But he's not an adult. Not really. He doesn't look like an adult. Not really. He's wearing a cap. And he's not sitting like an adult. Adults don't sit like that.

Her name is Irena Stanczyk. A Polish surname. She's from Poland. Or, not her, but her mom and dad. She's from Mariefred.

She has two sisters. Diana and Izabella. Older, almost married, they don't live at home anymore. She misses them; it was nice to have two sisters at home, but now she's alone with Mom and Dad, and they're more worried now, always asking where she's going, who she's meeting, what time she's coming home.

They need to stop that. She's nine years old now.

———

It's the dark one who does all the talking. The one with long hair held back by a pink headband. Almost as if she's talking back. Foreigner. With an attitude. She looks down on the chubby blond one. It's the dark one that decides—he sees that, feels it.

"Girls as little as you? I don't believe it. What could you be up to at this time of day?"

He likes the chubby blond one best. She has cautious eyes. He's seen those kinds of eyes before. Now she dares, she glances at the other one first, then at him.

"We were practicing, actually."

———

It's still just Irena talking. She always says what they think.

Now it's her turn. She's also going to speak.

He doesn't seem dangerous. Not angry. He's wearing a nice cap, just like Marwin, her big brother. Her name is Ida and she knows why. Her brother Marwin picked it. He read it in a book by Astrid Lindgren. So ugly. That's what she thinks. Sandra is prettier. Or Isidora. But Ida. That's the name of the girl Emile hoisted up a flagpole.

She's hungry. It has been a long time since she's eaten. School lunch today had been disgusting, some kind of meat casserole. She's always hungry after she trains.

They usually rush home to eat, but now Irena is just talking and talking, and the man in the cap keeps asking.

———

No animal. No car. No candy. He doesn't need that. They're talking to him. He knows it's settled now. If they talk to him, it's settled. He looks at the blond chubby one. She dared to speak. He didn't think she would. The one who is naked.

He smiles. He always does that. They like that. You put your trust in people who smile. You smile when someone smiles at you. Just the chubby blond one. Just her.

"So you were training? Doing what, if you don't mind my asking?"

The chubby blond one smiles. He knew it. She looks at him. She looks just above him. He knows. He grabs his cap, turns it half a turn until the brim appears. He bows, takes it off, lifting it up, holding it in the air above her head.

"Do you like it?"

She raises her eyebrows, glancing up without moving her head, as if she might bump it against an invisible ceiling. She hunches up, making herself smaller.

"Yeah. It's nice. Marwin has one like that."

Just her.

"Marwin?"

"My big brother. He's twelve."

He lowers the cap. The invisible ceiling, he passes through it. He swiftly strokes her fair hair. It's shiny and quite soft. He puts his cap on her head. On its shiny softness. The red and green suits her.

"You look nice. It suits you."

She doesn't say anything. The dark one is about to say something, so he continues hurriedly.

"It's yours."

"Mine?"

"Yeah, if you want it. You look beautiful in it."

She looks away. She takes the dark one by the hand. She wants to pull them away, away from the park bench, away from the man who has just given her a red-and-green cap.

"You don't want it?"

She stops, lets go of the dark one's hand.

"Yeah."

"Well then."

"Thank you."

She curtsies. It's so rare these days. Girls used to do that. Not anymore. Now everyone is supposed to be equal, no curtsying, no bowing either.

The dark-haired one has been silent longer than usual, now she firmly grabs hold of the blond one's chubby little hand. She almost jerks it, both stumble.

"Come on. Let's go now. It's just a fucking guy in a stupid backward cap."

The blond chubby one looks at the dark-haired one, then at him, then defiantly back at the dark-haired one again.

"Soon."

The dark one raises her voice.

"No. Now."

She turns toward him. Runs her hand through her long hair.

"And besides. It's ugly. Probably the ugliest cap I've ever seen."

She points to the red-and-green cap. Presses her finger hard against it.

An animal. Soon. A cat. A dead cat maybe. They are nine or maybe ten years old. A cat is fine.

"You never said what you did at the gym."

The dark one holds her hands at her waist. Like an old lady, a shrill old lady. Like the old lady at Säter Institution, the first time. The kind who wants to raise you and change you. He can't be changed. He doesn't want to be changed. He is who he is.

"Gymnastics. We've been practicing gymnastics. We do it all the time. Now we're leaving."

They walk away, the dark-haired one first, the blond one second, not as quickly, not as determined. He looks at their backs, their naked backs, bare buttocks, bare feet. He runs after them, past them, stands in front, stretching out his hands.

"What are you up to, fucking cap guy?"

"Where?"

"What do you mean, where?"

"Where do you train?"

Two elderly ladies are walking up the hill. They are almost at the flowers that aren't roses. He looks at them. He looks down, counts to ten hastily, looks up again. They're still there, but about to turn, take another path, toward the fountain.

"What are you up to, fucking cap guy? Are you having a stroke?"

"Where do you work out?"

"It doesn't matter."

The blond chubby one stares angrily at her friend. Irena is talking for both of them again. She doesn't agree. She doesn't think they need to be so mean.

"We practice at Skarpholm Hall. You know. The one over there."

She points to the hill, the direction they just came from. The cat. The dead cat. Fuck it. Fuck animals.

"Is it a nice gym?"

"No."

"It's even grosser than you are."

They're both taking the bait. Not even the dark one can stay quiet.

He's still standing in front of them. He lowers his arms. Runs one hand over his black mustache. Almost petting it.

"I know a new gym. A brand-new gym. It's close to here. Actually, over there, by the high rise, the white building next to it, do you see it? I know the guy who owns it. I usually go there myself. Maybe you can train there? Your whole club could, as well."

He points excitedly, and they follow his arm and finger, the blond chubby one curiously, the dark-haired slut with attitude.

"There's no gym over there, fucking cap guy. There isn't."

"Have you been there?"

"No."

"Well then. There is a gym there. A brand-new one. And it's not gross."

"You're lying."

"Lying?"

"Lying."

———

Irena just keeps talking. It's always her doing all the talking. She shouldn't talk for other people. She shouldn't be so mean. It's because she didn't get a cap.

She believes him. She got his red-and-green cap. He knows the guy who owns the gym. She doesn't like Skarpholm Hall—it smells old, the carpets smell almost like vomit.

"I believe you. Marwin said there's a new hall there. It would be nicer to practice there."

———

Ida really believes there's a new gym. She believes everything she hears. It's just because she got an ugly cap.

She knows what new gyms look like. She saw one in Warsaw when she was there with her mom and dad.

"I know there's no new gym there, cap guy. I know that you're lying. If there's no new gym there when we get there, I'm gonna tell my mom and dad."

———

It's a beautiful day. June, sunny, warm, a Thursday. Two little sluts are walking in front of him down a park path. The dark-haired one is everybody's slut. The blond chubby one is his slut alone. Sluts sluts sluts. With their long hair, their thin jackets, their tight pants. He shouldn't have touched himself.

The blond chubby slut turns around and looks at him.

"We have to be home soon. We have to eat. Mom and Marwin and me. I'm so hungry, I'm always hungry after gymnastics."

He smiles. They like that. He reaches for the cap sitting on her head, pulling gently on the brim.

"Come on, this will be super quick. I promise you that. We're almost there. So you can see if you like it; if you want to train there. It smells new, you know how it smells when something smells like new?"

They go in. He's been sleeping there for three nights. It was easy to break the door open. A basement filled with storage rooms full of useless crap: boxes of kitchen utensils and books, strollers, IKEA bookshelves, rugs, an occasional floor lamp. Just shit. Except the

second farthest from the back, number thirty-three, a black children's five-speed bike that he sold for two hundred and fifty kronor;
a full basement and one shitty kids' bike. He grabs them by the
arms when they walk through the cellar door. He holds tight, one
in each hand, they scream just like they always scream, he holds on
even tighter. He's the one who decides. He does the deciding, and
sluts do the screaming. He's been sleeping there for three nights,
he knows nobody goes down here, not to the cellar, not during the
evenings. Two mornings he heard people in the cellar entrance,
someone in a storage space, then silence. Sluts can scream. Sluts
should scream.

———

She thinks about Marwin. She thinks about Marwin. She thinks
about Marwin. About Marwin's room. Is he there now? She hopes
that he's there, in his room. At home. With Mom. He's probably
lying in bed reading. He usually does that in the evening. Mostly
Donald Duck comic books. Still. He read the Lord of the Rings trilogy not too long ago. But he likes Donald Duck comics the most.
He's probably there, she just knows it.

———

Fucking fucking cap guy. Fucking fucking cap guy. Fucking fucking
cap guy.
    She's not supposed to talk to his kind. Mom and Dad ask her all
the time, and she always says she never talks to someone like him.
And she doesn't. She just gets kind of cocky. Ida doesn't dare. But
she dares. Mom and Dad are going be angry when they find out she
spoke to a guy like this. She doesn't want them to be angry.

———

Number thirty-three is the best. That's where he found the bike.
That's where he's been sleeping.
    They're not screaming anymore. The blond chubby slut is crying,
snot running from her nose, her eyes red. The dark-haired slut stares
defiantly at him, challenging him, hating him. He binds their hands
to one of the white pipes running along the gray concrete wall. It's
hot, probably a water pipe, it burns the skin of their forearms. They

kick at him, and every time they kick, he kicks back. Until they learn. Then they don't kick anymore.

They sit still. Sluts should sit still. Sluts should wait. He's the one who decides. He takes off his clothes. T-shirt, jeans, underwear, shoes, socks. In that order. He does it in front of them. If they don't look at him, he kicks them until they do. Sluts should look. He stands in front of them naked. He's beautiful. He knows he's beautiful. A fit body. Muscular legs. Firm buttocks. No belly. Beautiful.

"What do you say?"

The dark-haired slut is crying.

"Fucking fucking cap guy."

She cries. It took some time, but now she's just like all sluts.

"What do you say? Am I beautiful?"

"Fucking fucking cap guy. I want to go home."

His penis is erect. He's the one who decides. He walks over to them, pushes it up against their faces.

"Beautiful, right?"

He did it twice this morning. He can only do it twice more. He masturbates in front of them. He's breathing heavily, kicking the blond chubby one when she looks away for a moment, comes onto their faces, in their hair, smearing it around as they shake their heads.

They're crying. Sluts cry so fucking much.

He takes off their clothes. Their shirts, he has to cut them off, since their hands are fastened to the hot pipe. They're smaller than he'd imagined. They don't even have boobs.

He takes off everything except their shoes. Not the shoes. Not yet. The blond chubby slut has pink shoes. Almost like patent leather. The dark-haired slut has white trainers. The kind tennis players wear. He bends down. In front of the blond chubby slut. He kisses her pink patent-leather shoes, on top, near the toes. He licks them, from the toes, along the length of the shoe, and to its heel. He takes them off.

The slut's foot is so beautiful. He lifts it up. She's about to fall farther backward. He licks her ankle, her toes, sucking on each one for a long time. He glances up at her face—she's still crying. He feels an intense desire.

SHE WAKES UP when the morning paper arrives. Every damn time. A thud against the wooden floor. Door after door. She's tried getting up to stop him, but always too late. She's seen his back several times. A young guy with a ponytail. If she caught up with him, she'd tell him exactly how people feel on a Sunday morning at five o'clock.

She can't go back to sleep now. She turns, twists, sweats, tries and tries and tries to fall asleep, but it's too late. It used to be no problem, but now her thoughts overwhelm her. She's tense by six in the morning—fuck the paperboy and his ponytail.

The newspaper is as thick as a Bible on Sundays. She lies down with a section, looks at a word here and there. Too much text, she can't make sense of it, all those interesting stories about interesting people that she should read but doesn't. She ends up putting them all in a pile intending to read them later and never does.

She's restless. Newspaper, coffee, teeth, breakfast, bed, desk, teeth again. It's not even half past seven on a Sunday morning in June. The sun whips through the blinds, but she turns her face away, not yet ready for the light. Too much summer, too many people walking hand in hand, too many people sleeping next to each other, too many people laughing, playing, loving—she can't take it, not yet.

She goes down to the basement. To her storage space. Where it's dark, lonely, messy.

She knows it will take her at least two hours to clean it. By that time it will be at least nine thirty.

The first thing she sees is that the padlock has been busted. On the storage pens next to hers, too. She should find out who owns them. Thirty-two and thirty-four. Seven years in this building, and she's never seen either of them. Now they have something in common, they all own a broken padlock. Now they can talk to each other.

Then she notices the bike. Or rather the lack of bike. Jonathan's expensive, black, five-speed bicycle. Which she was going to sell for at least five hundred kronor. Now she has to call him, at his father's house. Might as well tell him about it now, so he's calmed down by the time he comes back.

Afterward, she has a hard time understanding why she didn't see. That she could think about who owns storage spaces number thirty-two and thirty-four, about Jonathan's black mountain bike. It was as if she didn't want to see, couldn't. When the police questioned her, she started laughing hysterically when asked what she saw when she opened the storage door. Her first important impression. She laughed long until she started coughing, she laughed while tears ran down her face, she explained that her first and only thought was that Jonathan would be sad that his black mountain bike was gone, that he wouldn't be able to buy the video games she'd promised him with the money they were going to get for it, at least five hundred.

She had never seen death before, never encountered people who looked at her without breathing.

Because that's what they did. Looked at her. They lay on the cement floor, their heads cradled on flowerpots, like hard pillows. They were little girls, younger than Jonathan, not more than ten. One fair-haired and one dark-haired. They were bloody: face, chest, genitals, thighs. Dried blood everywhere, except on their feet, the feet were so lovely, almost as if they'd been washed.

She'd never seen them before. Or maybe she had? They lived so close.

Of course. She must have seen them. In the store or maybe in the park? There were always a lot of children in the park.

They lay there on the floor of her storage space for three days. That was what the coroner said. Sixty hours. They had traces of semen in their vaginas, anuses, on their upper bodies, in their hair. The vagina and anus had been subjected to what was called blunt force. A sharp object, probably metal, had been forced inside repeatedly, which caused major internal bleeding.

They might have gone to the same school as Jonathan. There were always so many little girls in the playground. All the little girls looked the same.

They were naked. Their clothes lay in front of them, just inside the storage door. Piece after piece, as if lined up in an exhibition. The jackets folded, pants rolled up, shirts, underwear, socks, shoes, headbands, all in a neat row, carefully arranged, two centimeters between each one, two centimeters to the next garment.

They looked at her. But they weren't breathing.

close to now

I
(one day)

HE'D ALWAYS FELT silly in masks. A grown man in a mask should feel silly. He'd seen other men do the same thing. Winnie the Pooh or Scrooge McDuck or something similar, they'd done it with a kind of gravitas, as if the mask didn't bother them. I'll never understand, he thought. I'll never get used to it. I'll never be the kind of father I wanted and decided to become.

Fredrik Steffansson fingered the plastic in front of his face. Thin, tight-fitting, colorful. A rubber band on the back, pressing hard against his hair. It was difficult to breathe, smelled of saliva and sweat.

"Run, Dad! You're not running! You're just standing there! The Big Bad Wolf always runs!"

She stood in front of him with her head tilted back, her long blond hair full of grass and dirt. She was trying to look angry, but an angry child doesn't smile, and she was smiling as a child does when the Big Bad Wolf is chasing her around a small-town house lap after lap, until he's completely out of breath and wants to be somebody without a mask, without a plastic wolf tongue or wolf teeth.

"Marie, I can't anymore. The Big Bad Wolf has to sit down. The Big Bad Wolf wants to be small and kind."

She shook her head.

"One more time, Dad! Just one more time."

"You said that last time."

"This is the last time."

"You said that last time, too."

"Absolutely last."

"Absolutely?"

"Absolutely."

I love her, he thought. She's my daughter. It took time. I didn't see it, but now I do. I love her.

Then he glimpsed a shadow. Right behind him. It was moving slowly, stealthily. He'd thought he was in front of him somewhere, over by the trees, but now he was behind him, moving slowly at first, then faster. At the exact same time, the girl with grass and dirt in her hair attacked from the front. They tackled him from opposite directions. He staggered and fell to the ground, and they threw themselves on top of him, lay there. The girl held her hand up in the air and a dark-haired five-year-old boy held up his. They high-fived.

"He gives up, David!"

"We won!"

"The pigs are the best!"

"The pigs are always the best!"

When two five-year-olds attack the Big Bad Wolf from either direction, he doesn't have a chance. That's just how it is. He rolled over with the two children still on top of him. He lay on his back and took the plastic off his face, squinting up at the bright sunlight. He laughed out loud.

"It's so weird. Somehow I never win. Have I ever won? Even once? Can you explain that, you two?"

He spoke, but the other two weren't listening. The other two held a prize in their hands, a plastic mask that they wanted to try on and run away with ceremonially—go into the house and up to the second floor to Marie's room, put it on the dresser next to their other prize, stand in front of both for a while, the height of eternal glory in two five-year-old friends' Duckburg.

He watched their backs as they left him. He watched his neighbor's son and his daughter. So much life, all the years they held in their hands, months running through their fingers. I envy them. I envy them their infinite time: the feeling that an hour is long, that winter will never end. They disappeared through the door, and he turned his face to the sky, lying on his back and looking at the shades of blue. He did that as a kid, and he did it now. Skies are always made of more than one blue. He had a good life back then, as a child. His father was a career officer, a captain, a field officer with the potential for a career to be embroidered on his shoulder. His mother had been a housewife in the apartment he and his brother left each morning and returned home to at night. He never knew what she did in between, three bedrooms on the third floor of an apartment complex. He'd thought about it often, how she could stand those repetitive days.

Everything changed when he turned twelve. Or the day after, to be exact. It was as if Frans had waited until his birthday passed, hadn't wanted to destroy it, as if he knew birthdays were more than just birthdays for his little brother. Knew they were all his longing in one day.

Fredrik Steffansson stood up, brushed the grass from his shirt and shorts. He thought about Frans a lot, more now than ever. One day he was just gone—his bed made and empty, their conversations over. Frans had hugged him that morning for a long time, longer than he usually did, hugged him and said goodbye and went to Strängnäs station and took the train an hour into Stockholm. When he arrived he continued on toward the subway, bought a ticket and sat down in a subway car on the green line south toward Farsta. At Medborgarplatsen he'd stepped off, jumped down from the platform, and slowly walked along the rails in the tunnel toward Skanstull. Six minutes later a subway driver saw a man in the headlights of the train, threw on the brakes, and screamed in panic, agony, and terror as the first car crashed into a fifteen-year-old's body.

After that, they left Frans's bed untouched. The bedspread stretched, the red blanket weighing on the foot of the bed. Fredrik didn't know why then; didn't know now either. Maybe they'd left it to welcome Frans if he ever came back? For a long time, Fredrik had hoped to see his big brother standing in front of him again, hoped it was a big mistake. Mistakes do happen sometimes.

It was as if the rest of his family died on the tracks that day too, in a tunnel between Medborgarplatsen and Skanstull. His mother was no longer waiting at home all day. She never said where she went, just came home after dark, regardless of the season. His father had collapsed—the captain's straight back was bent now. He'd never talked much, but now he was almost mute, and he never hit again. Fredrik couldn't remember any more punches.

They stood in the doorway again. Marie and David. They were the same height, the height of five-year-olds. He'd forgotten the precise figures but had received a note with weight and height from her nursery school. They are as tall as they are—he wasn't much for printouts of statistics.

Marie still had grass and dirt in her long blond hair, David's dark hair lay plastered to his forehead and temples. He'd worn the mask inside. Fredrik could see that, and it made him laugh.

"A bath is what you need. Pigs take baths, did you know that?"

He filled the old claw-foot tub with water—he'd found it at an auction in Svinnegarn, at an estate right off Road 55. He sat there for more than half an hour every night, letting the hot water refresh his skin, while he was thinking, just thinking, structuring the next day's writing, the next chapter. Now the water worried him. Not too hot, not too cold, and he adds white foam from a green Donald Duck bottle, to make the bath look inviting, soft. They climbed in voluntarily, to his surprise, sat at either end.

Five-year-olds are so small. It's only when they're naked that you realize it. Their soft skin, slender bodies, constantly expectant faces. He looked at Marie, white bubbles on her forehead, slipping down along her nose—he looked at David, the shampoo bottle in his hand, upside down and empty and even more bubbles. He didn't have any pictures of himself as a five-year-old, he tried to imagine his head on Marie's shoulders, they resembled each other, people often commented upon it triumphantly, which surprised him but embarrassed Marie. His five-year-old face on her body, he should be able to remember, to feel what he felt, but all that came back to him was the beating his father gave him in the living room, that big fucking hand against his back and bottom. He remembered that, remembered Frans's face pressed against the glass door to the living room.

"The foam is gone."

David held out the bottle, shook it a few times onto the water to demonstrate.

"I can see that. Probably because you used it all."

"Should I not have done that?"

Fredrik smiled. "No. Of course you should use it."

"Now you have to buy us a new one!"

He also used to watch when Frans was beaten. Their father never noticed them standing there behind the glass door. Frans was older. He took more punches, the beatings lasted longer, at least it seemed like it from a few meters away. Only as an adult did Fredrik remember. The beatings had ended more than fifteen years ago, and at some point just before thirty it suddenly hit him—the big hand and the pane of glass in the living room door. Since then he'd been overcome by memories of that living room again and again. He didn't feel angry, strangely enough, or vindictive, just full of grief; maybe grief was the best description of what he felt.

"Daddy, we have more."

He looked at Marie emptily. She was chasing it, the emptiness.

"Hello!"

"We have more?"

"We have more Donald Ducks."

"We do?"

"On the bottom shelf. Two more. We bought three."

Frans's grief had been greater. He was older, had time for more beatings. Frans used to cry behind the glass. But only then. Only when he was watching. He lived with his grief, hid it, carried it until it became his own, until at last he turned it on himself, into a giant blow from a thirty-ton train.

"Here."

Marie had climbed out of the tub, walked to the other side of the room to the bathroom cabinet and opened it. She pointed proudly.

"Two of them. I knew it. I knew you should buy three."

The bathroom floor was wet, foam and water flowing off her body, and she didn't notice of course, walked back with a Donald Duck in her hand and climbed into the tub again. She opened it with unexpected ease. David grabbed hold of it and emptied it without looking up, without hesitation. Then he shouted something that sounded like yippee, and they high-fived for the second time in an hour.

HE HATED KIDDIE fuckers. Just like everyone else. But he was a professional. This was just a job. He'd convinced himself of that. A job a job a job.

Åke Andersson had been transporting prisoners to and from Swedish prisons for thirty-two years. He was fifty-nine years old. His salt-and-pepper hair was still thick and well taken care of. A kilo overweight. Tall, taller than any of his colleagues, taller than any perp he'd transported. Two meters, he usually said. He was actually two meters and three centimeters, but people that tall are considered freaks, nature's defects, and he was tired of that.

He hated rapists. Little bastards who have to force their way into a pussy. But he hated the child rapists most of all. The feeling was so intense and forbidden, and it got worse every time they said hello to him—the only time he felt anything at all during the day, an aggression that scared him. He suppressed the urge to turn off the engine, jump between the seats, push the bastard into the rear window.

He revealed nothing.

He'd transported worse scum. Or at least scum with longer sentences. He'd seen them all. He'd put every fucking headline in handcuffs, walked them to the door of his van, stared at them blankly in his rearview mirror. Quite a few of them were idiots. Fools. Some got it. They knew the costs. All that fucking talk from people on the outside about compassion and treatment and rehabilitation. Don't do the crime, if you can't do the time. As simple as that.

He knew who the kiddie fuckers were. Every single one. They had a look about them. He didn't need to see any sentence. Any papers. He saw it on them and hated them. He'd tried to say that a few times at the pub over a beer. That he could see it, and when they wondered how, he hadn't been able to explain. They'd mistaken he was homophobic, prejudiced, not a humanist, and so he never said it again, didn't have the energy, but he could see it and those pervs knew it, no matter how they tried to hide it when he met them.

He'd transported this one at least six times before—in '01 a few trips back and forth from the court of appeal and Kronoberg jail, then again when he'd escaped in '07, in '09 from Säter Institution to somewhere else, and now in the middle of the night to Söder Hospital. He looked at him—they looked at each other, a meaningless stare-down in the rearview mirror. He seemed normal. They always did. To other people. Short, not fat, a crew cut, quiet. Completely normal. The type of man who raped children.

They hit a red light at the hill that led up toward the hospital. Sparse late-night traffic. Then a siren and blue lights came from behind him. He stopped while the ambulance passed by.

"We're here, Lund. Thirty seconds. Get ready. We called and a doctor will be here soon to take a look at you."

He refused to speak to a kiddie fucker. Always had. His colleague knew that. Ulrik Berntfors thought the same way he did. They all did. But Ulrik didn't hate them.

"So we won't have to wait for breakfast. And you won't have to sit in the waiting room wearing those."

Ulrik Berntfors pointed at the man called Lund. To the chains on his stomach. At his belly chains. He'd never used them on anyone before. But those were his orders. Oscarsson had called specifically about them. When he'd asked Lund to take off his clothes, he got a smile and a slow thrust of the hips as his answer. A metal belt around his stomach, four chains down his legs fastened to shackles at his ankles, two chains across the upper body fastened to handcuffs. He'd seen them on the news and on professional visits to India, but never here; Swedish prison services controlled their inmates numerically, more guards than perps, sometimes handcuffed, never with chains under their shirts and pants.

"How thoughtful. I'm very grateful. You're good guys."

Lund spoke quietly. Barely audible. Ulrik Berntfors couldn't decide if he was being ironic. Until Lund leaned forward, the chains making a metallic sound as they rubbed against each other, and rested his head on the edge of the window separating the front seat from the back.

"Seriously, guards. This isn't working. Chains are a pain in the ass. If you take this damn metal dress off me, I promise not to run away."

Åke Andersson stared at him through the rearview mirror. He accelerated violently up the hill toward Emergency and then hit the brakes. Lund struck his chin hard on the edge of the window.

"What the hell are you doing, you fucking pig? Are you as retarded as you look?"

Lund was calm, spoke with care. Until he was crossed. Then he screamed and swore. Åke Andersson knew that. They don't just look alike. They are alike.

Ulrik Berntfors laughed. Inside. Fucking Andersson, he wasn't quite all that he should be. He did that sort of thing.

"Sorry, Lund. Sorry. Orders from Oscarsson. You're classified as dangerous, so that's just how it is."

Ulrik had trouble controlling his words. The words did as they pleased, pushing their way out of his mouth, even though he could control his face, afraid of the boisterous laughter that might slip out, further antagonizing the person they were being paid to transport. He spoke, but he stared straight ahead, just like Andersson did.

"If we remove that crap against Oscarsson's orders, we'd be in breach of our duty. You know that."

The ambulance that had just overtaken them was standing at the doors of Emergency. Two paramedics were running with a stretcher between them, up two steps, toward the entrance. Ulrik Berntfors caught a glimpse of a woman, her long, bloody hair clinging to one of the orderly's legs. It occurred to him that the orange of the uniforms didn't match the red of the blood and wondered why not since they must get blood on them now and then. Strong emotions always filled his head with pointless thoughts.

"Damn! Fucking Oscarsson! What the hell! Can't he just trust me when I say I won't go anywhere! I told him that at Aspsås!"

Lund shouted through the window into the driver's compartment, then whipped back his head and threw himself headlong toward the windowless wall of the driver's side. The chains at his waist clanged against the metal wall, and for a moment Åke Andersson thought that he'd driven over something and looked around for a vehicle that wasn't there.

"I told him, pigs. And now you don't trust me either. Well then. Then we'll say this. If you don't take this fucking metal off my body, I will leave. Do you understand that, pigs? Leave. Are you sure you understand that?"

Åke Andersson searched for his eyes, adjusting the rearview mirror to find them. He felt the hatred wash over him. He had to hit something. The bastard had gone too far—one *pig* too many.

Thirty-two years. A job a job a job. He couldn't take it anymore. Not today. Sooner or later, it all goes to hell. He tore off his seat belt. He opened the door. Ulrik Berntfors knew but wasn't fast enough. Åke was going to whip that perv like he'd never been whipped before. Ulrik sat there smiling. He didn't have anything against that.

IT WAS THOSE most silent few minutes after four. After the last patrons of the Hörnan bar had made their way noisily from the harbor, along the water, toward the old bridge to Tosterö, but before the newspaper deliverymen on Stor Street started opening front doors and mailboxes to drop off the *Strengnäs Times*, an edition of the *Eskilstuna Courier* with the front page and page four replaced with pictures of local life.

Fredrik Steffansson knew what time it was. It had been quite a while since he'd slept through the night. He lay with the window open listening to a small town fall asleep and wake up again, filled with people he probably knew or at least recognized. That's just what it's like to live in a small town—it's not far to the other side. He's lived here for most of his life. He'd read Ulf Lundell and Jack Kerouac and moved to Stockholm, studied the history of religion then moved to a kibbutz in northern Israel not far from the border with Lebanon. But he always came back here, to the people he knew, or at least recognized. He'd never really moved on from his home, from his childhood, his memories, the loss of Frans. He'd met Agnes, fallen violently in love with this urbane, black-clad woman who was always searching for something more. They'd lived together and were about to separate when Marie arrived, and then they'd lived as a family for about a year before splitting for good. She lived in Stockholm now with her beautiful friends. She fit in better up there. They weren't enemies, but they didn't talk much anymore either, except about picking up and dropping off Marie.

Someone was walking outside. He looked at his watch. A quarter to five. Fucking nights. If only he could think about something useful, like the next two pages of his book, but it was as if he had no thoughts at all, just listened to time passing through the half-open window while doors closed and cars started. He could barely write anymore. The days just stood there. Marie left for preschool, and he sat in front of the computer overcome by fatigue, hours without sleep, three chapters in two months. It was a disaster. And his publisher had already guessed what he wasn't doing.

A truck. It sounded like a truck. They usually didn't arrive until five thirty.

The thin wall of Marie's room. He could hear her through it. She was snoring. How could a child of five, cute, with a high voice, snore like an old man? He thought it was only Marie who snored like that, but then David slept over and together they were twice as loud, filling the silence between each other's breathing.

It wasn't a truck. A bus. He was sure of it.

He turned away from the window. Micaela lay there naked, as always, with the blankets and sheets in a pile at her feet. She was so young, only twenty-four years old, she made him feel horny and loved and now and then very old—when they talked about music, and books, and movies, when one of them referred to a composition or text or scene, it suddenly became clear: she was a young woman and he was a middle-aged man. Sixteen years is a long time when it comes to film quotes and guitar solos.

She lay on her stomach, her face toward him. He caressed her cheek, kissed her lightly on her bottom. He liked her a lot. Did he love her? He couldn't think about that right now.

He liked the fact that she was lying there next to him, that she wanted to share his hours. He hated loneliness, because it felt meaningless and suffocating, because not being able to breathe meant death. He lifted his hand from her cheek, stroked her back. She moved restlessly. Why was she here? With an older man, who had a child? He wasn't particularly good-looking, not rich, not even that much fun. Why did she choose to spend her nights with him, when she was so beautiful and so young, with so many more hours to live? He kissed her again on her hip.

"Are you still awake?"

"I'm sorry. Did I wake you?"

"I don't know. Haven't you slept at all?"

"You know how it is."

She pulled him close to her, her naked body against his. She was warm from sleep, awake but not quite.

"You need to sleep, old man."

"Old man?"

"You'll be exhausted otherwise. You know that. Sleep now."

She looked at him, kissed him, held him.

"I'm thinking about Frans."

"Fredrik, not now."

"Well, I think about him. I want to think about him. I listen to Marie in there, and I think about how Frans was just a child when he took those beatings, when he saw me take a beating, when he got on the train to Stockholm."

"Close your eyes."

"Why would you hit a child?"

"If you close your eyes long enough, you'll fall asleep. That's how it works."

"Why hit a child who will one day grow up to judge the person who hit him or at the very least judge himself?"

She pushed him, turned him on his side with his back against her, lying close behind, like two large branches beside each other.

"A child who will think the beating is a father's duty? A child who will tell himself that he bears some part of the blame?"

Micaela was asleep. Her breathing came slow and regular against his neck, so close it was wet. He could hear a bus stopping outside, backing up, stopping again, backing up again. Same as yesterday, maybe a tourist bus, a fairly large one.

WHEN ANDERSSON OPENED the front door of the prison transport van and hastily stepped out, he felt something he'd never felt before. His rage, his accursed hatred felt beyond his control. For over thirty years he'd taken shit from inmates. He'd hated them, but sat in silence, driving them from prisons to district court, from hospitals to institutions. He'd let his colleagues do the talking, transported the dregs, stared straight ahead, and did his job. But he just couldn't take this fucking child rapist. He'd been on the verge of losing control in the past with this guy. He knew what he'd done and what the girls looked like afterward. After his most recent run-in with his sneer and lack of empathy, he'd dreamed of him for several nights, his same offense repeated over and over, and in the morning he'd woken up and couldn't make it to the toilet before throwing up on the hall floor, as if the control accumulated in his stomach, and when there was no more space, it had to escape somehow.

He had no idea what he was going to do. He was no longer in control. When he heard *pig* for the third time, duty and consequences ceased to exist, only pictures of naked little girls and the injuries left by sharp metal objects. His lumbering body was almost running toward the back door of the van.

———

Berntfors had only transported Lund once before—the second trial date for the girls found in the basement storage room. He'd been fairly new to the job back then, and the trial was the biggest one he'd been involved in. It had been the kind of trial where journalists and photographers gathered in rows, jostling one another, in front of each other, because the story of two nine-year-olds moved people and sold. He was ashamed of his own reaction at the time. He hadn't thought about those girls at all, hadn't understood. He'd been so inexperienced, and it made him feel special, almost proud, to be walking beside Lund on TV. The reality came later, when his daughter asked him why Lund killed two girls, why he destroyed them—she'd only been a year older than they were and carefully read every news article and always came with new questions—because her father really knew him, had walked beside him on television several times. Of course, he'd had no answers. But slowly he started to understand. His daughter, with her questions and fears, had taught him more about his professional role than any class he'd taken.

He knew Andersson hated them all. They'd never talked about it, but he'd seen, heard, and comprehended. Maybe that would happen to him, too. When a man like Lund shouted at you a sufficient number of times. So he did all the talking. Someone has to speak to them. That was their job. Transporting them.

When Lund screamed *pig* for the third time, he knew. There was no room for more. Even as Andersson got up, he knew.

If he kept his eyes on the Emergency entrance in front of the bus, he wouldn't see. If he didn't see anything, he couldn't lie to an investigator.

———

It was empty in the Emergency parking lot. No cars and no people. That was what Åke Andersson said afterward. He also said that even if it hadn't been empty, even if other people had been there, he wouldn't have noticed them—he'd run toward the back of the vehicle filled with fury and hatred, and it had clouded his sight.

He pulled the door open. A small handle, his hands were as big as the rest of him, and he could barely fit his right hand between the metal of the car and handle.

That's when everything went to hell.

Bernt Lund screamed *pig* in a falsetto several times. And then attacked. He held his chains in one hand—the ones under his pants and his shirt, which were bound together by handcuffs and shackles around his ankles. Andersson didn't even see anything before the heavy iron links tore his face, and he fell to the ground. Lund jumped out of the open bus door, hit Andersson's head again and again, kicked him in the stomach, in the hip, in the groin until the tall guard lay completely still.

———

Berntfors had been staring straight ahead for a long time. Andersson was giving that pervert quite a whipping. He listened. Lund was still screaming *pig*, must be suffering quite a bit. He waited, until he started to feel uncomfortable. Andersson had gone on for too long. Surely Lund had had enough. If Andersson didn't stop soon, things might turn out bad. Berntfors was just about to open the door and step out, on his way to stop Andersson from making a mistake, when he saw Lund standing beside him. Lund threw his long chain through the window, hitting Berntfors in the face before pulling him out and beating him. The only thing Berntfors would remember afterward was the terrible screaming, and how Lund pulled off Berntfors's pants, whipping the chain against Berntfors's penis, screaming that he would have fucked them both in the ass if they hadn't been so big. Big people didn't deserve his love, only small people felt longing, only they deserved to have him inside them.

ONE HUNDRED AND eighty steps from the front door to the iron gate in the middle of the gray concrete wall that dominated their small community. Lennart Oscarsson always counted them. Once, it took him only one hundred and sixty-one steps. That was his record. It was a few years ago, and he'd been working out a lot at the time with the inmates at the institution's gym. He'd worked out with them until the assault—a long-timer split open by some inmates one morning. They'd used dumbbells and weight plates, according to the doctor—the marks clear and easily identifiable. And nobody had seen anything, nobody knew anything. He couldn't go there anymore. He wasn't afraid, no one was stupid enough to risk another legal process for the sake of a principal officer such as himself. It wasn't fear, but disgust. He would never be comfortable in a room where a man he was responsible for had been deprived of his life.

He rang the bell and waited for a voice from the speaker, while having the feeling of being watched by the little camera just above his head. As he stood there, he turned around, back toward the home he'd just left, searched the windows of the living room and the bedrooms. Darkness. Shades pulled down halfway. No glimpses of a face, no back near the phone shelf.

"Yep?"

"Oscarsson here."

"I'll let you in."

The gate opened and he entered. He blinked at the prison walls around him, two different worlds, and he was able to walk between them, just a couple of minutes separating them. He approached the next door, knocked on the window of the guardroom, waved to Bergh, who waved back and pressed a new button. The door buzzed, he opened it, the hallway smelled of scouring liquid and something else.

Lennart Oscarsson always felt proud when he arrived for another day of work at Aspsås prison. Principal Prison Officer. He had ambitions for further advancement. He took every course, took any chance to study correctional treatment. If you want to get somewhere you have to show it, so he did and knew someone was taking note. He had been named head of the Aspsås Department for Sexual Crimes seven years ago.

He spent his days with people who were locked up for violating those who were dependent on their protection. People who had broken the only taboo society had left. He was responsible for them and for the staff who took care of them and punished them. That was what they were supposed to do. That was their only task. Care for and punish and know the difference between the two. He thought what he thought, felt how he felt, but he showed that he was willing, and someone would take note of it.

But this—this was a pretty dismal day. Unit meeting. Department meeting. They were building a labyrinth of meetings around themselves, meaningless decisions about meaningless routines, clinging to the structure. Solving problems required sharp minds and energy, but these meetings did nothing but make them feel secure in their repetition while preserving the nothingness.

"Good morning."

The conference room—long tables, whiteboards, and overhead projector—could be any government department. They greeted each other, eight principal officers and Arne Bertolsson, the governor. These were Oscarsson's closest colleagues, who he spent time with every day but didn't meet much outside work. He'd never been in any of their homes, and they'd never been in his. They'd met for a beer in town, or a football game, but never at home. Could you really know each other then? They were all around the same age, looked similar in a uniform of blue pants, a tie, white shirt—a room full of limo drivers.

Bertolsson turned on the overhead projector. It made a sound. Made a sound but projected nothing. He squatted down and pushed every button he could find. Finally, he gave up.

"Let's forget about this. Forget the agenda. Who wants to start?"

Nothing. No one said a word. Gustafsson drank his coffee, Nilsson wrote in his notebook, Lundström looked out of the window, and the rest stayed silent. Someone had taken their routine away from them, and they were all lost, without their data.

Oscarsson cleared his throat.

"I can start."

The others breathed out. Now there was at least a temporary agenda.

"I've brought this up before, but I know what I'm talking about. Has anyone forgotten the assault on Salonen? Inmates from the regular units are running from the gym to the kitchen at the same time as my people. We had another incident yesterday. Something unfortunate might have happened if Brandt and Persson hadn't intervened."

Oscarsson was observing each of them as he talked. Mostly looking at Eva Bernard. He really couldn't stand her. She didn't understand the prison rules of tradition and time, the rules found outside their folders that just existed and were followed.

"You're talking about—"

Bertolsson understood that accusatory gaze and didn't want any fights, not now, not again, and so he interrupted.

"—coordination?"

"Yeah. This is not general society. Not reality. Everyone in this room knows that. Everyone here should at least know that much."

Oscarsson didn't take his eyes off Eva Bernard. Conflict-averse Bertolsson was not going to be able to avoid this, not going to hide from this problem again.

"If the wrong person from the general units were to run into one of mine, there might be hell to pay. Everybody approves of killing a pedophile."

He pointed at her.

"The son of a bitch who incited yesterday's incident is exactly the type. And he's in your unit."

Eva Bernard met his gaze.

"If you mean 0243 Lindgren, just say so."

"Yes, Lindgren."

"Stig 'Tinyboy' Lindgren is a bastard. At least, when he wants to be. When he doesn't, he's a model prisoner. Calm. Does absolutely nothing. Lies around in his cell smoking hand-rolled cigarettes, never reads, never watches TV, just lets the hours go by. He's served twenty-seven years. Forty-two separate convictions. He's one of those who speaks Romani. He only acts up when someone new enters the unit, and he has to show them who's been there longest. It's about the hierarchy. And respect."

"This isn't about a new inmate. This is about yesterday. He would have killed my guy if he hadn't been discovered. And you know it."

Gustafsson had put down his coffee cup. Nilsson had flipped to a blank page in his notepad. Lundström was staring out through another window. Bertolsson stayed silent, as though he thought this was interesting. As though he didn't feel up for it.

"Can I finish speaking? He goes after sex offenders. And only them. He gets . . . well, what he feels for them is more than hate. I've gone through his records. There's a reason why he wants to kill them."

Lennart Oscarsson knew very well who Tinyboy Lindgren was. A small-time crook who'd become institutionalized, who got so scared every time he was released he'd piss on the wall outside hoping one of the guards would see. And if that weren't enough, he'd knock down the driver of the first bus on his way from the prison. That's what he'd done the last time around. He usually made sure that within a month or two he was back in the only society he knew how to live in, the place where people knew his name.

"You said Romani."

Månsson, the new temp from Malmö, whose first name he couldn't remember, looked at Eva Bernard.

"Yes."

"You said Stig Lindgren spoke Romani."

"Yes."

"What do you mean by that?"

Eva Bernard smiled superciliously. It was that smirk that made people dislike her. She didn't have to discuss the attack with Oscarsson anymore, now she had the upper hand. Now she was in charge. She turned to Malmö-Månsson.

"Yes, how could you know about it?"

Månsson may be new, but he'd just learned a valuable lesson. He wouldn't show his ignorance in front of her again.

"Forget it."

She continued.

"It was common in the past. The inmates spoke it to each other—a prison language—not the Romani that the Roma speak, another one, used exclusively in prisons. Now it's almost disappeared. Only people like Lindgren still know it—the inmates who've lived longer inside these walls than out of them."

She was pleased. Oscarsson had jumped on her and insinuated her lack of knowledge of prison traditions, and she'd proved he was wrong.

Meanwhile, Bertolsson finally managed to get the projector to function. An image, an agenda, he looked relieved. They'd been about to derail, but now he could start over. He was about to thank the eight principal officers for their ironic applause when he heard a telephone ring. Not his, it was turned off, as all the others should be.

"It's me. It's mine. Sorry. I forgot to turn it off."

Oscarsson had stood up, was searching the inside pocket of his jacket.

Two rings. He didn't recognize the number. Three rings. He shouldn't answer. Four rings. He answered it.

"Oscarsson here."

Eight people were listening to his conversation.

"Yes?"

He sat down.

"What the hell are you saying?"

His voice was faint.

"Not . . . him."

Now he was shouting. But you could barely hear him. His faint voice had lost even more of its force.

"Not him! Do you hear what I'm saying, not him!"

His colleagues sat completely still. Oscarsson was always so proper. Now he was standing in front of them shaking.

"That was the guards' station."

He shut off the phone, red in the face, breathing heavily.

"There's been an escape. One of mine. At Söder Hospital. Bernt Lund. He overpowered both of the guards and stole the bus."

THE POLICE STATION on Bergs Street in Stockholm was filled with the music of the '60s Swedish pop star Siw Malmkvist, at least as far as the hallway on the second floor. It was like this every morning, and the earlier it was, the louder it was, a C-120 cassette tape, the big kind, common in the '70s. The same plastic cases, the same tapes for thirty years, three mixed tapes of her songs in various orders. This morning, "Mother Is like Her Mother" and "Nothing Comes Close to Old Scania," Metronome 1968, the A- and B-sides on the same single. A black-and-white picture of Siw in front of a microphone, wearing a short housecoat and holding a broom.

Ewert Grens, who had received the stereo as a birthday present when he turned twenty-five, took it to work and put it on his bookshelf. He had switched offices a few times before he became a detective superintendent and every time he did he carried the tape deck himself, in his own arms. He always got to work first, never later than five thirty in the morning—two hours with no idiots at his doorway or on the phone. At half past seven, he lowered the volume, because of the fucking whining of the other people around him. He always made them wait a while though and never lowered the volume of his own accord. If they wanted him to do something, they had to ask.

It was as if he lived in black and white, like one of Siw's key changes.

Large, heavy, tired. A strip of gray hair wrapped around Grens's skull. He walked with a striking, jerky gait, almost a limp. His neck stiff because a few years ago he'd ended up in a noose-snare while the

SWAT team he was leading was apprehending a Lithuanian hitman. He spent quite a bit of time in the hospital after that.

Grens had been a good cop. He didn't know if he was one anymore. If he even wanted to be. Did he keep working because he didn't know what else to do? Had he turned work into something more than what it was, something that seemed important for a while? Why the hell should anyone even remember him after a few years? New people kept coming. They had no knowledge of history, no clue about anything important until recently, no idea who had informal power in the station or why. We have to teach ourselves. We shouldn't forget that. It should be part of our training, our deprogramming, being forced to understand how small this all is. You're here for a limited amount of time, no more. There were also those who'd come before him, and he hadn't cared about them either.

There was a knock on the door. One of the idiots. Someone coming to gently ask him to lower the volume.

Sven.

The only person in this building with any sense.

"Ewert."

"Yes?"

"Now, for Christ's sake."

"Yes?"

"Bernt Lund."

He woke up, stretched, stopped what he was doing.

"Bernt Lund?"

"He's escaped."

"He's . . . ?"

"Again."

Sven Sundkvist liked Grens, tolerated his sarcasm, his unpredictability, his fear of being forced to retire and face the fact that thirty-five years is thirty-five years and no more. At least Ewert Grens wanted something. He was surly and grouchy, but he believed in what he did. Unlike many of their colleagues.

"Tell me more, Sven!"

Sundkvist explained the transfer from Aspsås prison to the Söder Hospital Emergency department. Explained how Bernt Lund used his body chains to attack two guards and steal their van. Explained that Lund was moving freely out there, probably already sitting somewhere, watching girls, small children, who were just getting to school.

Grens stood up, pacing restlessly back and forth across the room as Sven explained, limping around the desk, moving his big body between the chairs and flower pedestal. He stopped in front of the trash can, took aim with his good foot, and gave it a kick hard enough to send it through the air.

"How the hell could Bernt Lund be transported into the city with just two prison guards! How the hell could Oscarsson approve that? If he'd just picked up the phone and let us know, we'd have sent a car over, and Satan himself wouldn't have been set loose!"

The can had been full of banana peels and empty envelopes, now scattered on the floor.

Sven had seen this before. He just had to wait for a moment.

"Åke Andersson and Ulrik Berntfors. They're good. Andersson is tall, at least two meters, I think. Around your age."

"I know who Andersson is."

"And?"

"Another time. Not now."

Sven suddenly felt tired, and the feeling overwhelmed him. He wanted to go home. To Anita, to Jonas. He was already finished for the day. He didn't have enough energy to think of all the children who might be desecrated at any moment. He couldn't think about Bernt Lund. He'd switched to the morning shift. They were supposed to celebrate. He had wine and cake in the car. They were just about to toast him.

Grens could see that Sundkvist was somewhere else. His eyes were fading. Grens regretted kicking that damn trash can. Sven didn't like that sort of thing. He spoke again, more calmly this time.

"You look tired."

"I was about to head home. It's my birthday."

"Well . . . happy birthday. How old?"

"Forty."

Grens whistled loudly and bowed.

"Well, well. Give me your hand."

He held out his hand. Sven took it. Grens pressed it for a long time. Held him tightly as he began to speak.

"Unfortunately, young man, forty or not, you have to stay a little longer."

He pointed at his visitor's chair, impatient, urging with his index finger. Sven tore himself away from Grens's hand, sat at the very edge of the chair, still on his way out.

"Sven, I was there last time."

"Last time?"

"Two girls, nine years old. He'd tied them up, masturbated on them, raped them, cut them up. Just like the time before that. We found them lying on the basement floor, staring up at us. The coroner found traces of metal objects in the vagina and anus. I won't believe it. I can't believe it. Have you ever thought about that, Sven, that if you just make up your mind you can believe anything you want to?"

His wrinkled shirt, too-short pants, restless body. He scared a lot of people. Ewert Grens was loud. Sven himself had avoided him. Nobody deserves to be insulted—it was as simple as that. So he avoided him until, for reasons that remained obscure to him, he'd been accepted by Grens, almost chosen. Everybody needed somebody, and that somebody became Sven.

"I did the interrogation. I tried to look him in the eye. It was impossible. He looked above me, beside me, through me. But he wouldn't meet my eyes. I stopped the interrogation several times, asked him to look at me."

You don't understand, Grens.

Dammit, Grens.

I thought you'd be someone who would understand.

I'm not turned on by all little girls.

How the fuck can you say that?
I just like the ones who are a little bigger.
The chubby blond ones.
That type.
It's important, Grens.
Sluts.
Tiny sluts with tiny pussies.
All they do is think about cock.
They really shouldn't be doing that.
Tiny sluts with tiny pussies shouldn't walk around thinking about
cock.

"Sven, people look at each other when they talk. But it was impossible. Impossible."

He looked at Sven. Sven looked at him. They were people.

"I understand. Or, I don't understand. If he couldn't look you in the eye, if he was that type, why wasn't he put into psychiatric care? Säter? Karsudden? Sidsjön?"

"He was. The first time. Three years at the Säter Institution. But this last time his mental disorder was diagnosed as mild. And then they put you in prison. Not the loony bin."

Ewert walked over to the tape recorder, changed the cassette to another one by Siw. He stood in front of the speaker, stopped for a moment, eyes closed, "The Jazz Bug," 1959, original: "The Preacher." He raised the volume, squatted down, and picked up the banana peels and crumpled paper, put them back in the trash, took three steps back, getting a really good start, and kicked it even farther this time, against the wall and window.

"Sven, a *mild* mental disorder? Two nine-year-old girls. If that's a mild mental disorder, then tell me, what the hell is a *grave* mental disorder?"

THE WALL, GRAY concrete and two meters high, ran along the forest's edge for one and a half kilometers, encircling five low brick buildings.

The ones out there and the ones inside.

Aspsås prison was one of twelve with level-two security in Sweden. They put the murderers and the big-time drug dealers in Kumla, Hall, and Tidaholm, level-one security. Aspsås was full of small-time crooks, no life sentences, often just two to four years, prisoners who came and went. Eight departments, one hundred and sixty inmates. Most were drug-addicted professional criminals: a break-in, a little dough, get high, another break-in, cops, twenty-six months, get out, break in, a little dough, the cops, thirty-four months, get out, one more break-in.

Just like everywhere else. Me against you, you against the guards. Only two rules: you don't squeal and you don't fuck those who don't want it.

Aspsås also had two units for sex crimes. For those who did just that: fuck those who didn't want it.

Hated. Threatened.

It was as if all the shame and self-loathing of the inmates had to be directed somewhere—I can't stand to be despised by the society on the other side of the wall, so I hate someone who has committed an even worse crime than me; I can breathe easier if we all decide there's someone else even uglier than us, even more damaged, even more outside—an ancient agreement in prisons all over the world—I, a murderer, am hierarchically superior to you, the rapist; I, who have taken someone's right to live, have more dignity than you who forever took away someone's trust, my violation is less criminal than yours.

At Aspsås the hatred was perhaps even greater than at other prisons. Here they kept the normal units in the same buildings as the sex offenders. An eighteen-month term could be a potential death sentence if you ended up at Aspsås. Everyone here was suspected of sex crimes. Those who were transferred to another prison after Aspsås took a lot of beatings if their papers weren't in order. Without your verdict in hand you were considered a rapist until proved otherwise.

Unit H was one of eight normal sections for low-level junkies, burglars, assaulters, and the occasional swindler, those on their way up in the criminal hierarchy who'd end up with longer sentences the next time around, or the ones who just kept committing the same shitty offense again and again and couldn't serve with the drunk drivers and petty first-time offenders anymore. A unit that looked like all the other units in all the other prisons for all the other repeat offenders with medium-length sentences. A locked reinforced steel door to the stairwell. A corridor with yellow linoleum. Half-open cells on both sides, ten to the right, ten to the left. A small kitchen. A few dining tables. A TV corner. Right next to it, the green felt of a pool table. Back and forth, inmates moving slowly, headed somewhere to kill time, never think about the hours passing by and the hours that remain, there's only now, if you're longing for release you're longing your life away, and life is the only thing that exists when the doors are locked.

Stig Lindgren was sitting in the TV corner. The card deck in front of him on the table, the television muted on some channel, it was his deal, he and five other card players were waiting for queens and kings. Stig Lindgren was known as Tinyboy around here and in the rest of this country's other prisons—he'd served time at most of them.

He picked up the cards. Grinned. The gold tooth in front flashing.

"Damn, all the aces went to me again. You play like little bitches."

The others were silent. Shuffling their cards. Turning them.

"Don't show me your damn cards."

He was forty-eight years old, looked older, furrowed, worn. Thirty-five years of abuse left him with amphetamine-like tics that flashed unpredictably under his eye. His hair dark, ever thinner. Thick chains around his neck. Eighty kilos, muscular after his latest stretch of nineteen months at Aspsås. After he was released and had been using again for a while, he dropped to sixty.

He suddenly stood up, stumbling to find the remote control among the cards and newspapers on the table.

"Where the hell is it?"

"Play your cards now, dammit."

"Shut up! Where is it? The remote control. Dammit, Hilding, put down your cards and help me look!"

Hilding Oldéus immediately dropped his cards on the table, started nervously overturning newspapers that Tinyboy had just put down. Skinny, short, with a high-pitched voice. Ten stints in eleven years. A large sore on his right nostril, a chronic infection from incessantly scratching it while he was on heroin.

It wasn't on the table. Hilding searched aimlessly on the table and windowsills, while Tinyboy pushed the table aside, stepped straight between the irritated but silent card players, groping along the TV buttons to try to raise the volume manually.

"Shut up, girls! Hitler is on the tube."

Everyone in the TV corner, the kitchen, the hallway, they all stopped what they were doing and hurried toward Tinyboy, standing just behind him, watching the lunchtime newscast on the monitor. Someone whistled in delight as the screen switched to a new image.

"Shut up, I said!"

Lennart Oscarsson in front of a microphone. Aspsås prison in the background.

Oscarsson looked harried, he wasn't accustomed to TV cameras or to explaining why everything he was in charge of had gone to hell.

. . . *how could he escape*
. . . *as I said before*
. . . *the prison claims to be escape-proof*

. . . it didn't take place here

. . . what do you mean not here

. . . a guarded emergency visit to Söder Hospital

. . . what do you mean guarded

. . . two of our most experienced guards

. . . only two

. . . two of our most experienced guards and full-body chains

. . . who made that assessment

. . . he overpowered them both and

. . . who decided that two guards were sufficient

. . . and disappeared in the prison transport vehicle

A close-up on Oscarsson's face. Beads of sweat were running from the hairline above his forehead—the camera was enjoying his nakedness. Television was about surface and the moment, but you felt it in the gut, like now. His eyes roamed, he swallowed, he'd taken management training courses for the camera, but this was the real thing and he was thinking too long and stammering too much, forgetting to repeat the answers he'd practiced. Decide on a single answer and repeat it no matter what the question is. He knew the basic rules of the interview, but in front of a camera and those insistent reporters, and a microphone pushed into his face, that knowledge was drowned out by his fear of the people watching the news in Alvesta and Gällivare.

"What a fucking loser!"

Hilding's penetrating voice shattered the silence, but Tinyboy had given him a command.

"Hitler's fucking gone!"

Tinyboy took a hasty step forward, punched him hard, a fist to the back of the head.

"Shut up! Are you having trouble understanding me today? I'm listening to this!"

Hilding wriggled uneasily in his chair, ripped viciously at the sore on his nose, but said nothing. He'd learned this on his very first stint in here. Eight months for robbing a 7-Eleven in Stockholm.

Seventeen, stoned out of his mind, panic-stricken, he threatened a young shop assistant with a kitchen knife, took the two five-hundred-kronor bills from the cash register, then made a deal with a drug dealer standing just outside the store. Hilding was still there when the police arrived. He'd learned—when prison was still threatening and unfamiliar—to lick the ass of the person who was in charge of your unit; ingratiation meant safety, and he was tired of being afraid. He'd licked Tinyboy's ass twice before, once at Mariefred prison in '98 and again at Frituna outside Norrköping in '99. Tinyboy was no worse than anybody else.

The screen switched images again. Oscarsson's tormented eyes lingered, though for another reason: the Aspsås wall was in the distance, as the camera moved in slow motion over the edge of the wall to the sky and back again, the clichés of a quickly produced news report. A voice, factual bordering on dry, explained that Bernt Lund had escaped during a supervised furlough this morning, that he'd been arrested and convicted four years earlier for a series of brutal rapes of minors, which culminated with the so-called "basement murders" of two nine-year-old girls, that he'd served those years in isolation at Kumla and was recently moved to one of the special departments for sex offenders at Aspsås to serve out the rest of his time there, that he was considered very dangerous, and that in the interest of public safety they were showing pictures of him.

Bernt Lund was smiling. He was sitting in shirt and pants and smiling at the camera in black-and-white stills. Tinyboy took a few more steps forward, stood in front of the TV screen.

"Fuck. Fuck! It's that perv whose ass I kicked at the gym yesterday! It *is* that fucking bastard!"

Tinyboy screamed his anger, those closest to him jumped up, moved a bit farther away. They'd seen him flip out over the sex offenders before.

"What the hell are they even doing here? Why the hell do they have that fucking pervert unit here?"

Tinyboy screamed, pushing away memories. That's how *he* had done it. Every time. At home, in the house in Svedmyra. Those fucking images. His uncle. At his father's funeral. He was five years old and felt Per stroke his back, down over his butt.

"I'll cut their dicks off!"

The images blocked his thoughts. He had to think them, see them, live through them again and again. Per said they were going to go into Daddy's office. He held his hand on the outside of Tinyboy's suit pants. He pulled them down, first the pants, then the underwear. Then he pulled down his own pants. He pressed himself against him, touched his ass with his penis.

"One by one, goddammit, Hilding, help me cut their dicks off!"

He cleared his throat, collecting saliva, spat on the TV screen, on Bernt Lund's black-and-white face. He watched as the spit flowed slowly over the frozen smile, fell from the glass screen to the floor.

The crowd dispersed. One to his cell, one down the corridor, one picked up the cards from the table. Tinyboy sat down again, in the same chair, waved off Hilding as he handed him the cards. It was as if the images refused to leave, could not be resisted. He screamed and he focused and he hit his hands hard against his thigh as image after image pierced his defenses.

Per again. In their summer house in Blekinge. The big hands did what they'd done last time, and he was bleeding profusely from his bottom. He hid his underwear so that Mom wouldn't see—she never looked in the cupboard in the shed.

"Tiny, dammit, you should come and play."

"Lay off. You'll have to play without me."

"Forget about Hitler now."

"Leave me the fuck alone. Otherwise, I'll give you another beating."

He was thirteen years old. He was high as hell on speed and beer. Larren, who was big and never afraid, was with him. They hitch-hiked down to Blekinge and climbed into the cabin. Laila was in the kitchen washing the dishes, and Per sat in the living room. They didn't understand what was happening, even when Larren held him while Tinyboy hacked at Per's scrotum with an ice pick.

"Full house!"

"What do you mean full house?"

"Eights and sixes."

"That's not a fucking full house."

"It is too a full house. Tinyboy, explain it to this asshole."

"I'm not playing. Didn't I already say that? You'll have to play on your own."

Keys rattled. Two guards on the other side of the door.

Tinyboy looked in their direction. They had somebody with them. Somebody new. Surely here to fill Bojan's empty cell. He'd been moved to Hall yesterday morning—he had been in a precarious situation and someone had warned the guards, and management acted immediately. There'd been no blood in this unit, not for a long time.

The new guy was a big bastard. Shaved head, tanned as hell, a sunbed fag. Tinyboy sighed loudly and looked at him as he walked through the door, the guards on either side of him, as if he had his own escort. The new guy stared straight ahead, said nothing, saw nothing. The guards showed him to his cell, Bojan's old one, but left the doors wide open.

"What kind of clown is that?"

Tinyboy pointed in the direction of the new guy. Hilding took a deep breath, looked like he was thinking, searching through his previous stints.

"I don't know. Never seen the bastard before. Have you?"

Dragan shook his head. Skåne shrugged his shoulders. Bekir picked up two cards from the table.

"Forget him. Play now, I have good cards!"

Tinyboy didn't take his eyes off the new guy's door. He was waiting. He usually did that, waited until they came out and then told them the lay of the land.

———

An hour and twenty minutes. Then he came out.

"You, come here!"

Tinyboy waved his hand as a command. The new guy heard him, stared straight ahead, ignoring the voice that was demanding his presence at the end of the corridor. He walked slowly, almost deliberately, into the kitchen, drank some water from the tap, put his big shiny head under the stream of water.

"You there, come here!"

Tinyboy was annoyed. This was his unit. He decided if someone answered him or not.

"Come here!"

Tinyboy pointed at the floor in front of him. He waited. The new guy stood completely still.

"Now!"

The new guy didn't get it—he really didn't get it. The silence was almost palpable to Hilding, and he glanced uneasily at Tinyboy, picked up the deck, and raised a finger to the others, telling them to wait. Dragan and Skåne and Bekir had already understood. There was going to be a fight, and they weren't a part of it. They had front-row seats and high hopes, and they, too, could feel the silent tension.

The new guy started moving. Toward Tinyboy. They were hunting each other. He walked over to the place on the floor Tinyboy was pointing to, then past it, and stopped with just a few centimeters between them.

Tinyboy had never lowered his eyes. He wasn't about to do that now either. The new guy was taller than him. He had a huge scar, like a halter from his left ear to his mouth, sharp and deep. Tinyboy had seen similar ones made by a knife or a razor blade.

"My name is Tinyboy."

"And?"

"We like to introduce ourselves around here."

"Fuck you."

The images of Per and Larren and a scrotum bleeding like hell and Aunt Laila, who was screaming at the kitchen sink while he ran around with the ice pick asking if Per wanted more, if he wanted it somewhere else. Per had been weeping, Tinyboy was taking aim at his eyes, when Larren let go of Per. Not the eyes. That was Larren's limit.

Tinyboy shook. He tried to hide it, but everyone saw. He shook and hesitated and spat, but on the floor this time.

"Where you from?"

The new guy yawned. Twice.

"Jail."

"I know you fucking came from jail. Do you have your verdict with you?"

Three times.

"Tinyturd, is that what they call you? You know damn well I can't take my verdict with me into the unit."

Tinyboy starting rocking, weight on his right leg, weight on his left leg. Per had died a long time ago, and he had died without his balls, and the ice pick had been confiscated, evidence that went to the reformatory.

"I don't care whether or not you can take your verdict with you! I wanna know what the hell you're in for—I don't want any fucking pervs or snitches in here!"

It's strange how a room can seem cramped, how letters become words become messages and bounce off the walls, taking all the space, all the power, as if nothing else exists other than breath and silence and waiting.

The new guy couldn't get any closer, but somehow he did. He hissed small droplets of saliva between them.

"Are you looking for an adventure?"

Someone had to give in, look down at the floor, or turn away. But they just stood there.

"Because there's one thing I'm gonna make damn clear to you, Tinyturd. Nobody, and I mean nobody, calls me a snitch or a perv. And if some junkie loser does, then things won't turn out well for him."

The new guy poked Tinyboy in the chest with a long outstretched finger. He did it several times, and hard. He was still hissing, but speaking jail Romani now.

"*Honkar di rotepa, buråbeng.*"

He poked Tinyboy one more time in the chest and then turned around, walked back to his cell just a short distance away, and left the door wide open.

Tinyboy stood completely still. He followed him with a blank expression, watched him disappear behind the door, and then looked at Hilding and the others, shouting at a deserted corridor.

"What the fuck. What the fuck!"

An open door and a middle finger poking at his chest.

Tinyboy shouted again.

"Fuck, *racklar di Romani, tjavon?*"

FIRST THE BASTARD had looked him in the eye, then threatened him, then poked him in the chest. *Nobody calls me a snitch or a perv. And if some junkie loser does, then things won't turn out well for him.* And then he'd gone to his cell, leaving the door open, and refused to come out again. Tinyboy had waited in the corridor for an hour until Hilding ventured over, tapped him in the back, and whispered *it's here.* Now they were both sitting on a toilet with their hands on a piece of tinfoil, swatting each other's fingers out of the way.

Inside was a flat brown square of something.

They'd ordered Turkish Glass. It had one hell of a kick and the best high. They were trying to fly through Aspsås and Unit H and the hours of waiting. They were trying to get through it.

They'd ordered this from the Greek, and paid for half when he delivered. Now they owed him more than was good for them. They should have made do with Pressed Moroccan or Yellow Lebanese, but Hilding had nagged and pleaded and licked ass and Tinyboy had given in; they'd placed the order for Turkish Glass and waited three days. Now, they smiled at the small, glowing pieces of glass as they lifted the hash into the light of the bathroom.

"You see, Tiny?"

"Of course I see."

"It's so . . . beautiful."

Tinyboy held the lighter's flame underneath the foil. One minute was usually enough. The flat brown square turned into a soft mass, and he crushed and shaped it with his fingers. Hilding kept his tobacco in the outer pocket of his prison-issued coat. They usually made their joints 75 percent tobacco.

"Smells good."

"Fucking hell, Tiny."

Hilding stood on tiptoe and pressed his hands against one of the ceiling tiles, the one closest to the lamp. After a few seconds it gave way easily, and he reached in and fished out a corn pipe. Tinyboy packed his pipe, inhaled as he lit it, inhaled again, then handed it to Hilding, who hurriedly pushed it into his mouth.

They took two drags at a time, then passed the pipe, two more drags. It was quiet in the shower room, a couple of sinks dripping, one of the overhead lights blinking, *drip drip blink blink blink drip.* It was good Turkish Glass, even better than last time.

"Holy shit, Hilding Wilding, motherfucker."

Tinyboy took two more drags and passed the pipe. He giggled.

"You know what, Hilding Wilding? We're sitting in a fucking shower room smoking good hash and it didn't even occur to us that this is the perfect place to get rid of a perv."

"What are you talking about?"

"And we didn't even think about it."

"Are you talking about this fucking shower room? We sure as hell've whipped enough rapists and snitches in here. How new is that? In the joint in America, they butt-fuck each other by the sinks."

Tinyboy couldn't stop giggling. That's how Turkish Glass worked, first he got giggly as hell, then he got horny as hell, and if he hadn't smoked for a while he became terrified of seeing it all over again, Per and his penis, and he would start searching for the ice pick and a bleeding scrotum.

He inhaled deeply, pipe in hand, held on to it to annoy Hilding while patting him on the head.

"You don't understand shit, Hilding Wilding, we should be doing a lot more than just kicking their asses."

Hilding reached toward the pipe, but Tinyboy pulled it back, holding on to it stubbornly.

"Listen. Next time we get a pervert in this unit, we'll wait the bastard out—wait until he goes into the shower. When he's in here, water all over him, you'll create a diversion out in the yard so that all the guards end up there."

Hilding wasn't listening. He was trying to get hold of the pipe, reaching toward it again.

"What the hell, it's my turn now."

Tinyboy giggled and threw the corn pipe into the air, almost to the ceiling, caught it, then gave it to Hilding, who took two long drags.

"Listen, I said. Now we have him in the shower. Then either me or Skåne go in and shiv him till he croaks. Then, we butcher him. We cut up the fucking bastard into tiny little pieces and crush his bones. And then we'll lift up the whole fucking john and wash every little fucking piece of him down into the drain in the floor. Then we put the toilet back on again and flush a few times. Wash the blood away with the shower."

Hilding had forgotten to smoke or to pass the pipe back again. He looked offended. His face, normally stripped of emotion, undefined, like he was wearing a mask with a fixed rigid expression, was now wavering between disgust and delight. He was aware of Tinyboy's hatred, and it was a trip to hate along with him, but Tinyboy was the kind who was always walking the line. Hilding remembered how he beat that dickhead in the gym with the weight plates and dumbbells until he wasn't moving anymore.

"Fuck, Tiny, you're joking."

Tinyboy grabbed the pipe, so happy when he was smoking.

"I'm not joking. Why the hell would I joke about that? I wanna try it. The first perv who comes in here, I wanna try. I wanna see if it works. I want to feel again what it's like to shove in the ice pick and twist it."

LENNART OSCARSSON RUSHED past the guard, Bergh, who waved and gave him a thumbs up. And Oscarsson couldn't decide if Bergh was being ironic or just didn't realize that the TV cameras had stripped Oscarsson naked.

He hurried through the first corridor, then decided halfway to swerve to the right and take the shortcut through Unit H.

He took two steps at a time, thinking that they'd done everything they could: cognitive therapy, medication, group and individual therapy. Bernt Lund had been offered everything and still took the very first chance he got. He was thinking about Åke Andersson and Ulrik Berntfors, who Oscarsson had worked with for many years, and who, for some unknown reason, had opened the back door of the van and let out one of this country's most dangerous human beings. Thinking about Bernt Lund, who was free now and on the hunt for little girls, thinking about the press conference he'd been preparing for for years, the one that should have been his spring-board but instead felt more like a rape.

No one had touched his privates, but the camera and microphone still felt like a violation.

He had thought of himself as a willing participant, and so he believed he wouldn't be completely deserted, but now he realized he was being used by somebody else for somebody else's purposes.

He thought about the hours that had passed since he woke up this morning.

Thought, did life have to be so fucking complicated?

Sometimes it felt like he couldn't take it anymore. Middle age was pushing him toward old age, and he couldn't keep up. There was no time for reflection, it would always be later, later, often he would just close his eyes. He wanted to close his eyes now and know that everything was over, someone else had decided and everything was clear—like when he was little, he'd sat in the middle of the floor and closed his eyes while Mom and Dad worked on their home, and when he opened his eyes again, they were done. Something happened while he waited quietly, refusing to participate. Someone else had taken care of it, and all he had to do was close his eyes for a moment, and it would be over.

He unlocked the door to Unit H. He knew that both his colleagues and the inmates disliked it, no fucking unnecessary running, but it was a shortcut, and he was in a hurry. He said hello to one of the guards without remembering his name, nodded to some of the inmates who were playing cards in the TV corner. He passed the door to the shower room and was centimeters from running straight into Tinyboy Lindgren and his lackey. They were high as kites. Their staring eyes, their flapping movements, he could even smell it coming from the showers. The lackey mumbled *Howdy, Hitler* and Tinyboy Lindgren giggled and tried to congratulate him on his TV appearance. Lennart Oscarsson pretended not to see the outstretched hand. He knew as well as the rest of the staff that Lindgren had beaten up one of his inmates in the gym, but no one had seen anything or heard anything, so without proof they couldn't do a thing, not even in a prison.

Through the next locked door, down the stairs, out into the yard, over to the next building, up the two flights of stairs to Units A and B, the sex offenders, his domain.

They were waiting for him. In a line in the meeting room.

"Excuse me. I'm late. Far too late. I've just had so much on my plate today."

They smiled, wanting to express some kind of compassion, because they had also seen him on TV. It was still on when he walked by. Five new trainees who, starting tomorrow, would begin their jobs in the two units for pedophiles and rapists. They sat with pencil and pad at the oval table. This was the first day of their new lives.

"Perv."

He usually started that way. He pulled the cap off a green marker, which smelled strongly, and wrote in capital letters on the glossy whiteboard.

"P-E-R-V."

The five temps sat in silence. Fiddling with their pens, hesitating, should I write this down? Is it good to take notes or am I giving myself away? They were lost beginners, and he wasn't helping them. He continued talking and occasionally wrote something on the board, a main point, a number.

"They live here. For two to ten years, depending on what they've done, how sick they are."

Still silence. It was longer than usual.

"Fifty thousand convictions—the amount of criminal cases last year in this shitty little country. How do we keep up? I can't understand it. Out of those, five hundred and forty-seven were sexual offenses. Less than half made it all the way to prison."

A few took notes. Numbers were easier. Statistics demanded no opinion.

"If we know, then, that at any given moment there are approximately five thousand people in Swedish prisons, two hundred and twelve sex offenders shouldn't pose any problems. Right? Four percent. One out of twenty-five. But that's exactly what they do. They are problems. They are risk. They are hate. Therefore, they have their own units. Like here. But sometimes, sometimes there just isn't room. Then they end up on a waiting list, then we have to sneak them into a normal unit for a while. And if and when the other inmates realize there's a perv serving in their unit, they'll attack him. They beat him to a pulp until we intervene."

A man in his forties, retrained from something else, raised his hand as if he were in a classroom.

"Perv? You both said it and wrote it."

"Yes?"

"Is it important?"

"I don't know. We call them that here. That's what you'll be calling them within a day or two. Because that's what this is about. Wham bam thank you, ma'am."

Lennart Oscarsson waited. He knew what was coming next. He wondered which of them would start. He guessed it would be a younger woman near the front. She looked like the type. The young were the ones with the furthest to go. They still believed that change was possible. They didn't understand time, which took your life and energy and, in exchange, gave you experience and compromise.

He was wrong. It was the man again, who was retrained from something else.

"Why so cynical?"

He was upset.

"I don't understand. During our training, I learned what I already knew. That people aren't objects. That you, my future boss, have this kind of attitude scares me."

Oscarsson sighed. He'd been through this performance several times before. He usually ran across them later, a few years older and in some other prison after they'd advanced to a new job. They usually joked as they recalled it, and defended these exchanges as a beginner's unfulfilled ambitions.

"You can think what you want. That's your right. Call me cynical if that's what gets you going. But answer this first: Have you come to Aspsås prison's sex offender department because you want to see pervs as more than objects, because your dream is to change them?"

The man, who tomorrow would commence his duties in Unit A, slowly lowered his hand and sat quietly.

"I didn't hear you. Is that correct?"

"No."

"Then why?"

"I was ordered here."

The principal prison officer tried not to show how pleased he was. He felt the performance was over. That was his main role. He gazed at them in silence, all five, one by one. One fidgeted, one kept writing down numbers, diligently recording them in a notebook.

"Honestly now. Is there anyone here who joined this unit voluntarily?"

After seventeen years at Aspsås he had yet to meet a single colleague whose professional dream ended among the pedophiles in Units A and B. You were ordered here. You applied from here. He, himself, had become the boss. Better pay and the hope of advancing to the next management position elsewhere. He walked slowly behind the five new employees in the conference room, leaving the last question unanswered so that they would comprehend and formulate their own answers. Only then would they understand and accept their placement in the coming months. He stopped at the window with his back to his students. The sun was high. It hadn't rained for a long time. The inmates kicked up dust as they walked in the exercise yard. A few were playing football, others jogged along the barbed wire. In one corner, two were walking jerky and slow. He recognized Lindgren and his lackey, still high on hash.

MICAELA HAD LEFT early. He must have been asleep then. Night after night, the same ritual: just as the city woke up outside his window, right after he'd heard the first newspaper delivered and the first trucks arriving, he finally fell asleep close to five thirty. Hours of thoughts crowded into an exhausted body until, finally, the restlessness could no longer resist, and he fell asleep, dreaming in a void until late morning.

Fredrik had some bleary images of the morning: Micaela lying naked on top of him, and him not being up for it, and her whispering "bore" and kissing him lightly on the cheek before going to the bathroom. Marie's room was on the other side of the wall from the tub, and she usually woke up when Micaela showered. When the water pushed forward along the pipes, it made a screeching sound. This morning David had also been there. Micaela had made breakfast for herself and the two children while Fredrik stayed in bed, his legs refusing to get up and keep them company, until he slipped into the void and the dreams again. He didn't wake up again until just after eleven, when Marie changed the video and cartoon characters started screaming in falsetto.

He had to start sleeping at night. This wasn't working anymore. It just wasn't.

He wasn't writing, and he wasn't participating in other people's lives. The morning had been when he did most of his writing, from eight until just after lunch. There wasn't time now to drive from Strängnäs to his writing space in Arnö, a fifteen-minute drive every morning and afternoon. Marie had gotten good at spending the morning hours by herself, and Micaela, who thankfully worked at Marie's nursery school, made sure, day after day, that the other staff were friendly to the child who never showed up until lunchtime.

He was ashamed.

He felt like an alcoholic who'd sworn himself to sobriety the night before, then woken up the next morning with a hangover. He was tired, had a headache, and felt anxious to start another day with the promise that today things would change.

"Hello."

His daughter stood in front of him. He lifted her up.

"Hello, my darling girl. Do I get a kiss?"

Marie put a wet mouth against his cheek.

"David left."

"Did he?"

"His dad was here to get him."

They know me, he thought. They know I'll take responsibility. They know that. He shook off his uneasiness, sat Marie down on the floor.

"Have you eaten?"

"Micaela fed us."

"That was a long time ago. Do you want more?"

"I want to eat at school."

It was a quarter past one. How long was the school open? Were they still serving lunch? Getting dressed took ten minutes, and they could drive there. The journey took five minutes. One thirty. They'd be there by one thirty.

"Okay. Let's get dressed. You can eat at school."

Fredrik searched for a pair of jeans in his closet. A white shirt was lying on the chair. It was hot outside, but he hated shorts. His pale legs looked silly. Marie ran through the hall with a T-shirt and a pair of shorts in her hand. He gave her a thumbs up and helped her turn her shirt right side out.

"Good. What shoes?"

"The red ones."

"Then red ones it is."

He lifted her feet one at a time, unbuttoned two buttons on a decorative metal buckle. They were ready.

The phone.

"It's ringing, Daddy."

"We don't have time."

"Yes, we do."

Marie ran into the kitchen, just barely reached the phone on the wall next to the refrigerator. She said *hello* and lit up, someone she liked. She whispered to her father.

"It's Mommy."

He nodded. Marie told her mother about the Big Bad Wolf chasing her yesterday and about how the little pigs had won and the Donald Duck shampoo that had run out and how she'd known that there were two in the bathroom cabinet on the bottom shelf. She laughed and kissed the phone and handed it to him.

"For you, Daddy. Mommy wants to talk."

He still wasn't awake. He stood up and held the phone to his ear, but his body was having a hard time distinguishing between the voice of the woman on the phone, whose name was Agnes, who he'd once desired more than anyone in the world, who'd asked him to leave, and the woman who just a few hours ago had been naked on top of him, whose name was Micaela, sixteen years younger than him, and who'd just left. He could still feel Micaela's naked body and hear Agnes's voice over the phone and was both here and there, and it made him dizzy, he couldn't breathe, and he got hard. He turned around, so Marie wouldn't see.

"Yes?"

"When are you coming?"

"Coming?"

"Marie is supposed to be with me today."

"No."

"What do you mean, no?"

"She'll be with you on Monday. We swapped, right? Right?"

"No, we didn't. Not now. Not today."

"Agnes, I can't. I'm tired and in a hurry, and Marie is standing next to me. I'm not going to argue while she's listening."

He gave Marie the phone again, spinning his hands around, their sign for hurry.

"Mommy, I don't have time. We have to go to school."

Agnes was smart enough not to take her irritation out on Marie. She never had. He loved her for it.

"Now, Mommy."

Marie stretched up on tiptoe and hung up the phone. It fell down, banging against the microwave on the counter. Fredrik took a step forward, picked it up, hung it up on the wall.

"Okay, honey. Let's hurry."

They walked through the kitchen. He looked at the clock above the dining table. One twenty-five. They'd get there by one thirty. She could stay there until a quarter past five. Then she'd be able to both eat a late lunch and play outside for a few hours in the afternoon. She'd be satisfied—almost as if she'd been there a full day—by the time he picked her up again.

ONE THIRTY. SVEN Sundkvist looked at a green alarm clock standing on Ewert Grens's desk. His shift had been over a couple of hours ago. He had the wine and cake in his car. He just wanted to go home, to Anita and Jonas. Have a calm dinner. He was turning forty today.

It was as if his work, the days and nights he spent at the City Police, just wasn't that important anymore. Until recently, he'd been prepared to do his duty, even on his wedding night, to choose divorce rather than compromising on the evening shift. He'd talked a bit with Ewert about it lately. They'd become closer during this year. Sven had tried to explain this forbidden feeling, how he'd ceased to care about which madman did what and whether said madman was headed to prison or not. As if he was finished, at the age of forty, waiting for retirement, the rest of it. Now all he wanted was to lie on his patio and eat breakfast in peace and quiet, go for long walks along Årsta Bay, be at home when Jonas came running from school with his whole life in his backpack. He'd been working for twenty years. He was supposed to work for another twenty-five years. He sighed heavily. He just would not, could not, was not able to accept how his life was flying by in a lousy police station surrounded by increasingly thick binders of open investigations. Jonas would be thirty-two on the day his father retired. How the hell would they ever have time to spend together then?

Ewert understood. He had no family. His days in uniform were all he had. He ate and drank and breathed police work. But he also knew what Sven knew, saw the insignificance of giving yourself over completely to a job that would come to an end one day. He often talked about how he, too, would cease to be one day. He understood, but he didn't have the urge to care.

"Ewert."

"Yes?"

"I want to go home."

Ewert was kneeling on the floor for a second time picking up the contents of his trash can. Two of the banana peels had been crushed, leaving large stains on the beige carpet.

"I know you do. And you know we'll be going home when we have Lund in custody again."

He lifted his head, trying to see above the desktop's edge, looking for the clock.

"Six and a half hours. And we don't know shit. It may be some time before you get to eat your cake."

"Pick Up the Pieces," with a full choir and orchestra, recorded in Sweden in 1963. Siw Malmkvist playing from the third mixtape, the one with a photo of Siw on its plastic case, a big blurry smile aimed at the adoring camera.

"I took that picture myself. Did I tell you that? At Folkets Park in Kristianstad, in 1972."

He walked over to Sven, who was still sitting in the visitor's chair, leaned toward him, and threw up his arm.

"May I have this dance?"

Without waiting for an answer, he turned around for a few quick dance steps. A remarkable sight, the half-lame Grens swinging around his desk to the music of the early '60s and the heyday of the Swedish welfare state.

———

They took Sven's car. Grens had moved the cake box and the plastic bag with the expensive wine bottles from the passenger seat to the shelf in the rear window. They headed out from the police station toward route E18. The streets of the capital were empty. The heat had forced people to take their summer vacations at the beach with its cool water. The dark asphalt reflected what life there was, as if all breath were bouncing off its hard surface.

Sundkvist drove fast. First going through two yellow lights and then two red. The few cars waiting for the signal to turn green honked angrily. There was a nationwide alert. They had two dozen Stockholm police officers at their disposal. But they still didn't know a thing.

"He licks their feet."

Grens had been silent since Sven started the engine—now he stared straight ahead as he spoke.

"I've never seen anything like it before. I've seen children raped, children murdered, even children worked over by sharp metallic objects, but I've never seen this. They were thrown onto the concrete floor. They were filthy, bloody, but their feet were clean and the medical examiners determined that there were several layers of saliva on them—he'd spent minutes licking their feet before he killed them."

Sven increased his speed. The plastic bag slid from one side of the back window to the other, the bottles rattled monotonously.

"Every piece of their clothing was placed on the floor—two centimeters apart. The final pieces were their shoes. One pair of pink patent-leather shoes, one pair of white trainers. The clothes were as dirty as the girls. Dust, dirt, blood. But not the shoes. They shone. Even more layers of saliva. He spent a long time on those."

Not even E18 was especially busy. Sven stayed in the left lane, passing the few cars on the road at high speed. He didn't have the energy to talk, to ask any more questions about Lund; he didn't want to know more, not right now. He almost drove past the exit, slammed on the brakes at the last moment, rammed the car across three lanes and onto the smaller road to Aspsås.

Lennart Oscarsson was waiting in the parking lot for them.

He looked stressed, nervous, a little hunted. The scapegoat. He'd just been stripped naked on television. He also knew exactly how Ewert Grens felt about the decision to let two lone prison guards transport Bernt Lund through the capital in the middle of the night.

"Hello."

Grens waited a second too long to stretch out his hand, enjoyed letting one of the many idiots who surrounded him suffer for a moment.

"Hello."

Oscarsson met his hand, dropped it quickly, looked at the driver's seat.

"Hello. I'm Lennart Oscarsson. I don't think we've met."

"Sven. Sven Sundkvist."

They all walked toward the large gate of Aspsås prison, which opened as they approached it. The central guard recognized Grens and exchanged a nod with him, but ignored Sven.

"Where are you going?"

Oscarsson stopped, went back to the window, annoyed.

"He's with me. From the City Police."

"He hasn't been cleared."

"They're investigating Lund."

"I have no interest in that. What I am interested in is why he wasn't cleared."

Sundkvist interrupted Oscarsson, who was about to start yelling something he would probably regret later.

"Here. My ID. Okay?"

The guard studied the picture of Sven on his ID for a long time, then input his social security number into a database.

"It's your birthday today."

"Yep."

"Then what are you doing here?"

"Are you going to let me in?"

The guard waved him past, and they walked one by one into the first corridor. Grens laughed out loud.

"With that guy on duty, it's harder to get in than to get out."

They walked down the basement corridor. Grens looked around and sighed at walls that looked like every wall in every basement of every Swedish prison. Long murals of varying quality, art therapy projects for inmates done under the supervision of consultants. Always a blue background, always the same overexplicit symbols: prison gates flung open and birds in the sky.

Some dirty doodles signed by Benke Lelle Hinken Zoran Jari Geten, 1987.

Oscarsson was holding his key ring, opening metal door after metal door. They passed a rowdy crowd of prisoners on their way to the gym with two guards in front of them and two behind. Grens sighed again. He'd run into some of them before. Some he'd interrogated, others he'd testified against, and a few of the old ones he'd picked up back when he was still patrolling the streets.

"Howdy, Grens. You taking a walk?"

Stig Lindgren, one of the inhabitants in the Society of Outcasts, who'd never be able to live anywhere except behind these walls—might as well lock him up and throw away the key. Grens was weary of that type.

"Shut your mouth, Lindgren, or I'll tell your friends why they call you Tinyboy."

Up a flight of stairs, into Unit A. The sexual offenders' section. Lennart Oscarsson was a few steps ahead; Sundkvist and Grens walked more slowly, observing their surroundings. It looked like any other unit. Same TV corner, same pool table, kitchen, and cells. The difference was that the crime that landed you here provoked the same hate in the Society of Outcasts as it did anywhere else. For prisoners in this unit, ending up in the wrong part of this building might mean a death sentence.

Oscarsson pointed to a cell door. Number eleven. A blank surface. All the other doors had been decorated by whoever had been living behind them. Posters, newspaper clippings, an occasional photo. But not cell number eleven.

Grens felt like he should have been here already, behind that door, six months ago. In Lund's cell. He'd been investigating a child pornography ring, his first real glimpse into a new sealed kingdom of pedophiles, which existed among databases and network connections. He'd seen pictures of children, pictures he'd never known existed: naked children, penetrated children, humiliated, tortured children. A child pornography ring that he and his colleagues at the commission initially suspected was located abroad, pedophilia and profit and dark agreements, but soon proved to be far more limited, sophisticated, and challenging.

There had been seven of them.

An exalted company of repeat sex offenders. Some locked up, but most had been recently released.

They'd created their own virtual showroom. Collections that were channeled through computers and networks on a schedule, as if they were TV programs. Every week, at the same time, Saturday at eight o'clock. They'd been sitting at their computers, waiting for that week's set of photos with ever-increasing demands—each show had to be more extreme than the last, naked children weren't enough for them anymore. The children had to touch each other, the children who'd touched each other had to be raped, the children who had been raped had to be raped even more—each photo had to outdo the last. Seven pedophiles, a closed company, custom illustrations of the pedophiles' own crimes, neatly scanned and sent.

They'd been at it for almost a year before they were discovered.

It was as if they were competing at child pornography.

Bernt Lund had been one of the seven. The only one in prison and, therefore, allowed to send old, previously captured images from the computer in the library, using a mobile hotspot he smuggled in—given his crimes, his right to participate was indisputable. Since their discovery, three of the others had been sentenced to long prison terms. A fourth, Håkan Axelsson, was still being prosecuted. The evidence they had against the other two was weaker. They would probably be able to avoid indictment. Everyone knew, but it didn't matter—if you can't prove it, it didn't happen, and in the meantime, they could make new contacts in the shadow of the investigation, lay the groundwork for a new child pornography ring.

There were many of them out there, and if one left, a new one would step in.

Ewert blamed himself. He should have visited Lund's cell during the preliminary investigation. They'd been pressed for time, under the pressure of outraged public opinion, so against his better judgment, he'd refrained from personally going to Aspsås. Instead, he sent two younger colleagues to visit Lund in a cell containing a stash of CD-ROMs bearing thousands of images of violated children. If he himself had gone to cell number eleven in the sex offenders' unit, then he might know more right now. If he'd actually been in Lund's presence back then, maybe he wouldn't be standing here now, facing so much uncertainty, with no lead on him.

"Here."

Oscarsson turned the key, opened the door.

"As you can see, a methodical man."

Sundkvist and Grens entered the cell and stopped abruptly. A very strange room. Outwardly similar to the neighboring cells. A window, a bed, a cupboard, some shelves, a sink, roughly eight square meters. It was the rest. Candlesticks, stones, pieces of wood, pens, bits of string, clothes, binders, batteries, books, notepads. Everything lined up. Along the floor, on the crisply made bed, on the windowsill, on the shelves. Like an exhibition. Two centimeters between each object. Like dominoes in one never-ending line, where if one thing were moved, it would fall over.

Grens searched his jacket pocket. He had a short ruler on the side of his diary. He went over to the bed and laid the pocket diary along the row of stones. Two centimeters. No more, no less. He measured the gap from pen to pen on the windowsill. Two centimeters. On the shelves the books were two centimeters apart, on the floor the pieces of string were two centimeters from the batteries, two centimeters from the notebooks, two centimeters from the cigarette pack.

"Does it always look like this?"

Oscarsson nodded.

"Yes. Always. When he goes to bed at night, he puts every stone on the floor in a new line. Measures the distance. In the morning he does it again, makes the bed, lifts up every stone, puts them onto the cover again, exactly two centimeters apart."

Sven moved a few pens. Completely ordinary pens. He turned a few of the rocks this way and that. Common rocks, each one more meaningless than the last. The folders, the notebooks. Nothing. The folders were empty shells, the notebooks pristine, not a page had been used. He turned toward Oscarsson.

"I don't understand."

"What is there to understand?"

"I don't know. Something. Why would a man lick children's feet?"

"Why do you think you have to understand?"

"I want to know where he is. Where he's on his way to. I just want to get hold of the bastard, so I can go home and eat my cake and get drunk."

"Sorry. You'll never understand. There is nothing rational about it. Not even he knows why he licks dead feet. I don't think he has any idea why he puts things in a line two centimeters apart, either."

Grens held his diary, put his thumb behind the dash that marked two centimeters. He lifted it to face level, and they were all forced to look at his thumb and two centimeters.

"Control. Just that. That's how it is with all of them. They enjoy rape because they are in control. Power and control. This one is just more extreme. But that's what the stones in a row are all about. Order. Structure. Control."

He lowered his diary to the bed, held it behind the line of stones, then quickly pulled it forward, and they all fell down on the floor, one by one.

"We know that. He's a sadist. We also know that power gives Lund's type a hard-on. That's how it works. When he's in power, when someone else is powerless, when he's the one deciding whether he'll hurt them and how much. That's what gets him off. That's why he ejaculates in front of bound and bruised nine-year-olds."

At the windowsill, the pens in a row, he did the same thing as before, used his diary to push them down onto the radiator.

"By the way, the pictures in the computer. How had he organized them?"

Oscarsson looked at the pens on the floor for a long time, pushing them into a pile, disordering them, then at Grens, startled, as if the question were a strange one.

"Organized? What do you mean?"

"How were they sorted? I don't remember. I remember their faces, eyes, how alone they were. But not the distance between them."

"I don't know. I really don't know. But I can find out. If you think it's important."

"Yeah. It's important."

———————

They turned the cell upside down. They touched and sniffed every nook of Bernt Lund's home for the last four years.

There was no information there. He'd had no plan to escape.

He didn't know he was on his way to somewhere else.

FREDRIK STEFFANSSON OPENED the car door. He knew he'd been driving too fast through Strängnäs, seventy over Tosterö Bridge, where the speed limit was only thirty, but he'd promised Marie that they'd be there by half past one.

She had to go to nursery school so Daddy could work. A lie today and a lie yesterday. She was there to hold her place, because it was part of his image as a father who worked hard, who wrote and needed to be alone to think important thoughts. He hadn't thought any big thoughts in months. He hadn't written a word in weeks. He had a block and no idea how to solve it.

That was why Frans, and the memory of that beating, haunted him at night. It was why he couldn't make love to the beautiful young woman who'd straddled him naked in his bed this morning, why he couldn't stop comparing her to a woman he had already lost, Agnes. As if the work, the writing, had kept him from reflecting and he couldn't anymore—really he'd always done just that, worked and worked and worked to keep from feeling. He had an engine inside him burning and pushing him forward, because if he was moving forward he was moving away from his past.

He parked on the street outside the school entrance. A turning zone, he'd gotten a ticket parking there before, but he didn't have the energy to keep looking for parking. He helped Marie out of her seat belt, opened the car door. It was even hotter outside. The sun was at its highest, and it was more than eighty-five degrees in the shade. An unusual Swedish summer, warm since May, with just a few cloudy or rainy days.

They walked toward the entrance. Marie was skipping in front of him, both feet right leg left leg both feet together. She was happy—Micaela and David and twenty-five other children, whose names he really should try to remember, were waiting inside.

They passed a park bench just outside the gate where the father of one of the children sat waiting. Fredrik recognized him and nodded slightly, without being able to connect him with one of the little faces jostling around inside.

Micaela was standing by the cloakroom. She kissed him, asked if he was awake, if he'd missed her. Yes, he said. I missed you. Had he? He didn't know. He missed her soft body at night when he couldn't sleep, he usually curled up close to her, feeling her warmth, and it made him less afraid. But during the day? Not often. He looked at her. She was young. Too young. Too beautiful. As if he wasn't enough for her. As if he wasn't worthy. A couple should be the same age. A couple should be equally beautiful. Did he really believe that? There was doubt deep inside. Like the beating, it was also there, deep inside. He'd wanted to be close to her after the divorce. She'd been standing there when he came and left Marie, day after day, and one day they'd walked together for a little bit, and he'd told her about the pain, about the loss, and she'd listened and they'd gone on more walks, and he'd continued to confide in her, and she'd continued to listen, and one day they'd gone home together to his house and made love all afternoon, while Marie and David played together in the living room on the other side of the closed door.

He helped Marie change her shoes. He unbuckled her red ones, put them on her shelf labeled with a striped elephant. That was her symbol. Other children had red fire trucks or football players or Disney characters, but she'd chosen an elephant and that was that. He put on her indoor shoes, white fabric.

"You shouldn't go, Daddy."

She held him tightly by the arm.

"But you wanted to come here, didn't you? And Micaela is here. And David."

"Stay. Please, Daddy."

He lifted her up, held her in his arms.

"But, honey, you know Daddy has to work."

Her eyes stared into his. She scrunched up her forehead. She looked at him pleadingly.

He sighed.

"Okay, Okay. I'll stay then. But just for a little while."

Marie stood beside him. She kissed her elephant. Ran her finger up its legs, across its back, onto its striped trunk. Fredrik turned to Micaela, making a silent gesture of resignation. It had been like this since she started, almost four years ago now, since Agnes had moved. He hoped each time would be the last, and that the next time he left her, said goodbye, that he could walk away without any guilt.

"And how long are you planning on staying today?"

The only thing they disagreed on. Micaela thought he should just leave, prove once and for all that even if he left right away, he'd be back later that afternoon to pick her up. She felt he had to stand a few tears, a little agony, but then it would pass, and Marie would get used to it. He'd respond by telling her that she'd didn't have any children of her own, so she couldn't really understand how it felt.

"A quarter of an hour. At the most."

Marie heard him.

"Daddy's gonna stay. Here. With me."

She held on even tighter to her father's arm. Only when David came running by, wearing watercolors on his face as war paint, shouting *come on*, did she let go of Fredrik's arm and run after. Micaela smiled.

"See. It's never been that fast. Now she's forgotten you."

She took a step forward, stood close to him.

"But not me."

A light kiss on the cheek, then she left, too. Fredrik stood there, uncertain, watching Micaela, watching Marie. He stepped into the playroom. Marie and David and three other children lay in a pile painting each other's faces, pretending to be Sioux Indians or something else. Fredrik waved to Marie, and she waved back. He walked away. The Indian warriors followed him as he opened the front door.

The sun shone directly in his face. A coffee in the shade? A newspaper in the square? He decided to go out to the island instead, to

Arnö, to his office. He would sit there and wait. Probably not write a word, but at least he'd be prepared, start the computer, read through his notes.

He opened the gate, nodded again to the father still sitting on the park bench, and continued toward his car.

HE LIKED THIS nursery. It looked exactly the same as it had four years ago. The small gate, the white picket fence, the blue shutters. He'd been sitting outside for four hours now. There had to be at least twenty children inside. He's seen children with their fathers and children with their mothers come and go, one by one. No child had arrived by herself. It was a shame. It was easier if they were alone.

Three girls had trainers. Two had on some kind of sandals, the kind with long leather straps that went up their legs. Some had arrived barefoot. It was, of course, unbearably hot today, but going barefoot, he didn't like it. One had on red patent shoes with metal buckles. Those were the most beautiful. She'd arrived late, almost half past one, and she'd been with her father. She was a fair-haired little slut, with natural curls, who tossed her head as she spoke with her dad. Not a lot of clothes, a pair of shorts and a simple T-shirt, she must have dressed herself. She seemed happy—sluts are often happy. She'd skipped all the way up to the front door, alternating between two feet together and then one foot. Her father had nodded at him, greeting him. He'd nodded back, that's being polite. When he came back—he'd been inside a little longer than the others—he nodded again.

He tried to see the slut through the window. Several heads passed by the window, but not those blond curls. She was surely looking for cock. Sluts want a lot of cock. She was hiding inside the house, with her T-shirt, her shorts, her red patent shoes with metal buckles, her legs bare. Sluts like showing skin.

TINYBOY SAT IN the TV corner of Unit H. He was tired. He always felt tired after smoking. The better the hash the more tired he got, and Turkish Glass made him the most tired of all. That shit was fucking good. The Greek had delivered on his promise. He'd said it was the best shit he had, and Tinyboy believed it—he'd rarely smoked better, and his experience was extensive. He looked at Hilding, who'd just been Hilding Wilding, but who now lay half asleep. It had been a long time since his face looked that peaceful. He wasn't even scratching at that damn scab on his nose. The hand he usually had on his face lay still against his knee. Tinyboy leaned over to him, hit him on the shoulder. Hilding woke up, and Tinyboy gave him the thumbs up. Thumbs up and an index finger pointing at the shower room. They had more in there under the tile next to the ceiling lamp, at least enough to get high twice more. Hilding understood and smiled. He returned the thumbs up and then sank down into the chair again.

There'd been a hell of a lot of commotion in their unit today. First, the fucking new guy with the shaved head who thought he didn't have to play by the rules here, who stood there with that big scar on his face staring Tinyboy down like a prize boxer. He found out the bastard's name later. One of the young guards had kindly told him when he'd asked. Jochum Lang. What a fucking name. A fucking hitman, a fucking enforcer. Accused of a bunch of assaults and manslaughter, but only short sentences because no one ever dared to testify against him. But in this unit, he'd soon learn. In this unit, there were rules. Then Hitler, who wet his trousers on live TV and had still been stupid enough to take a shortcut through this unit on his way to the sex bunker. Guard Hitler with his wet trousers had

run into them when the effects of the Turkish Glass were at their
best but didn't dare to say a damn thing. He must have smelled it
and still decided to walk right past, headed to those sexual vermin,
who should all be killed. And then Grens. Damned if that bastard
didn't walk by too. Limping as usual. He should be dead by now, he'd
been around so long. Grens probably still got hard when he thought
about it—he'd been one of the Stockholm cops who had driven down
to Blekinge in 1989 to transport a crying thirteen-year-old boy from
the sight of Per's bleeding scrotum to the reformatory.

Bekir shuffled, cut, dealt. Dragan put two matches into the
pot and took up his cards, Skåne put two matches into the pot
and took up his cards, Hilding shoved his cards away, stood up,
walked toward the toilet. Tinyboy picked up the cards, one by one,
sneaked a peek at them. Shitty cards. Bekir shuffled like a bitch.
They swapped cards. He swapped them all except one, the king of
clubs, meaningless to save, but he never swapped them all, on prin-
ciple. Four new. Equally worthless. King of clubs and four low cards
gave no points. His move, he laid down his king of clubs and two of
hearts and four of spades and seven of spades. Final round. Dragan
played a queen of clubs and because both the king and the ace had
already been played, he banged his hand triumphantly on the table,
the matches were his, and the thousands they represented. He was
about to take the pile of sticks when Tinyboy raised his hand.

"Dammit, what are you doing?"

"Taking my pot."

"I haven't played."

"The queen is high."

"No."

"What do you mean no?"

"I haven't played my card yet."

He put his last card on the table. King of clubs.

"There."

Dragan started waving his hands.

"What the hell? The fucking king has already been played."

"I see that. But now I'm playing one more."

"There's no damn way you can have two king of clubs."

"Can and do."

Tinyboy grabbed hold of Dragan's hands and pushed them away.

"Those are my sticks. I had the highest card. You owe me some, girls."

He laughed loudly and hit the table. The guards in their station, three of them who mostly chatted through their workday, turned around, trying to see where the sound came from. They saw Tinyboy throw a pile of matches up at the ceiling and try to catch them in his mouth. They turned around again.

Hilding walked through the hallway on his way back from the toilet. He moved slowly, more awake than before, holding a paper in his hand.

"Hilding Wilding, who do you think took the pot? I'll give you one guess. Who do you think's sitting here waiting for his thousands?"

Hilding wasn't listening. He was holding a piece of paper, showed it to Tinyboy.

"Fuck, you better read this, Boy. A letter. Milan got it today. He gave it to me when I was on the crapper. He thought I should show you. From Branco."

Tinyboy gathered up the matches, put them one by one into an empty matchbox.

"Shut up, little pig. Why the hell should I read other people's letters?"

"I think you should. And Branco thinks so, too."

He gave Tinyboy the paper. Tinyboy stared at it, turned it this way and that, tried to give it back.

"No."

"You only need to read the last part. From there."

Hilding pointed to the fourth line from the end. Tinyboy followed his dirty finger.

"I . . ."

He cleared his throat.

"I had . . ."

He cleared his throat again.

"I hope . . ."

He rubbed his eyes, handed the letter back to Hilding.

"Pig, dammit, I can't really see that well, my eyes, they sting like hell. You read."

Hilding read while Tinyboy continued to scratch his eyes.

"I'm hoping to avoid any unnecessary misunderstandings. Jochum Lang is my friend. Here's some good advice: get along with him."

Tinyboy listened. Quiet.

"Signed, Branco Miodrag. I recognize the handwriting."

Tinyboy took the letter, looked at the signature. Yugoslavians. The fucking Yugoslavians. He folded together the words, sentences, threw them and the matchbox onto the floor, stomped on the paper and matches. He looked anxiously around the corridor toward the cells, then Hilding slowly shook his head at Skåne, at Dragan, at Bekir. They did what Hilding did, shook their heads for a long time. Tinyboy bent down and was about to pick up the paper with a black shoe print on it when a door farther away opened. It was as if he'd been waiting. Jochum Lang came out, walked toward the kneeling Tinyboy, who stood up and turned around.

"Dammit, Jochum, you don't need to show me any papers. Fuck, you understand, we were just playing around a little."

Lang didn't look at him as he passed by, just spoke, almost in a whisper, though they could all hear it. Even quiet, it felt like a shout.

"Did you get a letter, *tjavon*?"

THE NURSERY SCHOOL was called The Dove. It was called that because it had been called that from the beginning. A long time ago. A name difficult to place. There were no doves there. Not even close by. Doves of love? Nobody knew. One of the older ladies in the social welfare department had been around since then, and she'd been asked but didn't have much to add. She'd certainly been there for the opening and remembered it well, Strängnäs's first modern day-care center, but had no idea where the name came from.

It was afternoon, almost four o'clock, most of The Dove's twenty-six children remained inside but a few chose to go out. Sweltering heat as the sun attacked the day-care center. Usually, they made all the children go outside at this time of day, but the heat had been beating down on the unshaded yard for several weeks, and small bodies couldn't take those kinds of temperatures.

Marie had decided to go out. She was tired of playing Indians, tired of having her face painted—the other kids didn't paint very well, not any of them. They just put on brown and blue stripes and she wanted red rings. No one wanted to paint rings at all—she didn't understand why not. She almost kicked David when he didn't want to, but then she realized he was her best friend, and best friends didn't kick each other over that kind of thing. So she had changed into her outside shoes and walked out into the yard. She wanted to ride in the pedal car. It was so yellow, and no one was using it right now.

She drove it for quite a while, twice around the house and three times around the playhouse and back and forth on the big pavement and then into the sandbox, where she got stuck and had to drag it backward to try to get it out. But that stupid pedal car didn't budge, so she did what she'd wanted to do to David, she kicked it and said mean things to it, but still, it wouldn't come loose. Not until that other father came over, the one who'd been sitting outside the gate on the park bench when they'd arrived, who Daddy said hello to and who seemed nice. He asked her if she wanted him to lift the pedal car, then he did, and she said thank you, which seemed to make him happy, but he said that there was a baby bunny next to the park bench that was nearly dead, and he was worried about it.

INTERROGATOR SVEN SUNDKVIST (I): Hello.

DAVID RUNDGREN (DR): Hello.

I: My name is Sven.

DR: I (inaudible)

I: Did you say David?

DR: Yes.

I: Nice name. I also have a son. He's two years older than you. His name is Jonas.

DR: I know a Jonas.

I: That's nice.

DR: He's my friend.

I: Do you have many friends?

DR: Yeah. Kind of.

I: Good. Great. A friend named Marie?

DR: Yeah.

I: You know she's the one I most want to talk to you about?

DR: Yeah. About Marie.

I: Great. You know what? I want you to tell me how it was at school today.

DR: Good.

I: Was it like it usually is?

DR: What?

I: Was it the same as always?

DR: Yeah. Same as always.

I: Everyone was playing?

DR: Yeah. Mostly Indians.

I: You were Indians?

DR: Yeah. Everyone was. I had blue stripes.

I: Ahh. Okay. Blue stripes. And everyone was playing?

DR: Almost everyone. Almost all the time.

I: Marie? Was she playing?

DR: Yeah. But not at the end.

I: Not at the end? Can you tell me why she didn't want to play?

DR: She didn't (inaudible) stripes and stuff. But I wanted to. Then she went outside. When she didn't get rings. No one wanted to make rings. Everyone wanted stripes. Like (inaudible) I have. Then, I said you have to have stripes, too. No, I want rings, no one wants to paint rings. Then she went outside. No one else wanted to go outside. It was too hot. So we got to choose. We chose Indians.

I: Did you see when Marie went out?

DR: No.

I: Not at all?

DR: She just left. She was probably mad.

I: You continued to play Indians, and she went outside? Is that right?

DR: Yeah.

I: Did you see Marie again?

DR: Yeah. Later.

I: When?

DR: Later, through the window.

I: What did you see through the window?

DR: I saw Marie. She had the pedal car. She almost never had it. She was stuck.

I: She was stuck?

DR: In the sandbox.

I: She was stuck with the pedal car in the sandbox?

DR: Yeah.

I: You said you saw her. And she was stuck. What did she do then?

DR: She started kicking.

I: Kicking?

DR: The pedal car.

I: She kicked the pedal car. Did she do anything else?

DR: She said something.

I: What did she say?

DR: I didn't hear.

I: Then what happened? When she kicked the pedal car and said something?

DR: Then the man came.

I: What man?

DR: The man who came.

I: Where were you then?

DR: By the window.

I: Were they far away?

DR: Ten.

I: Ten?

DR: Meters.

I: From Marie and the man?

DR: (Inaudible)

I: Do you know how far ten meters is?

DR: Pretty far.

I: But, you don't really know?

DR: No.

I: Look out the window here, David, do you see the car out there?

DR: Yeah.

I: Was it that far?

DR: Yeah.

I: Are you sure?

DR: That's how far it was.

I: What happened when the man came?

DR: He just came.

I: What did he do?

DR: He helped Marie with the pedal car.

I: How did he do that?

DR: He lifted it. He was strong.

I: Did anyone else see him lift it?

DR: No. It was just me there. In the hall.

I: You were alone? No other kids?

DR: No.

I: No teacher?

DR: No. Just me.

I: What did he do then?

DR: He talked to Marie.

I: What did Marie do when they were talking?

DR: Nothing. She talked.

I: What was Marie wearing?

DR: The same thing.

I: The same thing?

DR: Same as when she got here.

I: Do you think you could describe her clothes? What did they look like?

DR: A green T-shirt. Like Hampus has.

I: Short-sleeved?

DR: Yeah.

I: Anything else?

DR: Those red shoes. The really nice ones with metal things.

I: Metal things?

DR: The kind you snap.

I: What about for pants?

DR: Can't remember.

I: Did she have on long pants?

DR: No. Not long pants. Shorts, I think. Or a skirt. It's hot outside.

I: The man then? What did he look like?

DR: Big. He was strong. He pulled the pedal car from the sand.

I: What was he wearing?

DR: Pants, I think. Maybe a T-shirt. He had a baseball cap on.

I: A baseball cap? Was it for a certain team?

DR: For his head.

I: A baseball cap?

DR: Yeah. A cap.

I: Do you remember what it looked like?

DR: The kind you buy at the gas station.

I: And then? What did they do? When they finished talking?

DR: Then they went away.

I: They left? Where to?

DR: To the gate. The man fixed that thing.

I: What did he fix?

DR: That lock thing on the gate.

I: The latch? The thing at the top that you lift up?

DR: Yeah. That. He did that.

I: And then?

DR: Then they went out.

I: In which direction?

DR: I didn't see. Just out.

I: Why did they go?

DR: We're not supposed to. Go out. We're not allowed.

I: How did they look when they left?

DR: Not mad.

I: Not mad?

DR: They were a little excited.

I: They looked excited when they left?

DR: Not mad.

I: How long did you see them?

DR: Not long. Not after the gate.

I: They disappeared there?

DR: Yeah.

I: Anything else?

DR: (Inaudible)

I: David?

I: You've been really really good. You're good at remembering. Can you sit here for a bit while I talk a little to the other guys?

DR: I can.

I: Then I'll go and get your mom and dad, they're waiting down there.

II
(one week)

FREDRIK STEFFANSSON MADE it to the two o'clock ferry—bright yellow and ocean blue, the national Transport Administration colors. The ferry only went once an hour between Oknön and Arnö: a four- or five-minute journey—the symbolic divide between the mainland and the island, between where time was in a hurry and where time was at rest. The red house with white trim was a fifteen-minute drive from Strängnäs. He'd bought it a month before Marie was born, when he no longer found it possible to write at home. It had been in ruins then, standing in the middle of a jungle. He and Agnes had used the first few summers to turn that ruin into a house, the jungle into a garden. Soon, he'd have been here six years. He'd written three books here, a trilogy that sold decently, soon to be translated into German. The publisher had made an economic assessment and found that it had the potential to make more than what the launch would cost. Nowadays, Swedish titles found their way onto foreign bookshelves, too.

He knew there wasn't going to be any writing done today, but he still turned on the computer, put out the stack of half-finished outlines, and stared into the electronic square. Half an hour, forty-five minutes, an hour. He turned on the television, just to have some company on the other side of the room, silent images and low volume. He turned on the radio, a commercial station; hits he'd heard several times before and didn't really need to listen to. He took a short walk down to the water, looking through his binoculars at the passengers on the deck of the ferry outside. People in boats were a play without a plot.

Not one word yet. But he was going to sit here until he wrote one.

The phone.

It was always Agnes nowadays. Everyone else had stopped calling. It took him a year to even notice. He knew he got angry as hell
when a call disturbed him in the middle of a sentence. He found it
hard to hide that fact when he answered, so he'd managed to scare
them off one by one, and then, when the block came and the screen
turned white, he realized how the emptiness had crept slyly in, both
beautiful and ugly.

"Yes?"

"You don't need to sound so annoyed."

"I'm writing."

"What, exactly?"

"It's going a bit slow right now."

"So you mean nothing."

"Basically."

He couldn't fool Agnes. They'd seen each other naked.

"I'm sorry. What do you want?"

"We have a daughter together. I wanted to know how she's doing.
That's what we call each other about sometimes. I tried to call earlier. You made Marie hang up. So I didn't get an answer. Now I
want one."

"Good. She's good. She seems to be one of the few people who
doesn't mind the heat. She takes after you."

He saw Agnes's dark body in front of him. He knew exactly what
she looked like, even now, the way she was sitting in an office chair,
curled up against the backrest, thin dress. He'd wanted her every
morning, every day, every night, but now he'd learned to shut it off,
to be brusque, and irritable, and free.

"And nursery school? How did it go leaving her?"

Micaela. You want to know something about Micaela. It felt good
to know that she was bothered by his relationship with a woman
who was much younger than she was. He realized it didn't matter.
She wasn't coming back just because he made love to a woman as
beautiful as her. But it felt good in a childish way, and he couldn't
keep himself from enjoying it.

"Better. Today, it took ten minutes. Then she ran off and started playing Indians with David."

"Indians?"

"That's what they're playing these days."

He sat down in the tiny kitchen at the table, his workplace. Then he stood up, took the cordless phone into an even smaller room, which he called the living room, and sat down in an armchair. She'd called at just the right time. He could look away from the blank screen. He was just about to ask her how things were in Stockholm, how she was doing for real, which he hardly ever did, afraid of the answer, afraid to hear she was doing well, and that she was also seeing somebody. He was trying to figure out a casual way to say it, and thought perhaps he'd found it, when a picture came on the muted television that he always kept on.

"Agnes, wait a moment."

A still image in black and white, a smiling man, dark, short-haired. He recognized that face. He'd just seen it. Today. It was the father on the park bench. Outside the Dove. They'd said hello to each other. He'd been sitting on the park bench just outside the gate, waiting.

Fredrik walked over to the television, raised the volume.

A new picture of the father. One in color. From a prison. A wall in the background. Two guards on either side of him. He waved toward the camera. At least it looked like he did.

A hurried reporter's voice. They sounded alike, all of them. Rattling on, stressing every word, neutral voices without personality.

The voice said that the man in the picture, the father from the park bench, was thirty-six years old and named Bernt Lund. That in 2006 he'd been sentenced for a series of rapes of underage girls. That in 2013 he'd been convicted again for the same crime, which culminated in the so-called Skarpholm murders, two nine-year-old girls brutally molested and murdered in a basement storage unit. That early this morning he'd escaped from custody while being transported to a hospital from Aspsås prison's unit for sex offenders.

Fredrik Steffansson sat, silent.

He couldn't hear it, raised the volume, but couldn't hear. The man in the picture. He'd said hello to him.

A prison administrator with a microphone in his face stammered while sweat ran down his forehead.

A senior police officer with a sullen countenance replied with a no comment and ended with a plea to the public to report any sightings to the authorities.

He'd said hello to him.

The man had been sitting on the park bench outside the gate, and he'd nodded to him once on the way in and once on the way out.

Fredrik couldn't move.

He heard Agnes shouting from the phone, her sharp voice tearing into his ear. He let her shout.

He shouldn't have greeted him. He shouldn't have nodded at him. He lifted the phone.

"Agnes. I can't talk now. I have to make a call. I'm hanging up now."

He pressed a button on the phone, waiting for the dial tone. She was still there.

"Agnes, goddammit! Hang up!"

He threw the phone on the floor, stood up quickly, ran to the kitchen, to the jacket hanging on one of the chairs, found his mobile, and called Micaela's number, called the nursery school.

LARS ÅGESTAM LOOKED across the courtroom. A mediocre collection of people.

The politically appointed lay judges with their tired, ignorant eyes; Judge van Balvas, who had already acted unprofessionally at the beginning of the case, clearly showing her prejudice toward people indicted of sex crimes; the accused, Håkan Axelsson, who had yet to show any emotional awareness whatsoever of how his alleged crimes affected the young children involved; the prison guards stationed behind him trying their best to look like they understood what was going on; the seven journalists on the press bench at the front taking notes continuously, but still incapable of getting even the outlines of a trial correct; the two women on a bench in the back, who came to all the trials because they were free entertainment and a civil right; and, finally, the group of pimply law school students in the very back that—as he himself had done just a few years ago—viewed a trial about the despair of abused children as homework and the chance for a good grade.

He wanted to scream at all of them, tell them to leave the courtroom or, at least, to shut the fuck up.

But he was a well-mannered, ambitious, and relatively new prosecutor who wanted more for himself than to spend his time prosecuting sex offenders and junkies, who wanted to move up up up, and who was smart enough to keep his opinions to himself. He made the indictment, prepared the prosecution, and when the trial came, he knew more about it than anyone else in the room. It would take one hell of a defense lawyer to even try to win the case.

And Kristina Björnsson was one. One hell of a defense lawyer.

She was the one person in this courtroom he couldn't call mediocre—experienced, brilliant, the only one he'd encountered so far on the opposing side who defended idiots over and over and still considered them more important than her lawyer's fees. And, therefore, one of the few who had the complete respect of her clients. One of the first stories he'd heard when he started at law school was about Kristina Björnsson and her coin collection. She was a numismatist, with apparently one of the better collections in the country—a collection that had been stolen sometime in the early '90s. It caused a lot of commotion in the country's prisons, and through the prisoner organizations a peculiar search was conducted in the underworld. After a week, two burly guys with ponytails showed up at Björnsson's home bearing flowers and an intact collection, wrapped in gift paper and curly string. Every coin was in its place, in plastic case after plastic case. Attached was a letter, painstakingly written by three professional criminals who specialized in art and antiquities, a long letter in which they begged for her forgiveness, swore they'd had no idea who the coins belonged to, and that they could help her complete her collection if she ever decided to consider methods that were not entirely legal. If Lars Ågestam ever found himself in need of a defense lawyer, he would turn to Kristina Björnsson.

She'd done a good job this time, too. Håkan Axelsson was an emotionally dead piece of shit who deserved a long prison sentence, and that's what the prosecution would insist on—given the pictorial evidence of abuse presented in CD-ROM form, the witness statements from two of the other seven pedophiles who participated in the bizarre distribution of child pornography at eight o'clock on Saturday evenings, and the defendant's own confession—but still that pig would likely end up with only a year or two. Björnsson had patiently responded to charge after charge. She claimed her client suffered from a serious psychological condition and, therefore, belonged in psychiatric care. She knew she'd never get that, but she'd opened the way for a compromise that seemed impossible when Axelsson first confessed to the crime, and she was close to getting it. She'd stuck to her defense, and the lay judges liked her. It became clear that they were probably heading toward a sentence of violation with mitigating circumstances when one of the lay judges pointed out that the children had dressed provocatively.

Lars Ågestam's blood was boiling. That fucking municipal politician had sat in front of him, in a gray suit, talking about children's clothing and about an encounter between people and about who shared responsibility. Ågestam had been closer than ever to punching those despicable lay judges and telling them, and his own career, to go to hell.

He'd followed the trials of three of the other child pornographers closely. They'd received long sentences, and Axelsson was just as guilty, but Kristina Björnsson and that piece of shit had formed their archaic pact, and if Bernt Lund hadn't escaped this very morning, there might have been an acquittal and a loss of prestige for an ambitious young prosecutor. Lund's disappearance had brought those journalists to the front bench with a sudden heightened interest in Axelsson's trial. Their stories would now move from page eleven to page seven; each link between Axelsson and Sweden's most hated and wanted man would result in double columns and, at least, a one-year prison sentence to avoid public scrutiny.

Ågestam did not want any more sex crimes for a while.

They took too much energy. It didn't matter if the perpetrator and the victim were no more than two anonymous names on a piece of paper, the crime got to him, made it hard for him to maintain his distance, his governmental calm, plus, an affected prosecutor risked becoming completely useless.

He wanted a bank robbery, a murder, a case of fraud. Sex crimes were predictable. Everyone had already made up their minds, honed their arguments a long time ago. Before the Axelsson trial, he'd tried to understand, read what there was to read on the dissemination of child pornography, had taken a course at the Crown Prosecution Service to learn the basics of dealing with sexual violence—four prosecutors and three lawyers spending their evenings trying to lay the foundation to build better sentences.

He didn't want to prosecute any more sex crimes and he definitely didn't want the Bernt Lund case whenever Lund showed up again. Lund provoked too many emotions. His crimes were so extreme Ågestam didn't even want to read about them, much less write about them for a case.

He'd be sure to stay far away when the time came.

FREDRIK STEFFANSSON OPENED the front door, searched for his keys, then left it unlocked and ran for the car.

Marie.

He ran and wept and jerked open the car door.

The key was in the ignition, with the rest of his keys hanging off it. He started the car and backed hastily out through the narrow entrance.

She hadn't been there.

Micaela had listened to his incoherent statements, put the phone down, and started searching for her. First indoors, then outdoors. Nowhere to be found. He'd screamed, and Micaela had asked him to calm down. He'd lowered his voice and then raised it again and screamed louder than before, about the park bench and what he saw on the news, and the father sitting on the park bench in photos in front of a prison wall.

He'd hung up, and now he sat in the car and drove the narrow, winding road in panic, still weeping, still screaming.

He was sure of it. The man on the bench was the man in those photographs. He held the steering wheel with one hand while calling the Stockholm police, screaming his message. After a few minutes, they put him on the phone with someone on duty. He explained what happened, that he'd seen Lund outside a nursery school in Strängnäs, and that his daughter, who should be there, was gone.

It was three kilometers from the house to the ferry. He sped past the abandoned school at Skvallertorget and a few meters later past a thirteenth-century stone church. Three people in the cemetery, one watering flowers, one standing quietly on the grass in front of a tombstone, one raking the gravel path.

He was a few minutes late, the ferry had just left and was already halfway across. It went from the mainland every hour and came back to the island ten minutes later. He looked at the clock, fourteen minutes past three, honked several times, flashed his lights.

Meaningless.

He called. The ferry pilot rarely heard the phone ringing, but it was quieter than usual, no wind, no boats in sight. Fredrik got hold of him and tried to explain, and the pilot promised to return as soon as he dropped off the cars he was carrying.

Why the hell had they gone to nursery school?

Why the hell hadn't they stayed at home when it was already half past one?

The ferry landed on the other side of the water, and for Fredrik time stood still. Marie wasn't inside, and she wasn't outside. He thought about how his daughter had become more than a human, he'd made her more, maybe too much more. After Agnes it felt as if Marie had become the guardian of all of his love—he bombarded her with it—she was also the guardian of all the love Agnes directed at her. She was responsible for both of them, and he'd often thought that it wasn't right, that no one should have to be more than just a human being, shouldn't be forced to bear more love than they could, and a five-year-old wasn't that big.

He called Micaela again. No answer. One more time. Her phone was switched off. He was transferred to an electronic voice, which asked him to leave a message.

It had been a long time since he'd wept. Even when Agnes moved out. He just wasn't able to anymore, and he had tried, decided to without success. It couldn't be forced, and when he thought back, he realized he'd never wept as an adult.

He was shut off.

Or at least he had been.

Therefore, he couldn't comprehend anything—the awful fear that had taken hold of him and the tears that wouldn't stop. He'd often imagined it would feel good to cry, but this, this was more a theft, something pouring out of him, while he sat in the driver's seat like a huge, lonely hole.

The bright yellow and ocean-blue ferry had turned around now, four cars had driven off on the other side, and it was on its way back to make an extra trip. It was balanced on two rusty wires, like a moving rail in the water, and they clanged rhythmically and loudly against the metal where they were connected, getting louder as the ferry approached. He lifted his hand up toward the cabin—they always greeted each other. And he drove on board.

Water surrounding him. The ferry lazily following its route. Fredrik kept seeing the photographs from this afternoon's news. First the mug shot in black and white. He'd been smiling. The moment in front of the prison wall. He'd stood surrounded by guards, waving at the camera. Fredrik tried to rid himself of that face, but it overwhelmed him, refused to stop. That smiling and waving man had raped children. One by one. He knew it now. He remembered. Two girls had been molested and murdered in a cellar. They'd been destroyed. Lund had left them cut, torn, beaten, like used-up dolls in a pile. He'd read about it back then. But he hadn't been able to comprehend it. It was unthinkable. He'd read about it, and shared in the public fury, but it still felt like something that might never have happened. What he read didn't seem real. The media coverage of the trial had washed over him day after day until he wasn't capable of seeing it.

There was an older man up in the cabin of the ferry. Fredrik had only seen him piloting in the mornings until now, a retiree who was filling in until someone younger could be transferred here from a route they were canceling up north. A wise man who could see Fredrik's desperation and chose not to go downstairs and shoot the shit like he usually did about the weather and housing prices. He'd listened when Fredrik called and signaled that he had wanted to know what this was about, but now he stayed away, and Fredrik would thank him for it, next time.

On the other side, the older man's German Shepherd was tied to one of the trees near the shore, barking with joy when his master waved. Fredrik revved the engine and left the ferry as soon as it reached land.

He was scared. So scared.

She never went anywhere without telling someone. She knew Micaela was inside and that she was supposed to tell her if she wanted to go out to the yard, beyond the fence.

The man on the park bench outside the gate. Cap, fairly short, fairly skinny. He'd greeted him.

Arnövägen, nine kilometers on a curvy dirt road, then Road 55, eight kilometers on narrow asphalt. There were few other cars on the road. He increased his speed, drove faster than ever before.

He'd seen his face. It was him. He knew it was him.

Five cars in front of him. They drove slowly, in front was a small red car with a huge caravan in tow. It lurched heavily at the sharp curves, so the cars behind kept a respectful distance. He tried to pass, once, twice, but couldn't as the next curve came and visibility was reduced again to nothing.

Next exit, toward Tosterö, a right turn just before Tosterö Bridge and central Strängnäs.

He could see them already in the distance.

They stood outside the gate, between the Dove's yard and the street outside.

Five nursery school teachers and two from the kitchen. Police, four dogs. Some parents he knew, and some he didn't recognize.

One of them, with a small child in her arms, who was pointing to the woods. A policeman walked in that direction with the dog, let it sniff, was joined by two more.

Fredrik drove up to the gate, sat there for a moment before opening the door and stepping out of the car. He was met by Micaela. He hadn't seen her at first. She'd come from inside the building.

THE COFFEE WAS black. No fucking milk, no latte or cappuccino or any other fancy shit, just pitch-black Swedish coffee with no grounds. Ewert Grens stood in front of the vending machine in the hallway. No fucking way he was paying anything extra to put dry white powder into his cup. It tasted bad, like emulsifiers and chemicals, but Sven, he had to have it. He wanted it to look like brown slush, so he gladly paid to dilute it. Grens held the clear plastic cups a good distance apart, as if the light brown liquid might infect the solid black, balancing them as well as anyone could balance something while walking down a newly waxed hallway with a limp. He walked into his office, handed one cup to Sven Sundkvist, who sat shrunken and powerless in the visitor's chair.

"Here. Your dishwater."

"Thank you."

Ewert stopped in front of him. There was something in Sven's eyes he didn't recognize.

"What's the matter with you? It can't be that fucking bad to have to work on your fortieth birthday, can it?"

"No."

"Well, then?"

"Jonas just called while you were fighting with the coffee machine."

"Yeah?"

"He asked why I didn't come home when I said I would. He said I lied."

"Lied?"

"He said adults lie."

"And? Get to the point."

"He'd seen reports about Lund on television. He asked why adults lie and tell children that they'll get to see a dead squirrel or a nice doll when all the adult wants to do is use his penis and hit you. That's exactly what he said. To the word."

Sven drank his coffee silently for a moment, collapsed again, turning slightly on the chair, without thinking, to the left, to the right. Ewert moved to the bookshelf, to the tape recorder, searching through his plastic folders.

"How do you answer something like that? Dad lies, adults lie, some adults lie and use their penis and hit you. Ewert, I can't do this. I can't fucking do it."

"Seven Beautiful Boys," with Harry Arnold's Radio Band, 1959.

They listened.

My very first friend was as slim as a saber
My second was blond and ever so dear

The lyrics were like ice hockey, banal and unimportant and, therefore, they offered an escape. Ewert swayed his head, with his eyes closed, to a different time, for a few minutes of peace.

There was a knock.

Sven looked at Ewert, who shook his head in annoyance. Once more, harder.

"Yes, come in, dammit!"

Ågestam. The perfectly combed hair, the ingratiating smile through the partially open door. Grens had little sympathy for over-achievers. He didn't like overachievers playing at being prosecutors, just trying to rise up the ranks faster.

"What the hell is it?"

Lars Ågestam flinched, whether from Grens and his irritation or from the singing of Siw Malmkvist.

"Lund."

Ewert looked up from his plastic cup, set it aside.

"Yes?"

"He's been spotted."

Ågestam explained that an officer had just gotten off the phone with someone who spotted Bernt Lund a few hours ago in Strän-gnäs, outside a nursery school. A father, sober and well spoken but scared, had called from a mobile phone and said he saw a face he recognized wearing a cap sitting on a bench. He'd left his daughter there, a five-year-old who is now missing, according to the staff.

Grens crumpled up the cup, threw it into the bin.

"Fuck. Fuck!"

The interrogations. The ugliest he'd ever had. A man who was something else, eyes that never met his.

Dammit, Grens.

Lund, I want you to look at me.

Grens, they're sluts.

I hear you, Lund, but I want you to look at me.

Sluts. Little tiny horny sluts.

Either you look at me or we cancel this interview, here and now.

You want to hear? About those little cunts? I know you do.

So you don't dare to look at me?

Pussy wants cock.

Good. Now let's look at each other.

Small little pussies want lots of cock.

How does it feel to look into my eyes?

That's what you have to teach them. Not to think about cock all the time.

Now, you aren't doing it anymore. Your eyes are cowards.

Little pussies are the worst. They're the horniest, that's why you have to be rough.

You want me to put the tape recorder to the side and lose control?

Grens, have you ever tasted nine-year-old pussy?

He shut off the music. Put the cassette gently into its plastic case.

"If he's so desperate that he's letting himself be seen before snatching another kid, then the risk is great that he's lost all inhibitions."

He walked toward the coat hanger wedged behind the door and grabbed the jacket that was hanging there.

"I've interrogated him. I know how he thinks. I've also read the forensic psychiatric report, and it confirms what I already know, what everyone knows: he has pronounced sadistic tendencies."

Grens hadn't just read the forensic psychiatric report; he'd made sure he understood every word. He'd been more affected in the presence of Lund, and after, than by any other interrogation. No one else had ever gotten to Grens like that before. Made him feel like that, a hate, a fear. Police work had made him pretty cold, he knew that, and had hardened him. It was hell feeling anything when his days were like they were, but Lund and his crimes and his estrangement had made Grens feel for the first time like giving up, sneaking away, quitting. He'd also talked to the psychiatrist who wrote the report, gotten him to say more than he should. They'd talked about Lund and the sadistic rapes he'd committed, about how rage was the same thing as sexuality for him, that harming someone had become desire, making someone powerless had become pleasure. Grens had asked if Lund understood what he'd done, if he understood how the child and the child's parents felt, and everyone else who was a part of this. The psychiatrist had gently shaken his head and told Grens about Lund's childhood, his early abuse, how he'd shut out other people to endure it.

Jacket in hand, Grens pointed first at Sven, then Ågestam.

"A mild psychiatric disorder. Can you believe it? He rapes little girls and that's a mild disorder."

Ågestam sighed.

"I remember that. I was at the university then. I remember how strange it was, how pissed off we were."

Ewert wriggled into his jacket, turned to Sven.

"Back to the car. Strängnäs. Fast as hell. You drive."

Lars Ågestam stood at the door, should have stepped aside, but hadn't.

"I'm going with you."

Ewert disliked the young prosecutor. He'd shown that before and would again.

"So, you're the investigator in this case now?"

"No."

"Then I think you need to move aside."

————

Even though the sun was slowly going down, it was still hot out, and the bright light was annoying as they sped south down the E4, out of the inner city, past the inner ring of suburbs, past Kungens Kurva, Fittja, Tumba, Södertälje. They veered off toward the west, took the E20 toward Strängnäs, and Sven breathed easier. Ewert's hints that he should speed up and his whining about the sun visor not helping enough ceased the moment they changed direction. He could drive even faster now. The traffic wasn't as heavy, and the sun not so intense.

They didn't say much to each other. Bernt Lund had been seen outside a nursery school. A five-year-old girl was gone. There wasn't much more to say. They each went through what happened, what could have happened, and each scenario ended with the hope that it was a false alarm, that the little girl would suddenly come out of an overlooked playroom, that the father who thought he'd seen Lund was the type whose fear ran away with his imagination.

Forty-three minutes from central Stockholm to the Dove, a nursery school in Strängnäs.

Just a few hundred meters away, they realized it wasn't to be. That this was no false alarm. This was something else, maybe the worst-case scenario. There stood the teachers and childcare workers, the parents and their children running around, two police cars with uniformed personnel and impatient dogs, and all of it signaled fear, confusion, and a kind of solidarity.

Sven stopped the car back at the fence. One minute. The calm before chaos. Silence before rapid-fire questions. He looked at the people walking around outside their car. They were in constant motion. Anxious people keep moving. That's what they do. He glanced at Ewert and realized he, too, was watching, interpreting, trying to become a part of the conversation out there without opening the car door.

"What do you think?"

"I believe what I see."

"What do you see?"

"That things have gone to hell."

They stepped out of the car. Two of the police officers headed their way. They walked toward one of them.

"Hello."

They shook hands.

"Sven Sundkvist."

"Leo Lauritzen. We got here twenty minutes ago. From Eskilstuna, we're the closest."

"This is Ewert Grens."

Lauritzen smiled, surprised. Tall, his dark hair in a crew cut, he had the naturalness that people his age, thirty or so, just have, a kind of delicate invulnerability. He held Grens's hand slightly too long.

"Well, I'll be damned. I've heard of you."

"Really."

"It sounds like something you'd hear in a movie. But I just have to say it. You're shorter than I thought you'd be."

The second officer, standing just a few steps away, overheard and hurried forward. She didn't introduce herself.

"An hour ago. A police officer in Stockholm called and explained that one of the children at this nursery school had disappeared. A few minutes later, we received additional information. Bernt Lund had been seen in connection with the girl's disappearance. We activated a general alert. Dog patrols and people from the local working dog club are searching the woods that lead from here toward Enköping. Two helicopters are searching along the roads and shores of Lake Mälaren. We are about to launch a search party. We wanted to wait a bit with that. The dogs need to be able to smell before half of Strängnäs starts running around in the woods."

She was sweating profusely, her blond hair glued to her temples. She'd been working in sweltering heat. She excused herself, went back over to a few of the dog owners wearing jackets with the emblem of the Swedish Working Dog Club sewn on the chest. Sven and Ewert looked at each other, as if neither of them really wanted to get started, an aversion to the darkness. Ewert cleared his throat and turned to Leo Lauritzen.

"The girl's parents?"

"Yes?"

"Have they been informed?"

Lauritzen pointed toward the fence, toward a park bench standing just outside the entrance to the Dove. A man was sitting on one end of it. Long hair, ponytail down his back, in a brown corduroy suit—leaning forward with his elbows on his knees, staring into the gate or the bush behind it. A woman was next to him, holding him, stroking his cheek.

"The girl's father. The one who called. He was the one who saw him on two occasions, about fifteen to twenty minutes apart. Lund was sitting there, conspicuously, on that very bench."

"Name?"

"Fredrik Steffansson. Divorced. The girl's mother is Agnes Steffansson, lives in Stockholm, Vasastan, I think."

"And the woman?"

"She works here at the school. Micaela Zwarts. She also lives with him. The girl lives part-time at both homes, but apparently in the last year she chose Strängnäs as a home base, with Steffansson and Zwarts. She mostly sees her mother on weekends. The parents agreed, whatever was best for the child. If she wanted to stay here in Strängnäs, she could. Wish everyone could have it that way. I myself am divorced and . . ."

Grens had already started to walk away.

"I think I'm going to go and say hello to him."

The man on the park bench sat bent over. His eyes stared blankly ahead.

He sat as if he were in pain. As if the hole in his stomach were leaking concentrated energy, his will to live dripping down on to the grass below, turning it ugly.

Grens had no children. He'd never wanted any. Therefore, he couldn't understand what the man in front of him was feeling. He knew that.

But he could see it.

RUNE LANTZ WOULD soon be sixty-six years old. A year since retirement and not a single male friend. Late one Friday in July of last year, he'd emptied the four-cubic-meter reservoir of the apple juice mixer for the last time. He'd turned it off and washed it out and prepared to be relieved by someone on the night shift, someone who would say hello and put on ear protectors and a hairnet and mix the right amount of sugar—a little bit less sugar for juice going to Germany, a little bit sweeter for Great Britain, unbelievably sweet to Italy, and so sweet as to be almost undrinkable for Greece. He left that factory after thirty-four years to find that the friends he'd seen daily were coffee-break friends, bad-mouth-your-boss friends, bet-on-horses-over-lunch-on-Friday friends. Nothing more. Not a single one of them had called or visited since. He himself was equally guilty, never sought anyone out, whether in the factory or at home, wasn't even sure he missed them. Strange, he thought, you live your life surrounded by people you don't need or care about, people who are like the TV you keep on in the corner of the living room. Ritual and habit hides emptiness and silence. They are a reflection of yourself that proves you exist, but they don't mean shit. Not to you, not to anyone else. You disappear, but everything else just keeps going on and on; they mix their juice and fill out their horse-betting slips and laugh over their coffee, and it's as if you never existed.

He held on to her hand more tightly now.

He saw her more clearly now.

Margareta was still working in the factory. She had two years left and was gone all day, and he'd never before realized how much he needed her. Together, they had the time and life and courage to grow old.

They walked close to each other, rather slowly, her bad knees and all. The same walk every late afternoon, from their house in the harbor, over the Tosterö Bridge, past the terraced houses, and into the woods. He was already dressed when she came home; the last hour alone in the apartment was the worst, he missed her terribly then, wanted to be walking slowly as one, stepping as one, breathing as one. There were several trails in the forest to choose from. A couple of them had been marked with green and yellow signs, put there for joggers, one hundred meters between each. When it was light, during the spring and the summer and early autumn, they liked to leave the established trails and look for new ones, through the dense spruce trees and the wild blueberry bushes. Finding your own way was a lot more fun as life started slowly to recede.

Tonight was one of those nights. They held each other's hands, left the marked trail after just a few meters, walking side by side in the dry forest. It hadn't rained for several weeks, the summer and high pressure weighing over the skies of northern Europe made the ground crunchy and the risk of fire high. It was going to be a lousy year for mushrooms.

A deer. A few rabbits. Birds, quite large, maybe buzzards. They didn't say much to each other. They didn't need to. They'd been married for forty-three years and had probably used every sentence they had. Usually one of them would stop, point, hold a hand in the air. They always looked at any animal until it ran off, they had plenty of time—it would soon be evening, and they were too old to hurry anywhere.

The terrain changed shape, suddenly hilly, and they breathed more heavily. It was nice to feel the blood rushing through your veins delivering oxygen.

They'd just scaled a small mountain of boulders when they heard the sound approaching.

They both heard it. A helicopter.

Above their heads. It flew close to them, close to the ground, dancing along the treetops.

It was followed by another one.

Police helicopters. Rune saw them, and Margareta saw them, and they didn't know why, but both felt an immediate discomfort and anxiety, the intense noise of the engine and the intrusive presence, police officers searching for something, in a big hurry, right here.

Margareta stopped. She watched the machines overhead until they disappeared behind the trees on the horizon.

"I don't like them."

"Neither do I."

"Let's not go any farther."

"Not until they're gone."

"Not even then."

She'd been holding her husband by the hand, and now she put his arm around her. That's where it should be, around her waist. He kissed her lightly on the cheek, it was the two of them against the world, against the helicopters and uniforms and engine noise.

She pulled him even closer. She was worried. He looked at her. She never used to be afraid. She was the brave one. Now she just wanted to get away, humming helicopters meant misfortune.

Far away, at the edge of the forest. He noticed him before she did. A police officer with a dog. They were moving along the trees, the dog was searching for something, moving to the west, away from them, toward the helicopters.

"That, too."

"It might not be related."

But it was related.

They knew now. Something had happened here, in their forest, during their break from everything else.

They hurried down from the hill, through the thick bushes. Gone were the slow steps, the communal breathing. They wanted to get away from somebody's hunt, from somebody's misfortune.

———

It was Margareta who saw it first.

So red.

A child's shoe. A little girl's shoe.

Bright-red patent leather and a metal buckle, the decoration that dominated.

They went as fast as they could, and the pain in her knees stabbed angrily, but she ignored it. When Rune asked if she was okay, she nodded and pointed forward, the fastest route back, a shortcut away from the usual paths, hilly or not. The helicopter was so close, the policeman and his dog, she didn't want to think about the darkness but was convinced it surrounded them. She just knew. She could see that Rune was worried by her reaction, and she shook her head. She couldn't answer. Sometimes there are simply no explanations.

She was forced to let go of his hand as they walked on either side of a big spruce. The path was covered with brush, and they couldn't fit beside each other. They'd moved quickly across almost a kilometer, and it wouldn't be long until they were back to their starting point, to the asphalt and the houses.

She glimpsed it underneath the broad branches of the spruce. Thought at first it was mushrooms, kicked it gently. She lifted it then, turned and twisted and understood. She looked around. Where is she? Is she here? The girl.

She didn't scream, she wasn't surprised, just held the red shoe gently and handed it to Rune when he arrived.

LENNART OSCARSSON SAT in his office watching Aspsås prison wake up through his window. A beautiful day, just as warm as yesterday, just as warm as every day of the last week. He sighed loudly. It *could* have been beautiful. But an extremely dangerous sex offender was moving freely out there—and it was his fault. He left his office and hurried down the stairs, down to his department, nodded toward two new recruits with six months of service in front of them. He knew they all wanted to end up anywhere but in the sex crimes department, that they rejected the people they were supposed to be caring for, he understood that and didn't make more of it than what it was—they all felt the same, spitting on the pedophiles all the way to the bank to cash their paycheck.

It was empty, quiet, a deserted corridor with closed cell doors—everyone was in the workshop, they had an obligation to work and got a few bucks an hour for making wooden rings and triangular wooden blocks, building parts for educational toys. Say what you want about sex offenders, they didn't make much fuss about doing their jobs, went there quietly and produced whatever inanities they were asked to, unlike the normal units' mix of junkie convenience-store robbers who alternated between going on strike or going to the infirmary.

He walked into the hallway, along a wall of metal doors. He came to a halt in front of number eleven. Bernt Lund's abandoned cell. Soon, Lund would be one and a half days on the run. They didn't usually last that long—without sleep, without betraying themselves, staying vigilant every moment. It took an enormous amount of energy and money to hide, and with a couple of dozen police officers on your tail and an informed public, the number of hiding places shrank with every breath.

Door, locked. The key ring was in his pocket—it was always there. He unlocked the door.

It looked the same as it did when they'd closed it the previous day: the entire room filled with objects in a row, two centimeters apart. A big pile on the floor, he could still see that madman Grens sweeping all the objects off the bed with his pocket diary. The lean one whose fortieth birthday it was, Sundkvist, had looked aghast for a moment. At first he'd glanced anxiously at his colleague and then sighed loudly as Grens did it again, measured and swept things down a second time.

Lennart Oscarsson sat down on the now crumpled bedcover, blurry streaks on dark ground. After a while he lay down, trying to see what Lund had seen every day, every night. He stared at the white, patchy ceiling, investigating the too-bright fluorescent lamp, his eyes wandering around the doorjamb. What had he done in here? Lain here masturbating, while he shut his eyes and thought of little girls? Planned and fantasized about dominating and controlling, about a child's naiveté, which he would end the moment he chose to violate it? Or, had Lund understood, had he dared to approach the consequences, a child's feelings, fear, humiliation? Locked up in this eight-square-meter room with his guilt, alone with it evening, night, morning, it would be suffocating, it might have been so suffocating that he had to run, had to escape, had to beat up two guards in front of the entrance to an ER.

His eyes rested on the closed door, from the inside. Someone knocked.

Who? The door opened. Bertolsson, the governor.

"Lennart?"

"Yes?"

"What are you doing?"

Lennart got up quickly, straightened the hair on his neck, which always got messed up when he lay down.

"I don't know. I came here. I lay down. I think I wanted to know more."

"Do you?"

"Not a thing."

Bertolsson stepped in. He looked around.

"What a lunatic."

"No, that's just it. I realized that just now. He doesn't understand at all. He feels no remorse. He is incapable of understanding any perspective other than his own."

Bertolsson kicked at the pile lying on the floor, then looked at the shelves, at what was left by the window. He couldn't make sense of it. The chaos on the floor and everything else lined up in the cell, conformity that had no end. He looked at Oscarsson, who turned away, too tired to explain.

"Forget it then. I sought you out to talk to you about another lunatic, one of his colleagues. One of the seven in Lund's pornography club."

"Yeah?"

"His name is Axelsson. Håkan. Convicted for small-time stuff before. He'll be sentenced tomorrow. And he'll be locked up. Not as long as he should, but enough to miss both Christmas and Easter."

"Yeah?"

"He's coming from Kronoberg jail, and he should, of course, be placed here. But you're full."

Lennart Oscarsson yawned long and loudly. He thought for a few seconds then lay down again.

"You'll have to forgive me. They tire me out."

Bertolsson pretended not to notice that one of his unit heads was resting on a bed that belonged to an escaped inmate.

"You've only got this cell. Which is empty. But Lund should be back here damn soon."

"You see. You see. Sex crimes are trendy. Perverts all lined up."

Bertolsson angled the blinds, letting in bright sunlight. Outside, a day was in progress. It was easy to forget. Inside the prison, time wasn't divided into days, everything flowed together, turning into waiting and clumps of months and years.

"We'll have to place him in one of our normal units. A few days, a week until we can find something out in the country."

Lennart winced. He was silent, then rose up on his elbow, facing Bertolsson.

"Arne, what the hell are you saying?"

"You know he doesn't have to take his sentence into the unit with him."

"They won't give a shit about that. They'll find out why he's there, and then you know how it goes."

"Just a few days. Then he'll leave them."

Oscarsson drew in his elbow and sat up.

"Arne. Stop it. I know you know. If he leaves a normal unit he'll be doing it by ambulance, nothing else."

IT DIDN'T SMELL like anything. He knew that. But it didn't matter. He'd been here before, and even now, on the steps outside, his nose, his brain could smell death.

Sven Sundkvist had visited Forensic Medicine in Solna more times than he could remember. A detective in Stockholm has to do this, he knew that, but he also knew that he would always hate this part of the work, never learn to look at a dead person lying on a gurney, who had just been breathing and talking and laughing, that a man—most were men—in a white coat had sawed, opened, used their hands to lift what was inside into the bright light of the lamps in order to investigate it and then throw it back into the hole in the chest, chaotic, before sewing it shut again, before the dead person was covered in fabric to seem less offensive to their families, who would soon come, who would soon see their loved one and explain that this shell lying before them was the very person they'd just spoken to, filled with hope.

Ewert Grens didn't work that way. He stood next to Sven, also waiting for the coroner who'd answered the intercom, and Sven thought about the times they'd been here together. It was as if Ewert didn't understand that this was about death, as if he couldn't see the bodies that way, as if, when death replaced life, they were no longer human beings to him. Every time they came here, he ended up lifting the fabric that covered them, searching the dead skin, pinching the body, and saying something funny, as if to prove that this was just a thing and nothing more than that lying in front of them, that it was impossible to hurt it.

The coroner stood on the other side of the glass door. He was looking for his keycard, found it in the inside pocket of his white coat, a clicking sound as the door opened. Ludvig Errfors, fifty-plus, one of their most experienced coroners. Sven was glad they'd chosen Errfors, a child must be much more difficult to dissect, or, at least, you'd have less practice. But, if anyone could do it, if anyone had been here long enough to do this, it was Errfors.

They said hello, Errfors asked about Bernt Lund, and they told him they still knew nothing. He shook his head and made some short reference to the last time, to four years ago. He'd been the one who worked on those two small girls from the basement murders. He spoke loudly, while Sven and Ewert followed him down the stairs, explaining that he'd never before seen such senseless violence, definitely not done to children.

He stopped in mid-step, turned around, serious.

"Not until now."

"What do you mean?"

"I recognize the injuries. It was definitely Lund's work."

They continued to the stairs that led to a short corridor. It was the first room to the right, where Errfors usually worked.

There in the middle of the room—the damn table. It smelled, it did, but not much. Sundkvist realized if he didn't know this was an autopsy room, he wouldn't know it was a dead body he was smelling. The ventilation system was effective. The muffled hum ran all the time, changing the air, changing the smell. They should have dressed in green sterile clothing, but Errfors had waved dismissively. He was old enough to know when he could break the rules.

He turned off two lamps on the long sides of the room, kept on a single, bright one in the middle, large enough to cover the entire table. It was dark behind them, concentrated light on a dark stage.

"We can see better this way, all those shiny instruments reflect the light and make it harder to see."

The child in front of them looked peaceful. Her face, asleep. They recognized her from her parents' photographs.

Errfors lifted up a plastic folder that was lying next to her. He opened a glasses case, powerful glasses in thick black frames.

He pulled out two sheets of paper.

"Well, she's not peaceful underneath the fabric."

It was quiet, an almost soundproof room. The sound of papers rustling took up space.

"Traces of sperm were found in the vagina, anus, on the body. The perpetrator has ejaculated on her after death as well."

He lifted the cloth to show them. Sven turned his face away, couldn't stand to look, while Ewert searched the girl's body, trying to follow Errfors's report. He sighed.

"Like last time."

"It was rougher, but yes, you're right, the procedure was the same."

The coroner took out the other paper.

"I've determined the cause of death. A sharp blow, presumably from the edge of the hand, directed toward the throat."

Ewert looked at her neck. A large mark. He turned to Sven, who was still looking away.

"Sven."

"I can't."

"You don't need to. I'll look."

"Thank you."

"But you should know that we have him."

"We don't have shit."

"When we pick him up it will be a sure thing. Semen everywhere. Just like last time. We still have that. Just a single DNA sample for comparison and we'll know that it was him."

She'd been lying there, in the woods. Sven saw Margareta and Rune Lantz ahead of him. Two elderly people, two people who loved each other, who held each other's hands, didn't leave each other, their eyes, the tears flowing the entire time they were being questioned—hers had been worse, coming quietly at every answer, every time she was forced to describe.

I think we should sit down here. On this stone.

Okay.

I want us to do the interview here, so we can see the site. Is that okay?

Yes.

I want to know everything. From the beginning.

Can he stay here?

That's fine.

I don't know.

Try.

I don't know if I can.

For the girl's sake.

We take a walk every evening.

Every evening?

If it's not pouring.

Here?

Yes.

The same route?

Different ones. We usually try to vary it.

This path?

Yes?

Do you usually take it?

No. This was probably the first time. Was it, Rune?

I'll talk to Rune later. Right now I just want to hear from you.

I didn't recognize it.

Why did you choose this one?

We didn't choose it. It just happened. When we heard the helicopter.

The helicopter?

I thought it was horrible. That and the police dog. We were in a hurry.

And that's how you ended up on this path?

It seemed the closest.

What happened when you got here?

Do you have any tissues?

Sorry?

Or a handkerchief.

Unfortunately not.

I'm so sorry.

No need to apologize.

We were holding hands.
When you were walking?
Yes. Until we got here. By the tree. Then we let go.
Why?
It was too big. We had to walk on either side of it.
Who went first?
We went at the same time. On either side.
What happened then?
I thought it was a mushroom. It was so red. I kicked at it.
It?
The shoe. I realized that when I kicked it. That it was a shoe.
What did you do then?
I waited. For Rune. I knew something wasn't right.
How did you know?
Sometimes you just know. The helicopter, the dog, a shoe. I felt there was something horrible about it.
What did you do?
Lifted it up. Showed it to Rune. I wanted him to see it.
And then?
Then she was just lying there.
Where?
In the grass. I saw that she'd been destroyed.
Destroyed?
That she wasn't whole. I saw it. Rune saw it, too. That she wasn't whole.
She lay in the grass? Did you touch her?
She was dead. Why would we touch her?
I have to ask.
I can't do any more.
Just a couple more questions.
I don't want to.
Did you see anyone here?
The girl. She was lying there looking at me. Completely ruined.
I mean someone else. Somebody besides just you and Rune?
No.
Nobody at all?

We saw the dog. And the policeman.
Nobody else?
I can't. Rune, tell him that I can't do this.

The coroner spent a long time looking for a third paper in his folder. He couldn't find it. He walked away from the mortuary gurney to a shelf behind him. He found what he was looking for there.

"There's one more thing. Another connection to the last time."

He covered her up again. Sven turned back toward the gurney and to the fabric covering the body.

"Notice that when she arrived her feet were completely clean, while the rest of her was bloody and broken. We tested her feet. We found traces of—"

Ewert interrupted.

"Saliva. Right?"

Errfors nodded.

"Saliva. Just like last time."

Ewert looked at her face. She didn't exist. She lay there, but she didn't exist.

"Bernt Lund's version of foreplay. He licks their shoes. And feet."

"Not this time."

"You just said he did."

"There was no foreplay this time. This was afterward. He licked this girl's feet after she died."

———

He hadn't seen her for several months. They talked to each other on the phone every day, but only about Marie, about what time she woke up, what she ate, if she was using new words, playing new games, if she cried laughed lived—each step in a child's development that the absent parent was robbed of, they tried to compensate for with those calls. If it had to do with Marie—and only then—there was no bitterness, no accusations, no lost love.

Her beautiful face, he knew what it looked like when she was crying, how it swelled, how her features smeared together. He put his hand on her cheek, and she smiled at him, hugged him.

They were let in by a police officer, one of the policemen who'd come to the Dove nursery school yesterday from Stockholm, an older man who limped slightly.

"Ewert Grens, detective superintendent. We met yesterday."

"Fredrik. I recognize you. This is Agnes. Marie's mother."

They greeted each other quickly, then went down one floor to a hospital corridor. He saw the other officer from yesterday, the one who had interviewed him. Behind him stood a doctor with a white coat and tired eyes.

"We haven't met. Sven Sundkvist, detective."

"Agnes Steffansson."

"This is Ludvig Errfors. The coroner. He's performed the autopsy on Marie."

Autopsy on Marie.

The words screamed at them.

Hateful, piercing, final.

———

Twenty-four hours of hell hope hell hope hell hope was aching inside their bodies—just after lunch one day ago, Fredrik had left the person they both breathed for at her school, and now, in a sterile room at a forensic medicine center, they both had to look at her destroyed body and confirm that it was her.

They held on to each other.

Sometimes people hold on to each other until they shatter.

THE SUMMER STOOD still.

The sultry air was difficult to breathe.

He didn't notice. He was weeping.

Sundkvist had concentrated on soon, soon air, soon life, soon soon soon. He couldn't break down in front of them, the parents who'd held each other in front of the hospital gurney and nodded affirmatively when they saw her face. The father had kissed the girl's cheek, the mother had collapsed on top of her, her head against the fabric covering the girl's body. They'd screamed like he'd never heard anyone scream before. They'd died together in front of him, and he'd tried to keep his gaze fixed somewhere above them, on a point on the wall, soon away from this fucking gurney, soon out of this fucking room, soon up up up the stairs and out into air that didn't smell like death.

They'd held on to each other as they left, and he'd run out of there as soon as they'd gone, the corridor stairs door. He'd wept and had no wish to stop.

Grens also came, passed him, took him by the shoulder.

"I'll be in the car. I'll be waiting there. This is your time, take as much as you need."

Ten minutes? Twenty? He had no idea. He cried until he was empty, until there was no more. He cried their tears, as if they didn't have room for all of them, as if they all had to share in the grief.

Ewert patted him lightly on the cheek when he sat down in the car.

"I've been sitting here listening to shitty radio. The news is all about Bernt Lund and Marie's murder. It doesn't matter which fucking station I choose. They have their summer murder and from now on they'll be following every step we take."

Sven grabbed hold of the steering wheel in front of him, pointed at it, then at his boss.

"Do you want to drive?"

"No."

"Just for now. I really don't want to."

"I'll wait here until you're ready to turn the key. We have time."

Sven sat still. A few minutes. The radio changed from one indistinguishable pop song to another. He turned toward the back seat.

"You hungry for some cake?"

He reached for the box, pulled it toward him. Farther in the back lay the plastic bag with wine bottles. He put what remained of his party on his lap.

"It's a princess cake. That's what Jonas wanted. With two roses on it. One for me, one for him."

He snapped the string, opened the box, put his nose close to the green marzipan.

"Twenty-four hours in this heat. It's worse than sour."

Ewert flinched from the sudden stench, grimaced, disgusted by the smell of rancid cream, pushed the carton from Sven's knee, as far away as possible. He turned the car radio up, changed the station, changed it again.

The same words, a mantra, in newscast after newscast.

Child murder. Escape. Rapist. Bernt Lund. Aspsås. Police hunt. Grief. Horror.

"I can't listen to this shit anymore, can't stand to have this in my face. Can't you turn it off, Ewert?"

Sven grabbed a bottle out of the bag, inspected the label, nodded, and uncorked it.

"I think I need a little of this."

He put the bottle to his mouth, swallowed. Once. Three times.

"Do you understand? I turned forty yesterday. I celebrated by going to Strängnäs to interrogate an elderly woman who'd found a raped and murdered girl in the woods. Then I came here today, looked at that little girl, was told she had traces of semen in her anus, that a sharp object had been rammed into her vagina. I saw her parents fall apart as they held her. I don't understand it. Not any of it. I just want to go home."

"It's time to go."

Ewert grabbed the bottle out of Sven's hand, held out his palm for the cork, pushed it into the neck again, and placed the bottle at his feet.

"It's not just you, Sven. We are all equally frustrated, equally destroyed. But what good does it do? We have to find him. That's what matters. Get him before he does it again."

Sven started the car, backed out carefully from the large parking lot at the roundabout between the Forensic Medicine Center and the Karolinska Hospital. The lot was crowded despite the summer holidays, cars parked tightly in the usual Stockholm manner, as close to the next car as possible.

Ewert continued.

"Because I know what it's about for him. I've interrogated him, and I've read everything. Every line that the psychologists and psychiatrists have written. He will do this again. It's just a matter of time. He's abandoned all self-control, so he'll keep doing this until he's apprehended, or until he destroys himself."

TINYBOY SOUGHT THE shade. The exercise yard had no trees, walls, fences to hide behind or to stop the sun. Sweat ran down his back, and the big gravel yard had turned into a dry dusty cloud bordered by walls of gray stone. They'd tried playing football, two five-man teams and five thousand kronor in the pot, but after the first half ended in a draw, they quit, shoulders aching, red, and every breath an agony. Both teams lay down behind their goals and hadn't gotten back up again. Two representatives, one from each side, met in the center circle, declared that they themselves would gladly continue, but, for the sake of their opponents, they'd stop the game and take back the bet. Skåne, one of the negotiators, came back, sat down between Hilding and Tinyboy.

"Just like we wanted. They're totally fucking exhausted. The Russian can hardly breathe."

"Good. Good."

"On Monday, we'll play the second half. I raised our stake. Doubled it. They can't fucking play."

Hilding winced, looked anxiously at Tinyboy while scratching the long deep sore on his nostril. Bekir sat quietly, Dragan, too.

Tinyboy spat in the dry gravel.

"What the fuck? You doubled it? And who pays if we lose?"

"Shit, Tiny, we won't lose. They have no real goalie."

Tinyboy raised his head, studying their opponents on the other side of the field—still lying down, trying to hide from the sun, drained of all energy.

"You must be fucking high, Skåne, you motherfucker. Have you seen them play? Were you here? We had some good fucking luck, that's it. But okay, Skåne. Okay. What the hell. Why the hell not? Let's do it. Double the fucking pot, because you'll cover it if we lose. You can cover it. If we win, we share equally. Two grand each. Fair and square."

Skåne defiantly shook his head and walked a few meters away. He lay on his belly in the dust, doing push-ups, counting aloud so the others could hear, ten, twenty, fifty, one hundred fifty, and two hundred fifty. His wide neck shiny with sweat running down. He groaned and emptied all the frustration of this summer, and of the four years he still had to go.

Tinyboy stared at the sun, opening his eyes to bright sunlight, then closing them, making pricks of light and colors and waves and rhythms behind his eyelids. It was something he'd done since he was a child. It was easier to escape when all you had to do was close your eyes.

"And the fucking hitman then?"

Hilding felt the question, didn't want to touch it.

"What about the hitman?"

"Haven't seen him today."

"Why the hell would I know that?"

"That's your fucking job. Jochum Lang and Håkan Axelsson, they're new, and they're your fucking job. You should explain to them how the hell it works."

"Like your conversation with Jochum?"

"Shut up."

"What the fuck should I tell him? I'm not saying anything, not after Branco's letter."

The wind was blowing gently. The first breeze they'd felt for several days. It came suddenly, like sand, caressed their faces, and they stopped talking for a moment. Tinyboy sat up, wanted to breathe in something for a moment other than this oppressive heat. When he turned toward the wall, he saw him walking along the concrete, sandy-haired and bearded, one of the two new guys who arrived this morning. He followed him with his eyes, every step. He took out a pack of cigarettes and a lighter, lit one of the many halves that lay there. He didn't stop looking at the solitary walker, and slowly became irritated and waved his arms.

"There he goes. Axelsson. No one has a fucking clue who he is. Says he's here for assault. What the hell, the motherfucker couldn't piss on a football! I bet anything that fucker is a perv. I can feel it. I can smell those fucking bastards."

Hilding had woken up from the temporary coolness. He sat up, too, next to Tinyboy and watched Axelsson's slow walk.

"I heard the guards earlier. They were talking about the creep unit. That it was full. Every fucking cell is filled with pervs. Maybe that's why he's here. They can't put him anywhere else."

Tinyboy kicked the gravel in annoyance. White dust rose toward blue sky. He threw his cigarette down. It glowed for a while, then slowly went out.

"Skåne."

"Yeah."

"Look at me."

Skåne turned toward him.

"Yeah?"

"You have a job."

"What the fuck are you talking about?"

"You have six hours' leave. Right?"

"Yeah."

"No guards. Right?"

"Yeah."

"Then you know what you should do. You should look up Axelsson's record."

"But I can't. I got other things to do. Six shitty hours, I have a fucking girl."

Tinyboy laughed.

"You can forget that. Idiots who double our bet after a draw don't get a choice."

He pointed at them, first Skåne, then Hilding, then Skåne again.

"Hilding Wilding, would you be so kind as to get hold of Axelsson's social security number? Then you give it to Skåne, who's gonna get his junkie ass to Stockholm District Court tomorrow and request to see Axelsson's record. Then, motherfuckers. Then, we'll see!"

Hilding ripped at the skin of his nose until it bled, clearing his throat for a long time, but was interrupted by Tinyboy before he could start talking.

"No goddamn arguments. Just do it."

———

Lennart Oscarsson often stood in his office in the same place, at the same window. Calm. That's what he felt here. He had a good view of the yard and the football field, where he could watch grown men who'd threatened, assaulted, killed, lie on their backs in the sun panting heavily. He recognized Tinyboy and his harem—how they pointed and stared at Håkan Axelsson who was walking along the sawdust trail. He swallowed nervously. He warned Bertolsson not to put a convicted child pornographer in with the regular population. This would end badly. He'd seen it before, and only those who didn't live in this strange reality could think anything else.

THE SLUT HAD screamed when he took off her red shoes. He'd pressed her to the ground then, to the grass. Sluts should scream, but there'd been too many other people in the area, joggers and retirees taking walks. She hadn't liked it when he kissed the red patent leather and the metal buckles. She'd screamed louder than the others, yes, she had, and her scream was beautiful. He had to kiss her feet later. Maybe he'd been too harsh on her, pressing her face for a long time against the dry ground. It's hard with sluts. If you're nice to them they just want more cock. She was the same.

She'd had beautiful feet. The skin so light, toes so small. He'd almost forgotten what small sluts felt like. Four years, he'd been waiting, and now he didn't need to anymore. Now, they were with him again.

Sluts were the worst afterward. Once they got their cock. Once they were silent.

He'd hidden her. A large fir, branches that reached the ground, he found her a place underneath it. She'd been dirty—it was stupid to press so hard. He licked her feet clean. They tasted like soil.

———

He'd been sitting here for three hours now. It was a good bench, not too close, but still he could see everyone coming and going. It seemed like a good nursery school. He'd been here before, and the kids always looked happy.

There were guards. Just ordinary cops, but they were in the way. He'd have to get around them. In Strängnäs there'd been two outside every building. But this was Enköping, thirty kilometers away. He hadn't anticipated that they'd be here as well.

———

Little tiny sluts.

He'd seen a few already.

Almost all blondes, he preferred light-skinned sluts. They were always softer, their skin. He could see their blood vessels clearly, and red spots appeared when you pushed hard with your fingers.

IT WAS A beautiful church. Proud, white, powerful, dominating the small town, much too big, too demanding. He wondered if it had been built for a congregation of that size or if it was just the standard size, built in a time when Christianity was the law, and humanity and the universe were on a different scale.

Fredrik Steffansson liked it a lot. It had been a long time since he'd left the Swedish Church. He believed in what he could see, and he saw no life beyond death. But this church, this cemetery, was much more than that. This was his life. His childhood. Summer after summer, when he'd devotedly followed his grandfather, the sexton, to his job here. He'd watched him dig deep graves, mow a lawn that went on forever, put up the golden metal numbers of the hymns on a blackboard. He'd helped his grandpa as much as he would allow: every Saturday pressing the button that rang the church bell, after every service gathering the Bibles and putting them on a wagon with a rusty wheel, putting long shiny white candles in heavy brass candlesticks on the altar and then making sure they stood in a straight line. He realized this was nostalgia, polished memories, but he didn't care. What he did care about was that his grandfather had become his idol instead of some football player, that he still loved this ninety-four-year-old silver-haired man who walked around in his kitchen on stiff legs sipping boiled coffee, that it had been a happy time; the only future he recognized today.

He saw Agnes in the distance. She wasn't dressed in black—they'd both agreed on bright summer clothes—and had her eyes on the ground. She looked haggard. She was forty years old but had never before looked more than twenty. Three days and the years had started catching up with her. Sooner or later time always catches up. He wanted to hold her. He wanted her to hold him. They needed each other now, and in just a moment they were going to die together. Without Marie they would be forever separated.

They'd chosen a small funeral. No announcement, no invitations. Fredrik and Agnes. Micaela. No one else. Nothing more. The two officers leading the investigation wanted to attend and justified it with investigative reasons. He'd hesitantly said yes, as long as they kept quiet and stood at the back, they could do what they wanted.

He walked alone across the lawn, crossing between well-tended graves with lots of flowers and graves that time had covered with black moss, making their inscriptions difficult to read. He'd walked here as a child, back and forth, looking at the headstones, reading the names, figuring out how old they had been, wondering about the woman who was born in 1861 and died in 1963, about the boy born in 1953 who died in 1954, about how life could have such varying lengths that one would have the chance to grow up and find their way and another didn't even get the chance to learn to walk.

His own daughter would soon be buried. She'd had five years.

"Fredrik?"

He hadn't seen her approach. She laid her hand gently on his shoulder.

"Fredrik, how are you?"

He spun around quickly.

"I didn't hear you."

She smiled. One of the good people. He'd known her as long as he could remember. Grandpa had thought highly of her, helped her out regularly. He'd kept working until he was seventy-five, and especially at the beginning, when she was just out of school, inexperienced, a woman in a domain of men, he'd supported, protected, and smoothed the way for her, the congregation's new priest. Fredrik realized later that she must have been very young back then, as a child he'd seen her as one of the elderly. As an adult, they were suddenly in the same age range.

"I will never be able to understand how you feel, but I've been thinking about you. Every second since last Tuesday."

"Rebecka. I'm glad it's you."

"I've been a priest for three decades. This is the worst fucking day of them all."

Fredrik winced. Her expletive ricocheted off him, off the gravestones, off her faith. He'd never seen her as anything other than a great comfort, but now her face was broken, the softness and calm had turned hard and tense and torn.

Fredrik looked at the coffin. Wooden planks with flowers on it, right there in front of him. He held Agnes. They stood in the front row, every movement echoing through the empty church. He couldn't understand that there was a child in there. His child. Who he'd been talking to, laughing with, holding just a few days ago. Agnes wept and shook. He pulled her closer, held her tighter.

He couldn't cry. Since last Tuesday the grief had invaded him, robbed him, leaving only a hole in his chest.

She no longer exists.

She no longer exists.

She no longer exists.

HE PROBABLY SHOULD have sung. The cantor had played something on the organ.

Together they exited the echoing building. Rebecka had poured the soil over the coffin, said what she had to say, hugged him and Agnes, trying to console them but not managing to. Her own grief and anger and frailty had made her rudely push them away, look at them, immediately pull them close and hug them again, and then just leave.

They stood quietly on the gravel path. The sun was like before, still summer outside, the same long summer as when he wandered around here with Grandpa.

Now she would be buried, with the others.

"I'm sorry."

Behind them, the policemen, the old one who limped and Sundkvist, the one who questioned them. They were dressed in black. He wondered if they had thought of it themselves or if it was police etiquette.

"I don't have any children so I can't possibly understand, but I've lost someone close and know how that feels."

The older, limping policeman looked down the path as he spoke. It sounded awkward, bordering on harsh, but Fredrik knew it was for real, that it cost more than it seemed to.

"Thank you."

They shook hands. Sundkvist said something to Agnes, he didn't hear what.

They fell silent. A slight wind swirled around them. It had been blowing for a few days now. Maybe rain was coming. It was three weeks since the last rain, and it felt as if everyone had forgotten that anything existed other than this unrelenting heat.

The older one cleared his throat and spoke again.

"I don't know if it matters to you, but we'll get him soon. We've got a lot of people on the job, hunting."

Fredrik shrugged.

"You're right, you don't know if it matters to us."

"Does it?"

"No. Our daughter is dead. Nothing you can do can change that."

The older man nodded slowly.

"I can understand that. I would have felt the same. But it's our job. It's about punishing and preventing more crimes."

Fredrik had just taken Agnes by the hand, preparing to go, so they could mourn alone for a while. Now he turned to the two policemen, looking at the older one.

"What do you mean?"

"Since last Tuesday we've been guarding every daycare, every school."

"Because that's where you expect to find him?"

"Yeah."

Fredrik released Agnes's hand, searched her eyes; she was waiting, but she could wait a while longer.

"Which schools?"

"Here. All around. Many locations, a large area."

"And you're guarding them because you think he'll do it again?"

"We're guarding them because we're confident that he will try to do it again."

"Why?"

"We know how he acted in the past. And we have a clear mental profile of him. He's been examined by more psychiatrists and psychologists than any other prisoner in this country. He will do it again and again until he decides to commit suicide."

"And you know that?"

"Just the fact that he let you see him before . . . before this, the psychologists say that means he's passed whatever limits he had left, the last, when there is nothing left but destruction and self-hate."

He took Agnes's hand again. The cemetery seemed large.

He was alone. She was alone.

They would carry on—he maybe with Micaela, Agnes maybe with someone else. But they would always be alone.

———

They had driven from the cemetery to a restaurant in Strängnäs. He'd dropped off Micaela at home first, held her for a long time.

He was going to stay with Agnes, just a little longer.

They'd sat in an ugly courtyard, which was turned into a café in the summer, at a table jammed between a carpet beater and a bike rack, but they were in the shade with a light wind cooling them, and they were alone.

They'd driven to the train after that, but when Agnes was about to buy a ticket in the tobacco shop/ticket booth, they changed their minds. Fredrik offered to drive Agnes home, to Stockholm. They could sit next to each other for an extra hour, not have to say good-bye right here and now. They'd have an extra hundred or so kilometers on a busy highway to try to understand that not only had they lost a child, they'd also lost their relationship to each other. Tomorrow they would be two adults who shared nothing more than grief.

They didn't say much. There wasn't much to say. He dropped her off at St. Eriksplan. She was going to buy some groceries. She didn't want to go directly home to an empty apartment. They held each other. She kissed him lightly on the cheek, and he watched her walk away down the pavement, until she disappeared behind the corner of Birka Street.

He drove aimlessly through the inner city. Summer had scared most people away, only the occasional tourist out sightseeing, an elderly person with a cane too tired to leave the city, or a young person too broke to afford to get away. Otherwise, there was only asphalt and the heat it generated. He bought an ice cream, sat down next to a young woman under an umbrella, and ate it while empty buses and a few cars drove past; stopped later to order mineral water from a bored café owner, and so on and so forth through a city that was slowly heading home, eating supper, going to bed. It never got completely dark. The short nights and the artificial city lights chased away the darkness. He slept finally in the front seat of his car, his head against the window, on a footpath in the green expanse of Royal Djurgården.

———

His clothes were like glue. His light suit was rumpled, and he really should have washed himself. He awoke to the sound of early-rising ducks combined with drunken teenagers on their way home. Stockholm was smiling, and he had to take a short walk to stretch his back, which felt sore after five hours of sleeping in a sitting position.

He got back in his car, drove over Djurgårds Bridge, past Berwald Hall, stopped in the parking lot outside the Swedish Television building. It had been three years since Vincent left the *Daily News* for television, started working as a news editor at *Newsnight* and the *Nine O'Clock News*. The last time Fredrik visited, Vincent sat at the end of a huge hall, distributing telegrams and short news features to buzzing reporters. He'd moved to the morning news about a year ago, chopping up and reheating last night's photos for a new soup—that's how he himself expressed it. From that day on, he'd become a homogenous cog in the huge news machine, and that, along with a wife and child, suited him just fine for the moment.

Fredrik waited at the security desk. He'd asked a guard in a tight uniform to contact Vincent Carlsson and been told it would take ten minutes, that Carlsson would then come down and meet him.

He was the same. He could see him already through the window, friendly and tall and dark, with a kind of gravitas that made women smile at him. He'd seen it many times when they were in journalism school; stopping by a pub on the way home, Vincent would suddenly exchange glances with a woman at the end of the bar and say, I want that one, and would go over to the most gorgeous woman in the place, start talking and laughing and touching, and would leave with her on his arm. He was that type, easy to like and difficult to be angry with, even when he deserved it.

Vincent motioned to the guard from inside to open the locked doors.

"Fredrik, what are you doing here? Do you know what time it is?"

"Five."

"Quarter past."

They were walking down an endless corridor with blue linoleum floors and chalky white walls.

"I'd been planning on getting ahold of you. Privately, that is. But I didn't want to intrude. I didn't know what the fuck to say. I have no idea what to say now that wouldn't sound . . . wrong."

"We buried Marie yesterday."

Fredrik saw how difficult it was for Vincent, how few words he had, how lost he felt in the face of something he could never understand.

"You don't need to say anything. I know you're trying. I appreciate it, but honestly, fuck it, that's not what I need right now."

The never-ending corridor turned into a new corridor.

"What do you need then? You look like shit. You know you can come here or to my home whenever you want, but why now, five o'clock in the morning the day after Marie's funeral?"

"I need your help. It's the only help I need right now."

One floor up. Past the big newsroom.

"I can't take you in there today. It's impossible. Half of the room is working on broadcasts about Bernt Lund and you and Marie and the police search. There'd be a lot of questions. Let's go in here instead. Nobody comes in here before eight."

Vincent showed him into a smaller office, three desks in three corners, and came right back with two coffee cups.

"Here. I think you need it."

Fredrik nodded.

"Thanks."

They drank in silence for a minute, avoided looking at each other.

"We have plenty of time. I asked the other morning editor to take over my work for a while. She's really good, much better than I am. If her work appears in my box, so much the better."

Fredrik stretched against one of the desktops.

"Look, found some cigarettes. Do you think I could have one?"

"You don't smoke anymore."

"I do today."

He took out a cigarette, no filter, a brand purchased abroad. He didn't recognize it.

He exhaled. White smoke surrounded them.

"Do you remember when you helped me last time?"

"Yes. With Agnes."

"I thought she was fucking that damn economist. I was wrong. But it was thanks to you that I found out who he was."

Vincent waved away some of the smoke pointedly. Fredrik stubbed it out immediately against the bottom of his cup.

"And now?"

"The same thing."

"Same thing?"

"Personal information. Anything you can get your hands on."

"Who?"

"790517-0350."

"Who?"

Fredrik took a note from the inside pocket of his jacket.

"Bernt Lund."

THEY'D RAISED THEIR voices, arguing for and against, and the battle was won through pity. Now they were close to an agreement.

"I'm not breaking the law. But I'm trampling on everything I've believed was friendship."

"That's not true."

"Don't you understand? If I help you find personal data on your daughter's killer, I'm basically doing the one thing I shouldn't do."

"But this is the only thing I need."

"You're on a very unsteady, precarious path."

"Please don't talk so fucking much, and just help me."

Vincent stood up, mostly as emphasis, sat down again, turned on the computer in front of him.

"Well?"

"Yeah?"

"What do you want?"

"Everything. Anything you can get your hands on now."

Vincent moved the incoming news reports aside and minimized the morning news schedule on the screen. He pressed a few times, a name, a password, then got to the database's front page. Heading by heading. The Registrar of Companies, the Trade and Organization Registry, Address Registry, Swedish Information Service, Department of Motor Vehicles, the Land Registry.

"The number. The one you said. The social security number."

"790517-0350."

The screen blinked. A hit.

"You want to know where he lived. Then we'll find that out."

The morning sun streamed through the wall of windows. It was hot, the air still.

"Can I open the window? It's hard to breathe."

"Open them."

Fredrik opened two windows wide. He hadn't noticed he was sweating through his light suit. Two deep breaths, then Vincent's arm in the air.

"Bernt Asmodeus Lund. Last entry is a care-of address."

"Yeah?"

"Twelve Skeppar Street, care of Håkan Axelsson. In Östermalm. But that was a few years ago. He's probably been serving time since then. But no other address is specified. Skeppar Street is the last official address."

Fredrik stood behind Vincent. His back was still sore from last night, and the fresh air passing through the open windows felt good.

"Any other addresses?"

"Two earlier ones. Before Skeppar Street, there was Three Kungs Street in Enköping. Before Enköping, there was Nelsons Street in Piteå."

"Is that all?"

"That's what I can see here. If you want even older information you may have to call the local tax authorities in Piteå."

"That's enough. But I want more facts. Other facts."

Fredrik waited behind Vincent for almost an hour. He took notes on a piece of blank Swedish Television letterhead from the same desk that he'd grabbed the pack of cigarettes from, and he summarized points from each directory entry.

A property in Vetlanda registered to Bernt Lund; an apartment building with oddly high taxes, at an address just outside the city. From his credit history, a long list of unpaid debts, overdue tax accounts, overdue student loans, several failed asset-seizing attempts.

A suspended driver's license.

Two dormant limited companies for trading stock. Four previous board memberships in sports clubs.

Lund's life before prison was difficult to follow. He'd moved often, had constant financial problems, he occasionally made obvious attempts to connect with people. Fredrik wrote it all down, trying to figure out what it was he needed, trying to read what he couldn't see.

Vincent turned around, looked at Fredrik.

"I wish you'd forget about this."

Fredrik didn't answer. He clenched his jaw, stared at his friend, and said nothing.

"You can glare at me as much as you want. I think what I think."

He took the two cups of coffee and went out into the corridor. Fredrik watched him go, then he leaned over to pick up one of the desk's two telephones. He dialed her number.

"Hello. It's me."

He'd woken her up.

"Fredrik?"

"Yes."

"I'm too tired. I took a sleeping pill."

"I just want to know one thing. Where did you put those two duffel bags that we packed up when we cleaned out your father's apartment?"

"What are you talking about?"

"I just want to know."

"I didn't take them. They're still in the storage room upstairs. In Strängnäs."

Vincent came back into the room, full cups in his hands. Fredrik hung up.

"Agnes. It's tough."

"How's she doing?"

"Terrible."

Vincent nodded, gave Fredrik his cup, lifted his to his mouth.

"Let's finish this now. Then I have to go back to the news desk. It's a little crazy out there, a plane crash outside Moscow."

He searched for the screen, the main menu, Companies Registration: partnerships and sole proprietorships. He filled two rectangular boxes with Lund's social security number, the key to all the public records of Sweden. How strange, he thought, the right to chart another person's life with only a number, so convenient and so unbelievably strange.

"B. Lund Taxi."

Fredrik heard, but asked anyway.

"What did you say?"

"A taxi company. Registered as B. Lund Taxi. It hasn't been unregistered."

He walked over to the desk, sat down next to Vincent to read for himself.

"When?"

"Formed in 2002."

Fredrik laughed abruptly. Vincent looked up from the screen.

"What is it?"

"Nothing."

"You're laughing at nothing? Who the hell do you think you're talking to?"

Fredrik laughed again.

"Absolutely nothing."

"Nothing? Come on. You're sitting here less than a day after burying your daughter, your funeral suit still on, laughing. At what? Nothing? Shut up."

"Calm down."

"Calm down? What the hell? That's rich. That's fucking rich. Anything more you want? The company's finances?"

"I'm satisfied."

"Signatories? Reference numbers?"

"I'm good for now."

———

It was raining outside.

Three weeks without precipitation and suddenly drops fell on his head. He opened the door and sat down in his car. The windshield wipers slid across the front window. It took no more than a few wipes to move all the rain aside.

He drove through the city fast. It was still early Saturday morning, and there was no traffic. Out through Hornstull, over Liljeholms Bridge, toward Strängnäs. He put his handwritten notes on the dashboard, glancing cautiously at them as he drove.

An apartment building in Småland. Failed asset-seizing attempts. Addresses in Piteå, Enköping, and Östermalm. He skipped them. That wasn't where he'd find his lead. It was further down, in the trade registry, in B. Lund Taxi. A company that had existed for several years.

Fredrik leaned forward, put his hand under the driver's seat, rooting in the basket there. He wanted to listen to music. From the ugly suburbs of Stockholm to Strängnäs. He wanted to listen to Creedence and "Proud Mary" and sing loudly and forget that grief refused to sing along.

———

It was pouring when he arrived. As if someone was slowly peeling away the membrane that lay above humanity, buildings, life. It was a delivery and a joy, and although water washed over the city, he saw no umbrellas, no one running for shelter. The man and woman in front of him both walked slowly, their clothes getting soaked, while smiling and looking up. Fredrik could feel his suit coming loose from his body, could feel himself getting lighter, the air more rich in oxygen. He walked from the car to the house, lingering on every step, letting the rainfall wash away three weeks of heat and sand.

She was standing in the hall when he opened the door. She held some masks in her hand, a Big Bad Wolf and a Pig. She shouted Daddy and wanted to go outside, wanted to play. Hurry, hurry, she was so eager, as five-year-olds are.

He sat down at the kitchen table. A carton of juice in the fridge, he emptied it into three large glasses. The house, so quiet, so heavy.

He moved the chair, from the table to the phone that hung on the wall. Micaela would soon come home, he had to hurry. Two calls. Then he'd be done.

He was searching for the Enköping phone book, knew he had it in the bottom of a drawer, below the local Strängnäs book. He searched through the yellow pages. He found the number, figures he recognized next to the company's big logo. He'd called them several times before.

A female voice.

"Taxi Enköping."

"Hello. My name is Sven Sundkvist. The personnel department, please."

"One moment please. I'll connect you."

A few seconds, Fredrik cleared his throat, took a deep breath.

"Taxi Enköping, Liv Steen speaking."

"This is Sven Sundkvist, police detective at the Stockholm Police Violent Crime department."

"How may I help you?"

"I'm looking for information concerning a former driver that you worked with by the name of Bernt Lund. Social security number 790517-0350. A company called B. Lund Taxi."

"Okay."

"This is urgent."

"What is it you'd like to know?"

"I want to know what his regularly scheduled trips were when he was driving for you."

"Yes . . . there were quite a few."

"I just need the regularly scheduled trips that went to daycares and schools."

"Well . . . I don't know, we don't usually disclose that kind of information."

Fredrik hesitated. The woman was doing what she was supposed to do. He wasn't accustomed to lying, didn't like it. He'd always found it difficult to decide where the line was and whether or not he'd passed it.

"I'm investigating a murder."

"I don't know if that makes any difference."

"You might have read about it. The five-year-old girl. Raped and murdered."

It was hard to say. He couldn't do much more. The woman hesitated.

"Sundkvist, was it?"

"Yes."

"Can I call you back?"

"Of course."

A long pause.

"Well, I don't want to bother you. We'll do this now."

"Thank you."

Fredrik could hear her looking through folders. The snapping sound as the metal rings that held the papers in place opened and closed. His rain-soaked suit stuck to his skin, like before, when he'd been sweating.

"Eight regularly scheduled trips to nursery schools. Four in Strängnäs and four in Enköping."

"The addresses, please."

She flipped through a few more. She gave him the addresses. He recognized the four in Strängnäs. One of them was the Dove . . . Lund had been familiar with the school. He'd been there many times before, had made trips there for almost a year. He'd returned to where he felt safe, where he knew how the children moved, what the entrances and exits looked like.

Fredrik thanked her for the help, hung up. One more call. To Agnes.

"It's me again."

"I'm still too tired for this."

"I know. I just need the key to the storage. Do you know where it is?"

"There is no key. Because there is no lock. I never cared about that stuff. Those were my father's things. They had nothing to do with me."

"Thanks."

He wanted to end the call. He knew what he needed to know now.

"What are you going to do there?"

"Some of . . . Marie's stuff is there. Things she made at school and gave to him. I want to get them."

"Why?"

"I just do. Do I need to justify that?"

Fredrik stood in front of the refrigerator. He was thirsty. One more glass of juice.

He wrote a note, a few lines, explaining that he'd be gone for a bit but would soon come back. He put it on the refrigerator, a ladybug magnet on top.

It was still raining, a little less now. He walked across the street to the house there, eight apartments behind a villa-style façade. He took the elevator up to the top floor.

HE STOOD UP from the bench.

It was made of hard, thick wooden planks covered with graffiti. He'd been sitting there since this morning, four hours. He was stiff and sore in his body.

He'd seen the sluts several times now. He knew how they moved, how they looked, how they talked with each other. They were beautiful sluts, like the others, not much on their chests, but long slim legs and eyes that had seen cock.

There were two who he liked the most, two blondes, equally happy. He knew their names. They spoke so loudly. He'd taken photos of them when they arrived and when they left. He'd looked at those pictures a lot. It almost felt like he knew them.

———

They were pretty big.

Sluts that age know what they want.

When their parents dropped them off, they barely waved. He thought often about those kinds of sluts, the ones who believed they got to decide; thought about what he would say to them, how he would touch them.

———

He felt alone. He'd been watching for so long. He wanted them to be together, all three.

The parents would come late. That's what those kinds of parents did. He checked his watch. Five past eleven. He had nearly six hours to go.

———

In the afternoon.

Just like with the others.

Sluts were usually outside then. It had been hot before, but now, after the rain, they would be outside even longer. They always were. It was going to be chaotic, everybody in the yard at the same time. The cops wouldn't notice anything.

He knew exactly how he was going to do it.

IT WAS DARK. Fredrik had been here once before, when they'd cleaned out Birger's apartment and put whatever few possessions he had that weren't trash into the storage room. Birger had stopped mid-breath. From one moment to the next, he'd left life for death—they'd found him naked in bed with the *Boating News* still in his hands, half-sitting, half-lying, the bedside lamp lit on the table next to a diary bearing the current date, where he'd recorded the temperature and precipitation, noted a visit to the grocery store, a trip to hand in lottery tickets to the tobacco shop on the corner, and a few lines beneath that remarked that he felt tired and wasn't sure why, but had taken two Tylenol to avoid an incipient headache.

Fredrik had never really gotten to know him. He'd been a man who was difficult to connect with, tall, heavy, aggressive. It was hard to understand that he could be Agnes's father. They were so incredibly different, in both manner and appearance.

He opened the unlocked storage room door. A few boxes of clothing, a floor lamp, two armchairs, four fishing rods, a bicycle cart. At the far end, some duffel bags. He was stepping into the narrow space, squeezing past the two armchairs, when he heard the door open.

He stopped. Waited quietly in the dim light. At least two voices. They were whispering.

The high voice of a boy.

"Hello!"

New whispers.

"Hello! Here we come! And a lot more people too!"

He recognized the voice and smiled. He was about to shout when the other visitor, until now silent, started to speak. A little older, a little tougher.

"Ha! There, you see! I knew it. It always works."

The two boys started to move forward, searching through the storage space. They breathed deeply, said nothing. A few minutes, then Fredrik saw them, they were close, a few units away. He didn't want to scare them.

"Hello, David."

Too late. They were frightened, startled, looking around desperately.

"It's just me. Fredrik."

Now they saw him, too. Followed his voice in the darkness to where he stood waving between the two armchairs. David, short and dark with messy hair, a head shorter than his companion—a strong, ruddy boy Fredrik didn't recognize. They stared at him, at each other, they'd just met the ghost they'd been searching for and were, therefore, disappointed when they found that the awful and horrid thing was just somebody's father in the wrong place.

David pointed at Fredrik.

"Ah. It's just Marie's dad."

David had been Marie's best friend. They'd known each other since their first steps, same playground, same nursery, they'd eaten dinners together, stayed at each other's houses, woken up before the other one. They'd been like the siblings neither of them had. David had just said, *It's just Marie's dad*, then suddenly fell silent, looked away ashamed. He shouldn't have made Marie's father sad, he shouldn't have said Marie's name, she'd become dead now. She wasn't going to exist anymore.

He pulled at his companion's arm, wanting to go, wanting to get away from there and from dead Marie's father.

"Boys, stop."

David was crying when he turned around.

"I'm sorry. I forgot."

Fredrik stepped out of the storage space. He wondered if five-year-old children understood the concept of death. Did they understand that a dead person didn't exist, didn't breathe, couldn't see, couldn't hear, that a dead person would never be able to go to the playground again? He didn't think so. He didn't understand it himself.

"David, come here. And you, too. What's your name?"

"Lukas."

"Come here, too, Lukas."

Fredrik got down on the floor, a reddish-brown brick, filthy and uneven. He pointed to the floor beside him, wanting the boys to sit down.

"I want to tell you something."

They sank down on either side of him. He put his arms around them.

"David?"

"Yes?"

"Do you remember when we played last time?"

David smiled.

"You were the Big Bad Wolf. We were the Little Pigs. We won. We always win."

"You won. As usual. But was it fun?"

"Yep. Really fun. Marie is fun to play with."

She stood there. She smiled. She said they should play one more time. He sighed, like he always did, and she laughed, and they played one more time.

"She was. She was fun to play with. And she laughed a lot. You know that, David."

"Yep. I know that."

"Well then, you also know that you don't need to be afraid to say Marie's name. Not when I'm here and not otherwise."

David gazed down at the brick floor. He tried to understand. He turned to Lukas, then to Fredrik.

"Marie is fun to play with. I know her. I know she's become dead."

"She has."

"You aren't sad because I say her name."

"No, I'm not."

They stayed on the floor for another half hour. Fredrik told them about the funeral, that a priest had poured earth on the coffin, that it had been lowered into the ground. David and Lukas, a thousand questions about why a person has blood in their stomach, about why a child could die before an adult, how it's strange that first you can talk to someone, and then you can't.

He hugged them both, realized when they'd left that this was the first time he'd spoken about her death. They'd forced him. He'd explained, and they hadn't been satisfied, and he had to explain again. He'd even talked about his grief, told them he hadn't cried yet, and they'd indignantly asked him why, and he said he didn't know, that it was incomprehensible, that sometimes a person has so much sadness inside, they can't get it out.

They closed the door behind them, and he was alone again. Completely silent for a while. He took off, into the storage bin, between the armchairs, all the way in to the two duffel bags. He lifted them, turned them upside down. A big pile—books and pots and old clothes. It was in the second bag. It was huge, got stuck in the fabric, he had to shake it loose.

It was a good rifle. That's what Birger had said. He'd hunted quite a bit in his last years—moose, deer, rabbits. He'd been proud of it, took care of it. That was one of the images Fredrik had of him—Birger at the kitchen table in the evening, dismantling his rifle, tediously cleaning every part of it, then reassembling it, in order to sit for a long time and take aim at everything and everyone.

Fredrik picked the rifle up from the floor. He put it in the empty duffel bag, carried it under his arm as he walked away.

SIW MALMKVIST SANG so loudly the walls shook. "You've Only Been Playing with Me," a cover of "Foolin' Around," 1961. As if her voice ricocheted across the room, capturing itself and becoming a duet, even stronger, even more insistent.

I know that you've been foolin' around on me right from the start
So I'll give back your ring and I'll take back my heart

Ewert Grens had hissed at his visitors, telling them three's a crowd, and they could only stay there if they kept quiet. This was the third time he'd played it for them, the volume slightly higher each time. Sven Sundkvist and Lars Ågestam looked at each other, Ågestam questioningly and Sven shrugging his shoulders. This was just how it was. They'd have to sit there until Siw finished singing. Ewert held her photo in his hand, one he'd taken himself in Kristianstad in 1972, while singing along with every word, louder during the chorus. Siw fell silent, a few seconds of the crackle of an LP, Ågestam was about to speak when the intro began again. The detective superintendent raised the volume slightly and waved irritably at Ågestam to sit back down and keep his mouth shut.

But when it's you, a fool I'll always be

Lars Ågestam couldn't take any more Siw. He was in a hurry, he was the one in charge.

He didn't want any more sex crimes, any more flashers, or pedophiles, or rapists. He wanted more than that, wanted to move up up up.

So yesterday he'd been assigned to this. Another sex crime.

But, also, the ticket to his future.

He'd found it difficult not to laugh out loud when he'd been assigned officer in charge of the pursuit of Bernt Lund. Every newscast, every front page, the country was standing still, the murder of a five-year-old girl by a pedophile serial killer who'd escaped from prison dominated the media. This was his opportunity. His breakthrough. Suddenly, he'd become one of the most interesting people in Sweden, at least for the moment.

So honey fool around, you know right where I'm at
Don't worry if I'm lonesome 'cause I'm used to that

No more, not now. Not another line of these clumsy lyrics.

He stood up, walked over to Ewert Grens's bookcase and the bulky tape recorder and pressed the stop button.

The room was completely silent.

Sven stared at the floor. Ewert started to shake, his face turning red. Lars Ågestam knew he'd just broken the police station's oldest unwritten rule, and he couldn't care less.

"You'll have to excuse me, Grens. But I can't listen to any more of those bad rhymes."

The detective superintendent screamed.

"Get the fuck out of my office!"

Ågestam had made up his mind.

"You're sitting around listening to cheesy music rather than doing your job."

Grens continued screaming.

"I was listening to this and working harder than anyone else, when you were still shitting yourself! Get the hell out of here before I do something I regret!"

Ågestam went back to the chair he'd just left, sat down defiantly.

"I want to know where we stand now. And once you tell me what I want to know, I'll give you a lead you don't have yet. And if it's a good one, I'll stay. If not, I promise to go. Agreed?"

Grens decided to throw the little fucker out. He despised opportunistic prosecutors, university boys who'd never taken one on the jaw. This one would have to crawl away. He was on his way toward him when Sven stood up.

"Ewert. Calm down. Let him do what he says. Let him try to give us a new lead. If he doesn't have one, he'll leave."

Ewert hesitated. Ågestam took advantage of the pause, turned abruptly toward Sven.

"So, where are we?"

Sven cleared his throat.

"We've investigated all previously known addresses. And we continue to monitor them."

"His pedophile friends?"

"We've visited them all. They're under surveillance."

"Tips?"

"Streaming in. Newscasts. Newspapers. The public is listening, looking, and we're drowning in information—he's basically been seen all over the country. We're going through them one at a time. So far they've led to nothing."

"Possible next targets?"

"We're guarding as many as we can, we're in touch with every daycare and every school within a fifty-kilometer radius of the last sighting."

"Anything else?"

"Not much."

"So you've hit a dead end?"

"Yes."

Ågestam waited silently. Grens threw his diary onto his desk, raised his voice.

"Say what you have to say, you little prick. Then leave."

The prosecutor stood up, walked slowly around the room. From wall to wall.

"I've driven a lot of taxis. That was how I financed my studies. For five years I drove people around this whole city. Good money at the time. That was before deregulation, before there was a taxi on every street corner."

Grens shouted from his chair.

"And?"

Ågestam ignored the aggression, the hatred.

"I learned a lot. I know how taxis work. I started up a website with taxi info, you know, all possible information that wasn't gathered elsewhere: phone numbers, business structures, price comparisons. The works. I became a kind of expert, the kind tourists and the press turned to for answers."

It was hard to tell if Grens was listening, until he hit the table, breathing raggedly. Sven had seen him grumpy, even savage, but never like this, undignified and out of control.

"And, you little shit, *and*?"

"Bernt Lund drove a taxi. Right?"

Sundkvist nodded affirmatively. Ågestam continued.

"He even ran his own business. B. Lund Taxi. Correct?"

He now turned toward Grens, waiting quietly for him to answer. Four minutes.

A long time when a room is out of balance, when thoughts, feelings, bodies are out of sync.

Grens hissed.

"That he did. A shitload of years ago. We know that. We've turned that devil's bankruptcy inside and out."

Lars Ågestam let his thin legs lope freely across the room. He no longer walked from wall to wall, but instead almost ran, as if he were in a hurry. His fair hair fluttering, his huge glasses fogging up, he looked more like a schoolboy than ever, a schoolboy who'd made up his mind to rebel and was sticking to it.

"You've checked the company's finances, structure, scope. That's good. But you haven't investigated what it was he did."

"It was a taxi. He drove idiots around and got paid for it."

"Who did he drive around?"

"Those records don't exist."

"Not for individuals. But for regularly scheduled trips. Agreements with local governments."

He stopped. Ågestam stood between Grens, behind his desk, and Sundkvist, in the visitor's chair. And then continued the conversation with both of them, making sure to turn from one to the other, emphasizing the fact that he was speaking to both.

"Every small company has a hard time surviving on private customers alone. Most seek out scheduled trips, we called them school runs. The pay is lower, but the income is dependable. You often take children to nursery schools on your school runs. If you had a taxi as long as Lund did, the chances are high that you made school runs, especially if you were a sick man like him. I think if you were to look closely at Lund's business, you'll find contracts for those runs, you'll find schools he drove to regularly. The ones he knows. The ones he's fantasized about. The ones he'll return to."

The prosecutor took a comb out of his pocket, put his short hair back in place. His appearance was so proper—a tie, white shirt, gray suit—he liked feeling elegant, complete, ready.

"Have you investigated it?"

Ewert sat quietly, staring straight ahead, anger that either needed to come out or be smothered. He'd rarely been this provoked, in his office, over his music, his working methods. Either you respected his way, or you stayed in the hallway with the other idiots. He didn't know where this accumulated anger came from, why it was so intense, but now it was, had become so, over time, and with age everyone earned the right to be left alone, to avoid having to explain yourself. Others seemed to have a word for this feeling: they called it bitterness. He was completely uninterested, they could call it whatever the hell they wanted to. He had no need to be liked. He knew who he was and tried to bear it.

He realized the young prosecutor had pointed out something that could be a next step, but he had no desire to show that to him. Sven, however, sat up straighter, seemed appreciative.

"That seems sensible. That could be something. At least the area of surveillance would be drastically reduced. We lack the time and resources. We're doing our best, but it's not easy. If you're right, we'll gain time, and we can focus our resources and get closer to him. I'll look into it immediately."

Sven left the room, hurried steps down the corridor. Ågestam and Grens remained where they were, saying nothing. Grens was too tired to yell, and Ågestam could see how tired he was, how tense he'd been.

Stillness, a break. Until the prosecutor left the center of the room, walked toward Grens, past him, to the bookcase, turned on the tape recorder again.

"Lucky Lips," 1966.

Now you may not be good-looking, and you may not be too rich
But you'll never ever be alone, 'cause you've got lucky lips

Raspy, half-rhymes, jaunty. Ågestam left the office, closing the door behind him.

IT HAD STOPPED raining. The final drops hit the ground as he exited through the stairwell door. The air was clear, easy to breathe. The clouds were already lighter—the sun about to penetrate them—and it would soon be hot, dry, and stagnant again.

Fredrik Steffansson held the duffel bag in his hand, walked across the street to his car, put the bag in the empty back seat. The conversation he'd just had with two little boys about their perspective on death was still inside him. David and Lukas had been sitting close to him on the hard floor listening, understanding, and answering his answers with new questions, the musings of a five-year-old and a seven-year-old on body and soul and the darkness no one can see.

He thought of Marie. He'd thought of her every single moment since last Tuesday, the image of her in death, her still face had blocked any attempt of his to see something else, but now he wanted to think of her as not dead, as she'd been when she lived. He wondered about her concept of death. They'd never spoken about it—they'd never had any reason to.

Had she understood? Had she been afraid?

Had she submitted or had she fought?

Had she known in any way that death might happen at any moment, and that it was the same as eternal solitude in a white wooden coffin with flowers under a freshly mown lawn?

He drove through the narrow streets of Strängnäs, glancing at his address list: four nursery schools in Strängnäs, four in Enköping. He was sure that he was right. Lund was sitting outside one of them. He was waiting there, just as he had outside the Dove. Fredrik thought about the limping policeman in the cemetery, about how convinced he'd been that Lund would strike again and again until somebody stopped him.

The Dove first. Marie's nursery school was on the list, and Lund could just as well be sitting there as anywhere else, like an animal did when it found food. Fredrik had driven the same route for almost four years, knew every house, every street sign, and he hated it. It looked like safety and habit, but was a slowly suffocating grief. He was home, but there would never be home.

He parked a hundred meters away. In front of the gate stood a car labeled Security and security guards carrying batons, a bit farther away a police car with two uniformed police officers. It felt strange to sit outside the same school where he'd left his daughter six days ago, for the few hours between one thirty and five. If only he hadn't taken her there! They were so late already. Marie had been nagging, and he felt guilty for sleeping for such a long time. If only he'd stayed at home, if only he had taken her by the hand and walked to town, bought her an ice cream in the harbor like they used to do. If only he'd told her that she, like the other kids, had to stay inside when the heat was so extreme. He sat in the car, waiting. He walked into the woods outside the gate and looked back and forth until he was convinced that Lund wasn't nearby, wasn't watching this nursery school.

He started the car, backed out, drove toward the Grove nursery school, a few kilometers closer to town. He turned on the car radio, it was almost twelve thirty, the news. First, the plane crash outside Moscow, one hundred and sixteen dead, probably a mechanical problem, a Russian plane whose maintenance had been neglected. Then Marie. The hunt for her killer continued. A prosecutor appointed to lead the investigation was interviewed but didn't have much to say. A police officer, the older one from the cemetery who was apparently named Grens, loudly asked the reporters to disperse. And, finally, a forensic psychiatrist who'd examined Lund on several occasions warned that his behavior included compulsive repetition, because of an internal pressure that could only be satisfied by giving in to violent impulses.

He stopped and searched the area around the Grove, then drove to the other side of town to the Park and the Creek nursery schools.

Security services, police cars.

Lund wasn't there, hadn't been there.

Fredrik left Strängnäs, taking route 55 to Enköping. He drove fast—four addresses to go.

He looked at the duffel bag. He didn't hesitate.

What was right was right.

THE TREELESS EXERCISE yard was suddenly bearable. The rain had swept in over Aspsås prison and for a few hours dozens of inmates stripped to the waist in prison blue shorts and ran back and forth across the gravel, roaring. For a little while they didn't have to squint or cower from the dust, or sweat profusely from every move they made.

Last Thursday's football match had continued, the second half, and the pot had doubled, ten thousand kronor. Full time and still tied. They lay down like last time, one team behind each goal, but now in the rain with their faces to the sky—immediate coolness.

Tinyboy lay between Hilding and Skåne. He changed his position and those beside him followed suit, moving a bit farther away.

"How the hell could you be so stupid, Skåne? How the hell could you double the pot when we never had a chance, not at all?"

Skåne fidgeted, looked at Hilding, but received no support.

"It's . . . a draw. What are you talking about? It's not like we lost."

"Not yet, you fucking junkie. Have any of us had the ball during this half?"

He raised his head, looked around.

"Is that right? Is there anyone here who's done anything besides running and chasing? Extra time, dammit! Don't you get that? We'll keep chasing, and they'll keep kicking the ball to each other."

Hilding stared up at the raindrops, finding it difficult to lie still, to keep his finger off the wound on his nose. He was worried, his thoughts far away from some lousy football game with a few thousand riding on it. He kept glancing at Skåne, trying to get his attention. They were the only ones who knew so far, and they were the only ones who knew Tinyboy well enough to know he was capable of killing that pervert.

Skåne had had his six-hour release this morning. From seven to one. Permission to go to the city without guards. He'd fixed his brother's car and hurried to Täby to see his woman. They'd had coffee in her kitchen and then almost timidly undressed each other, and afterward he'd lain still against her naked body and she had caressed his face and said that she'd been waiting, that she'd fantasized and longed for this and knew she could wait four more years. He'd stayed half an hour too long and driven faster than he should have into the city. There'd been a traffic jam at the entrance, and he'd lost his patience, parked the car behind a hot dog stand and continued on foot, ran to the bus on Oden Street and hopped off at Fleming Street, ran into the courthouse, where the officer had been slow as hell but finally found the goddamn sentence. Then he'd run back again, to the car and back to Aspsås. He'd made it back with seventeen minutes to spare on the prison clock.

The sentence contained exactly what he'd feared. He'd returned to the unit just before the football game, told Tinyboy that after the final whistle he'd go through what he'd learned, what he'd already suspected: Håkan Axelsson had been convicted for possession of child pornography. Axelsson had been one of seven in a ring of pedophiles who streamed pictures and video of serious abuse online at a predetermined time. Bernt Lund had been one of the seven; two of the others had already been convicted and sat in the pervert unit at Aspsås. During the match, when for a moment they stood next to each other, Skåne had told Hilding what he knew, what he'd anticipated. Hilding had started tearing at his nose. He knew if Tinyboy found out any of this before Axelsson was moved, there would be an execution. And they didn't want that, none of them did, an execution tightened security and legitimized extended searches. It would bring in a shitload of guards, and they'd turn cells upside down until they realized they weren't going to find out a goddamn thing.

Hilding shook off the gravel that the rain had glued to his body. Tinyboy snapped irritably.

"Where the hell are you going? We're still playing."

"To the crapper. We won't start for a few minutes. I can't take a shit out here. Right?"

He walked toward the gray building and the door on the gable wall, opened it, and ran toward Axelsson's cell. Empty. He ran into the john, into the shower, into the kitchen. Empty. He tore at his nose until it bled, and he ran on toward the weight room. He spent a few seconds outside, looking around, then went inside.

There he lay. On his back on a bench, his hands wrapped around a barbell raised above his chest. He lowered it, raised it again. Bench-pressing eighty kilos. Hilding waited. Axelsson took a deep breath, lowered the metal bar again. With a few quick steps, Hilding arrived before the bar was pushed up completely. He grabbed it, putting the weight of his body onto the barbell and onto Axelsson, pushing it down toward his neck.

"I'm not doing this because I like you."

Axelsson kicked his legs, turning red in the face, having trouble breathing.

"What the hell is this about?"

Hilding pushed the bar even harder against his throat.

"Shut your fucking mouth, pervert!"

Axelsson quit kicking, stopped resisting. Hilding reduced the pressure slightly.

"I just talked to Skåne. He looked at your record today. You're a pervert who fucks kids!"

Axelsson was scared now. He couldn't say anything, but his eyes showed he knew what this was about.

"But this is your lucky day, pervert. You see, I don't want any murders in this unit. It's a pain in my ass. So I'm gonna give you one chance. In ten minutes I'm going to tell what I know to Tinyboy. If you're still here when he finds out, you'll be fucking lucky to make it out of here in an ambulance."

Axelsson's red face drained of color and he started trembling, spoke forcefully, and tried kicking his way loose again.

"Why are you telling me this?"

"Weren't you listening? I don't give a shit about you. But I don't wanna have to deal with any murders."

"What the hell do I do? I serve time where they fucking put me."

Hilding pressed one last time against his neck. Axelsson coughed, gasped for breath.

"If you want to survive this day, you better fucking listen. Understood?"

Axelsson nodded.

"I'm gonna leave now. Then you take your little pedophile ass over to the guards in this unit and ask to be put into solitary. Request voluntary isolation and tell them we have your records. But you better not say who warned you! Do you understand me?"

Axelsson nodded, eagerly this time. Hilding stood over him, gave a short laugh, collecting all the saliva in his cheeks, moved his mouth, and stopped just above Axelsson's face before slowly letting the spit trickle down.

GRENS DIDN'T WANT to go home. He was tired, had been sleeping in his office since Lund escaped, as he always did when something unusual happened. He was older now, he knew that, a gray-haired man approaching sixty who had a hard time keeping up with youngsters. His body was moving slower, his arms punching softer, but he still carried the same damn compulsion in his chest. That's what kept him moving forward and that compulsion didn't give a shit how many months had been taken from his life. It haunted him and only one answer would suffice: putting a fucking maniac behind bars. The power was there, but his thoughts were increasingly focused a few years ahead, on retirement, endings, death. He'd replaced a real life with this pretend one—he was his profession, and nothing else, no private life, not a father or grandfather or son. He was Detective Superintendent Grens, and he enjoyed the respect and dignity that often entailed but was frightened by how paltry it truly was, how alone he would be, the kind of loneliness that would not be chosen and, therefore, so much more brutal.

He wasn't going home this afternoon either. He would wander the corridors and sit in his office listening to Siw, and when the day ended, he'd lie on his sofa and sleep for a while, uneasily as usual, for four or five hours, until the light came back, the desire, the compulsion. A short walk now, when the air was clear and easy to breathe for a moment. He took his beret and walked out of the room, headed to the small park next door, the one with no name. He was about to close the door when Sven came running toward him.

"Ewert, wait a minute."

He looked at his younger colleague, his thin face tense, his cheeks red.

"You look stressed."

"I *am* stressed. I've run into a new problem."

Ewert pointed toward the end of the corridor, toward the exit.

"I'm going out. Need air. If you want to talk, come with me."

They walked side by side, Ewert slowly, Sven impatiently, using short steps to maintain the same pace.

"You had a problem."

"I did as we agreed."

Sven took a deep breath, looking for something to hold on to, somewhere to begin.

"Get to the point, boy!"

"Ågestam's taxi theory. I called around to all the taxi companies in the Mälardalen region."

"And?"

"I just talked to someone at Enköping Taxi."

They stepped out onto the pavement, choked with the exhaust of trash trucks, but Ewert breathed deeply, it had been a long time since air tasted this good.

"Well, I'll be damned."

"The problem is, I spoke with a very clever woman, who really knew the business inside and out—she claimed I'd already called and asked her the same questions. Early this morning."

Across the street and into the park. Some trees, a lawn, two playgrounds, not much of an oasis, but quite a bit of shade.

"I'm not sure I follow."

"Ågestam knew what he was talking about: Enköping Taxi confirmed that Lund did have school runs. I got eight addresses to nursery schools, four in Strängnäs and four in Enköping. The Dove was one of them."

"The bastard. Bastard!"

"I've already contacted the security companies and our guys. We've increased our security."

Ewert stopped in the middle of the park path.

"Then it won't be long now. He can't control himself. He's a sick bastard, and sick bastards need their medicine."

He was about to start walking again, down the path, but stopped mid-step.

"What did you mean you'd already called earlier this morning?"

"Exactly what I said. Someone had called this morning and asked the exact same question. Someone calling himself Sven Sundkvist. Someone who also realized Lund probably made school runs. Someone who was also looking for Lund and probably not trying to get him in front of a court."

They walked in silence, side by side. Ewert felt Sven had more to say, but he'd left his office for a break and a break he was going to take. He whistled loudly and off-key as they walked. "Seven Little Girls Sitting in the Back Seat," he whistled and breathed and knew that this all would soon be over—the school runs, Lund's desperation, and the passage of time weakening a quarry—it was coming to a close, as it always did. He'd lived in that other world for so long, met them again and again, he knew what only those who already lived know, that there wasn't too much more to it.

"Now, Sven. Now you tell me the rest."

Sven stopped in front of a bench, and they both sat and watched three toddlers play in a sandbox.

"It's Ewert Grens who you see on TV. It's Ewert Grens who's been interviewed. My name hasn't been mentioned. Only to a few. People here know, of course, and maybe few at Aspsås, the coroner, and those close to Marie Steffansson, who I interrogated at the murder scene. And from that group, only a few have any motive. I focused there. I started with the father. I didn't need to go any further."

Ewert nodded, waved his hand impatiently, wanting him to continue.

"I spoke to Fredrik Steffansson's current girlfriend, Micaela Zwarts, who works at the Dove. She hasn't seen him since the funeral. He was, of course, in bad shape, you couldn't expect anything else, but she's worried. He hasn't mourned, not really, hasn't let it get to him yet. She's tried to get hold of him—they've been living together for a few years—but described him as unreachable, someone she no longer recognized. He was home this morning, apparently. He'd been there while she was at work and left a brief note on the refrigerator, apologizing and saying he'd be back soon."

Ewert rotated his hand, impatient.

"I also spoke to Agnes Steffansson, the girl's mother. She's a clever woman, absentminded with grief, yes, but still she understood immediately and confirmed Zwart's impression. Fredrik Steffansson has not only failed to grieve, he's behaved erratically, called her twice after the funeral asking irrelevant questions. She'd taken it as an attempt to stay in contact and talk, but now she's upset."

"Go on."

"She was on her cell, in Strängnäs to pick up Marie's things at the Dove, but suddenly wanted to stop our conversation and call back again. I waited. She called after twenty minutes. She'd left the Dove and had gone to the apartment building where her father lived until his death. She explained that Fredrik's questions made her go upstairs, to her father's old storage room, which they still had. They'd packed up the rest of his things in sacks and left them there."

Sven cleared his throat. He was upset, finding it difficult to get the words out.

"The deceased father's hunting rifle had been there. A 30-06 Carl Gustaf, sharp optics, laser sight—why the hell would you keep a rifle in an unlocked storage room?"

Ewert sat still, waiting. Sven hesitated, as if saying it was going to make it happen.

"She was scared. Weeping. It wasn't there."

LARS ÅGESTAM WISHED he could throw up, leaning over the sink in the bathroom at the Swedish Prosecution Authority. It had all been so simple before. He'd been given the big assignment he'd been dreaming of. He had fought and defeated one of the bitterest souls of a used-up generation; the knowledge of Lund's taxi business had been enough to both shut up Grens and cut into Lund's lead.

That was before Sven Sundkvist's call. Now, he was alone.

He didn't want to deal with a father avenging his daughter's murder.

He understood what that would entail. A pedophile who killed a five-year-old girl was black and white, easy. It meant media attention, right against wrong, leading public opinion to where it already stood. But this. If the father got there first, if the father used a weapon powerful enough to hit a person three hundred meters away, that was something else entirely. It meant hell and madness, it meant spitting on goodness. He would have to bring charges against a parent acting under the shroud of grief, and, in that moment, he would be acting on behalf of society against the little guy—his big chance would also be his downfall.

He put his fingers down his throat. He had no choice. It had to come out, he had to think clearly, and this was usually how he did it.

IT WAS ALMOST five. The Freja nursery school in western Enköping would be open for another hour. It was located in a beautiful valley with a few small hills on either side, encircled. Fredrik had been waiting in his car for thirty minutes. He'd parked in a field, at the highest elevation, in order to have a clear view of his objective. When he arrived, he did what he'd done at the other addresses: left the car, carefully searched the terrain, making wide circles around the buildings.

It was only when he got back, was about to open his car door again, that he discovered him.

He'd been slightly crouched over, almost right in front of him.

Partly obscured by a small shrub with his back against the root of a fallen tree, slightly downhill from Fredrik, a few hundred meters from the two white buildings. Wearing a green tracksuit, with a pair of binoculars in one hand. He was still, and after half an hour still hadn't moved, facing the playground and the children inside the fence. Fredrik had verified it with his own binoculars—it was Lund. He'd greeted him six days earlier, and it was the same face, the same posture.

A beast who'd murdered his daughter, taken her away from him, and now he was sitting just a short distance away.

Fredrik tried not to feel, tried to chase or scare the pain away.

Just in front of the entrance to the building stood a police car. Two people in uniforms sat in the front seat, watching, counting down the long, weary hours of duty while staring at a locked gate. It was hot, even hotter inside a stationary metal shell. In the short time Fredrik had been watching them, they'd both stepped out of the car twice, leaning against the hood while smoking a cigarette. The smoke—there was no wind down there—was easy to see.

The occasional bird, now and then the sound of a distant high-way, otherwise a quiet, drowsy calm.

Fredrik got out and headed toward the front of the car. He got down on his knees, and his light suit turned a pale green on the legs as he crept along. Elbows on top of the hood, he took aim, leaned against the black metal, moving and pretending to aim until he found a position that was comfortable.

A deep breath. He felt alert, his body limber—it was easy to move.

He took the duffel bag from the back seat, emptied it. It was a heavy rifle, and he hadn't shot it for at least seven or eight years. He'd gone hunting with Birger, before Marie was born, when they were still desperately trying to find some common ground. Hunting was probably the only conversation they could have, pretending they functioned as son-in-law and father-in-law, that they shared anything more than their mutual love for Agnes.

Fredrik weighed the weapon in his hand, tossing it up and down a few times. He got back on his knees as he'd done earlier, the rifle between his two hands, leaning against the hood and taking aim for real now. He studied Lund's back through the crosshairs.

He waited. He wanted to take him from the front.

A quarter of an hour. Then Lund stood up, the tree roots and bushes not hiding him for a moment. He started stretching, leaned forward a few times, loosening his stiff joints.

The laser made its way down onto his body, moving restlessly over a breathing human being. Fredrik lingered a moment near his fly, held it still there a few seconds, then moved on, higher.

Suddenly Lund noticed the red dot wandering along his body and started beating it, as if it were a wasp, aimlessly waving.

Fredrik fired the first shot.

And the sound of a projectile, of death, took over the silence. The waving hands disappeared, Lund was hurled violently backward, fell heavily against the ground.

He tried to get up, slowly, as Fredrik moved the laser point to his forehead, rested it there. It didn't look the way he'd imagined it would when a head exploded.

That silence again.

Fredrik put the gun down on the hood of the car, fell to the ground, first sitting, then lying, holding his head and curling up into the fetal position.

He wept.

For the first time since Marie had been taken from him, he wept and let it hurt, the terrible grief that wanted to get out, that had got stuck, grown, and now was squeezed forward. He screamed, as you do when your life runs out of you.

INTERROGATOR SVEN SUNDKVIST (I): You can sit there.

DEFENSE LAWYER KRISTINA BJÖRNSSON (KB): Here?

I: That's fine.

KB: Thanks.

I: Interrogation at Kronoberg police station of Fredrik Steffansson. Present in addition to Steffansson are the interrogator Sven Sundkvist, head of the preliminary investigation Lars Ågestam, and defense lawyer Kristina Björnsson.

FREDRIK STEFFANSSON (FS): (inaudible)

I: Excuse me?

FS: I need some water.

I: Right in front of you. Help yourself.

FS: Thanks.

I: Fredrik, could you tell me what happened?

FS: (inaudible)

I: You have to speak louder.

FS: Just a moment.

KB: Is everything all right?

FS: No.

KB: Are you able to participate?

FS: I am.

I: One more time then, can you tell me what happened?

FS: You know what happened.

I: I want you to describe it.

FS: A convicted rapist and serial killer murdered my daughter.

I: I want to know what happened today, in Enköping, outside the Freja nursery school.

FS: I shot my daughter's killer.

KB: Excuse me, Fredrik, wait a moment.

FS: Yes?

KB: I need to consult with you.

FS: Yes?

KB: Are you sure you want to describe today's event in that way?

FS: I don't know what you mean.

KB: I get the feeling that you're going to talk about what happened today in a very particular way.

FS: I intend to answer their questions.

KB: You know that a premeditated murder carries the risk of life imprisonment.

FS: It's possible.

KB: I advise you to be careful how you choose your words. At least until you and I have had time for a long, private conversation.

FS: I haven't done anything wrong.

KB: You choose.

FS: I choose.

I: Are you done?

KB: Yeah.

I: Then I'll continue. Fredrik, what happened today?

FS: You were the one who informed me.

I: Informed you?

FS: In the cemetery. After the funeral. You were there, you and the limping one.

I: Detective Superintendent Grens?

FS: If that's his name.

I: At the cemetery?

FS: One of you said it was extremely likely that he'd do it again. I think it was the limping one who said it. I decided right then. It wasn't going to happen again. Not another child, not another loss. Can I get up?

I: Sure.

FS: I assume you know what I mean. He's locked up. He manages to escape. You're not able to catch him. He rapes Marie, then murders her. You still can't manage to catch him. You know he'll kill again. You know it. And you've proved that you can't prevent it.

LARS ÅGESTAM (LÅ): May I?

I: Go ahead.

LÅ: You took your revenge.

FS: If a society can't protect its citizens, then citizens need to protect themselves.

LÅ: You wanted to avenge Marie's death by killing Bernt Lund.

FS: I saved the life of at least one child. I'm convinced of that. That's what I was doing. That was my only motive.

LÅ: Do you believe in the death penalty, Fredrik?

FS: No.

LÅ: Your actions suggest otherwise.

FS: I believe that you can save a life by taking life.

LÅ: So you mean you're capable of determining whose life is worth more?

FS: A child playing outside her school or an escaped serial killer who is planning to desecrate and humiliate and then kill that child? Are their lives of equal worth?

I: I wonder, why didn't you let the police arrest him?

FS: I considered it. I decided against it.

I: You could have gone over to the police car that was standing just outside the gate.

FS: He managed to escape from prison. He'd previously managed to escape from a mental hospital. If I'd let the police arrest him, and he was sentenced to prison or a new psych department, why wouldn't he just escape again?

I: So you chose to be both judge and executioner?

FS: There was nothing to choose. There was nothing else. I had only one thought: kill him so that he would never again, under any circumstances, have the opportunity to do what he did to Marie.

LÅ: Are you done?

I: Yes.

LÅ: Very well. Then it's like this, Fredrik.

FS: Yes?

LÅ: I have to be formal now.

FS: Yes?

LÅ: I must inform that you are now in police custody, on suspicion of murder.

III
(one month)

THE NAME OF the village was Tallbacka. Or maybe not really a village, more of a small town: population two thousand six hundred, a supermarket, a small convenience store, a local bank open Tuesdays and Thursdays, a simple restaurant serving lunch during the day and alcohol in the evenings, a closed-down railway station, two small churches and a big empty renovated one.

One day at a time, it was that kind of place.

A place with a present.

With people who started out here.

That was good enough, no smart alecks trying to make their mark. A day was never more than a day, not even here, with two newly built exits from the highway.

Despite this, or maybe because of it, Tallbacka was perhaps to become the best example of what transformed Sweden for a few months into the void between the law and the people's interpretation of it.

It was a strange summer, a summer anyone would sooner forget.

———

Flasher-Göran. That's what they called him. He was forty-four years old, had studied to be a teacher, but never worked as one. He'd done one term of student teaching, with six months left at teacher's college, at a secondary school a few kilometers from Tallbacka. Twenty years ago now, almost half his life, and he still had no idea why. It just happened. One afternoon, on his way home, he suddenly stopped at a playground and took off his clothes. Piece by piece. He'd stood naked a few meters away from the students' smoking area, singing loudly. Facing the window where the principal was sitting, he'd sung the national anthem, both verses, loud and off-key. He'd then gotten dressed again, walked home, prepared tomorrow's lessons, and went to bed.

He'd finished his education and got his certificate. He'd applied to every job within a hundred-kilometer radius, advertised and not. He'd copied his grades and professional certificates every week for a couple of years until he realized that he was never going to get a teaching job. He'd never had to send in a copy of his sentence, but it lay on the top of his stack of papers anyway, hiding the rest, his fines and eternal shame for exposing himself in a playground to minors. He'd considered leaving the neighborhood, looking for a job in another part of the country, beyond his sentence and reputation, but he was, like so many others, too much of a coward, too much of a small-town boy, too much of a Tallbackan.

It was still warm. Not like in the Småland highlands, he'd been there buying tiles yesterday, but hot enough to not be able to wear long pants, to make him sweat profusely, to find the three hundred meters separating his home from the store a long stretch.

He heard them as soon as he crossed the street. They were usually standing there at the kiosk. He'd watched several of them grow up. They were big now, fifteen, sixteen, their voices no longer the voices of young boys.

"Show us your balls!"

"You, pedo, show us now, dammit!"

They had Coca-Cola cans in their hands, a few of them emptied the contents quickly, threw the cans on the ground. They grabbed their crotches with both hands, stood in a line, thrusting their hips.

"Show your balls, pedo! Show us your balls, pedo!"

He didn't look at them. He'd decided that under no circumstances would he look at them. They screamed louder, and someone threw a soda can at him.

"You fucking pedo flasher! Go home and take your clothes off. Go home and jerk off!"

He continued walking for a few more meters, around the old post office. They couldn't see him anymore, and they weren't screaming. The small store stood in front of him, the store that drove the other two out of business, now covered in red price tags with today's deals.

He was tired. As tired as he'd been every day of this long, hot summer. He sat down on the bench outside the store, breathing heavily from his brisk walk. He watched people he knew go in and out, heavy bags in their hands on their way to a bike or car. A little farther away, on the next bench, sat two girls, twelve or thirteen years old. The neighbor's daughter and her classmate. They giggled as girls that age do, laughing as if they couldn't stop. They'd never shouted at him. They didn't even see him. He was a neighbor who cut the grass sometimes, nothing more.

The Volvo.

On the road outside the store. His stomach always ached when he saw it. He knew it meant trouble, someone on the hunt for him.

It braked abruptly. A short skid, then stop. Bengt Söderlund opened the door and rushed out. A large, powerful man, forty-five, wearing a baseball cap with Söderlund's Construction on it and blue work pants with ruler, hammer, and knife hanging on them. He reached the girls' bench, yelling at them, at Flasher-Göran, at Tallbacka.

"Into the car! Now!"

He grabbed both girls by their shoulders, they cringed when they realized his rage, wanted to get away. They ran to the car, got in the back seat, and locked the door.

He continued on to the next bench, grabbed Flasher-Göran's collar, pulled hard on it, forcing him up.

He shook him, and it hurt, the collar burned against his neck.

"For fuck's sake. Now I got you, caught you in the fucking act!"

The girls in the car looked at the two men and then turned away as they usually did.

"You're fucking disgusting. That's my daughter. I bet you wish you could get your hands on her, right?"

The teenage boys had heard the car screech to a halt, heard the bellowing. They could see Söderlund and Flasher-Göran were in the middle of a fight and fights were fun. They came running. Not much happened around here, so you had to be there when something did.

"Kill the pedo!"

"Kill the pedo!"

All in a line, hands on their crotches, thrusting their hips.

Bengt Söderlund didn't look at the crowd, just gave Flasher-Göran another thorough shake, then pushed him away, down onto the bench. He walked to the car, opened the locked door with a key, then turned around and shouted.

"I'm not sure you understand, you fucking pervert! Two weeks. That's what you get. Two shitty weeks. If you haven't disappeared by then, I'll kill you."

He got in the car, started it violently, and it howled in protest. The boys still stood there, a few meters away. They'd seen Bengt Söderlund. They immediately stopped thrusting and shouting.

They'd understood his words. He meant them.

———

It was a beautiful evening. Seventy-five degrees, no wind. Bengt Söderlund left his home, looked at his neighbor's house, which he'd come to hate, spat at it. He was born here, had gone to school here, had started working at his family's construction company and taken it over just a few years later, only weeks before both of his parents started to slowly waste away until one day they disappeared completely. He'd never thought about death before. It wasn't his. Then he'd stood in it and squelched it with his feet, got stuck in it, buried both his mother and father, and realized that he was his own past, him and nobody else. This was his daily life, his party, his security, his adventure. He'd been in the same class as Elisabeth. They'd been going steady since ninth grade, and now they had three kids, two who'd left home and the baby of the family, who was hovering in that realm between girlhood and womanhood.

He knew how it smelled here.

He knew how it sounded when a car passed by on its way somewhere else.

He knew what an hour felt like. How it lasted longer here.

The lunch joint next to the grocery store was filled with the young men of Tallbacka at this time of day, the ones who weren't at work and who'd never learned to cook for themselves. They bought lunch coupons—buy ten, get one free—ate simple food, and tried to visit each other, watching as morning turned to afternoon. In the evening it turned into a bar, two poker machines in one corner, this week's beer special and peanuts at a bargain price. It was a shitty dive, but it was the only neutral place for the single men and women of Tallbacka to meet if they weren't members of one of the local evangelical churches.

Bengt asked them to show up there, called them when he got home feeling angry and scared and uncompromising. Elisabeth hadn't wanted to come along—she didn't approve of their hatred—but Ola Gunnarsson was there, and Klas Rilke, and Ove Sandell and his wife Helena. He'd known them all for their entire lives. They'd gone to school together, played football together, season after season, in the Tallbacka Football Club, drank alcohol for the first time together at parties at the community center—they'd been children who stayed here in order to have the time to grow up.

They'd talked about the flasher many times before.

But in every process there is always one crucial step, the moment when things either stop or go further. That was where they stood now. They had the future inside themselves.

Bengt Söderlund had bought everyone a beer and a couple of bowls of nuts. He was excited, wanted to tell them about this afternoon's confrontation with Flasher-Göran outside the grocery store, and he did, told them about the bench and the girls sitting close by, then looked at the others, raised his glass to his mouth, and let his lips turn white with foam. He held a paper in his hand, showed it to them, unfolded it.

"Here it is. I picked it up at the courthouse today. Enough is enough. I was so pissed off when I shook him, I drove like hell into town, and got there just before they closed. It took a hell of a lot of searching. This was before they used computers, archived everything by hand in folders in alphabetical order."

They all leaned forward, trying to read it, even upside down.

"That fucking pervert's record. In black and white. Showed his cock to children. Hell, there's no difference between him and that pervert they shot outside Enköping."

Bengt Söderlund lit a cigarette, passed the pack around.

"Your little sisters were there, Ove."

He looked at Ove Sandell. He knew he had him.

"He showed them his dick. My little sisters. I wasn't there. I would've killed the bastard. I don't give a shit. I'd have cut him."

They toasted.

The boys who'd been grinding their hips in a row went over to the already occupied poker machines. They watched, applauded the occasional win. They didn't try to order beer, they wouldn't get any, didn't even put any money into the change machine—they'd tried that enough times already. Eighteen was the limit, even in Tallbacka.

Helena Sandell was impatient, knocked the table to get everyone's attention. She examined them one by one, stopped at her husband.

"We have our own girls now, Ove."

"Yes, we do."

"When will it be their turn?"

"They shoulda castrated him. Back then. When he was convicted."

Bengt nodded, rose from the table, looked and pointed in the direction he'd come from.

"There are more than two thousand people in this fucking town. How the fuck did I end up with a fucking pedophile as my neighbor? Well? Can anybody answer that?"

The gang of boys had grown tired of watching people play poker machines. They'd borrowed the remote lying on the counter, turned on the television. Too loud, Bengt waved irritably at them until they lowered the volume.

"Nobody's answering. What should a person do? How the hell can we let his type live here? How the hell can we do it?"

Helena Sandell yelled until she was hoarse.

"He has to go. He has to go! You hear me, Ove?"

A few peanuts, Bengt chewed slowly, swallowed.

"He has to go. And he won't go unless we help him out. I promise here and now that if he's not gone in two weeks I will kill him."

One more round, Bengt paid again, he'd take it as a business expense, they usually just wrote food and drink on the receipt.

They drank the new round until Ove started to wolf whistle, the sound cut through the thick smoke, instant silence on the premises. He pointed at the television, at the boys with the remote.

"Hey, turn it up."

"Make up your damn minds."

"Now we want to hear it. Turn that shit up before you get a slap."

Fredrik Steffansson on the screen. Walking in slow motion through a corridor at the Kronoberg jail. A jacket over his head.

"Damn, it's the father. The one who shot that pedophile outside Stockholm."

Still silence in the bar. Several tables looked at the monitor, at Fredrik Steffansson as he waved at the camera, shook his head, and then disappeared, out of picture. In front of him stood a woman. The camera focused on her face, the defense lawyer Kristina Björnsson, a microphone in front of her mouth.

"It's true. My client does not deny the factual circumstances. He shot Bernt Lund and planned it for several days."

A close-up on her face as a reporter tried to interrupt with a question, but she continued, louder.

"But this is not about murder. This is something completely different. We maintain self-defense."

Bengt Söderlund hit his hand on the table.

"Fuck yeah."

He looked around and the others nodded slowly, followed each camera motion across the screen, each new statement.

"It was only a matter of time before Bernt Lund would repeat this crime. We know that. We can see this in the profiles made of him. My client Fredrik Steffansson, therefore, argues that by taking Lund's life he saved the life of at least one child."

"That's right. Damn right."

Ove Sandell smiled, leaned over, kissed his wife on the cheek. The reporter's voice again, the question she wasn't able to ask before.

"How is he?"

"Considering the circumstances, good. He has lost his daughter. He's disappointed that society could not protect her or other prospective victims. He's the one who's locked up now awaiting trial. He's the one who has to suffer the consequences of society's incompetence."

Helena Sandell caressed her husband's cheek, took him by the hand, stood up, and pulled him up, too.

"He's right."

She lifted her glass, toasted the television, then Bengt Söderlund, Ola Gunnarsson, Klas Rilke, and finally her husband.

"Do you know what he is, that Steffansson? Do you have any idea? A hero. Do you know that? A genuine hero. Cheers, cheers for Fredrik Steffansson!"

They all raised their glasses, drank silently until their glasses were empty.

———

They stayed there longer than they usually did. They'd made up their minds. They didn't know how yet, but they'd decided. They'd taken a step, allowed the process to continue. It was their Tallbacka, their life, their reality.

IT WASN'T THAT busy, it really wasn't, but all the same he couldn't find his way—he could never find his way around big department stores. Six floors, escalators and food samples and loudspeaker announcements and queue tickets and credit card machines and buy buy buy, and someone in line and someone smelling strongly of sweat and screaming children and the perfume department with its hollow-eyed saleswomen and the woman leaving clothes outside the fitting room and the man looking for swimming trunks and everything everything everything shipped and packaged and priced.

Lars Ågestam had tired of it before he even arrived. But he didn't know any other stores. He never bought music, had no time to listen to it, and, besides, he had a radio in the car. The record department was dizzying with its long rows of unknown quantities. It felt as if they were falling on top of him as he leaned back to avoid them. In the middle, a young woman—possibly beautiful, it was difficult to tell beneath heavy makeup and hair in her eyes—stood at the information desk.

He waited there for her to finally notice him.

"Yes?"

"Siw Malmkvist."

"Yeah?"

"Do you have her?"

The young woman smiled, with indulgence or maybe understanding—who knows why young women smile anyway?

"Of course we do. Somewhere in Swedish music. There has to be something there."

She exited the information desk through a little gate, motioned for him to follow her. He watched her back, his cheeks turning red. Her clothes were revealing. She searched through the rows, soon pulled up a cover with a picture of a woman who'd been young a long time ago.

"*The Classics of Siw*. That's what it's called. Is that what you were looking for?"

He held it in his hand, weighing it. This had to be what he was looking for.

She smiled broadly as she took his money. He blushed again, but also became annoyed, she was laughing at him.

"Is something funny?"

"No."

"You seem to be laughing at me."

"No, I'm not."

"Yes, you are."

"It's just that you don't look like the type to be purchasing Siw." He smiled.

"What do they look like? A little older?"

"They don't wear suits."

"Okay."

"And cooler."

He walked along Kungs Street with *The Classics of Siw*, an ice cream in hand, across the bridge to Kungsholmen, passed his office at the Prosecution Authority, and headed toward Scheele Street, toward the Department of Violent Crimes.

He felt tense, lingered a little too long outside the door, couldn't bring himself to knock.

That irritated voice. He went inside.

Grens was sitting just as he had been when Lars left here last time, behind his desk, on the edge of his chair, leaning forward with his elbows on his thighs. He stared at Lars, the same look that he gave to everyone: go to hell, you're not welcome here, no one is.

Ågestam stepped into the room. Into the contempt.

"Here."

He put the CD on the table.

"Because I was rude last time."

Grens looked at him but said nothing.

"I don't know if you already have it. I've only seen your tape deck."

Not a sound. Grens stretched his lips, remained silent.

"I'd like to speak with you for a moment. I'll be honest, just as I was last Monday. I think you're a surly, dreary boor, but I need you. I have no one else to test this against, no one else who can give me some perspective, ask the right questions."

He pointed to the visitor's chair, gesturing to ask if he could sit down. Grens was still quiet, a tired hand in the air, a kind of invitation.

Ågestam leaned back, searching for a good way to start.

"I threw up yesterday. I went to the toilet and emptied my breakfast and lunch. I was scared. I'm still scared. This might be the most important thing I have ever done. I have a pedophile serial killer shot dead by a grieving father on my hands, and it could go terribly wrong. I'm not stupid. I know it'll be a living hell."

Grens shook his head. He chuckled. For the first time since his guest entered the room, he spoke.

"That might have been good for you."

Ågestam counted. Quiet, inside. He counted the seconds, which was what he usually did, thirteen seconds. He'd humbled himself. Asked for help. The old bastard couldn't see that. He had to play his prestige game. Ågestam tried to ignore it.

"I'm going to ask for a life sentence."

That worked. He got his attention. That he had an opinion meant something.

"What the hell are you saying?"

"Just what I said. I don't want people running around taking the law into their own hands."

"Why the hell are you telling me this?"

"I don't know. I'd like to work through my thoughts. See if they're sound."

The detective chuckled again.

"You little fucking climber. Life?"

"Yes."

"They're all idiots anyway. I've always thought so. Half of the people serving time in our prisons have been convicted of violent crimes more than once. They're idiots, but that doesn't mean that they aren't human beings. Almost all of them have been the victims of violent crimes, often at the hands of their own parents. So even I can understand that sometimes it just ends up that way."

"I'm aware of all of that."

"You should learn it again, Ågestam, for real this time. Don't just read a few books."

The prosecutor pulled a black notebook out of the inside pocket of his jacket. He flipped back and forth, searching through his notes.

"Steffansson has admitted that he planned the murder. He had four days to come to his senses. He took it upon himself to act as police, prosecutor, judge, and executioner."

"He didn't know if he would be able to go through with it. He didn't know if Lund would show up."

"Steffansson had plenty of time. He could have contacted you. Your men were standing guard just a few hundred meters away. If he had contacted you, he could have refrained from shooting Lund."

"Sure, it's murder. No doubt about it. But life? Never. Unlike you, I've been working in this town for forty years. I've seen bigger fools than Steffansson get away with more. I've seen other prosecutors pretending to be hard men."

Ågestam breathed deeply, ignored the sarcasm, the personal attacks. He wasn't going to be pulled into that again, not going to fall for it. He flipped through his notebook again. He swallowed his anger and slowly began to smile. This was exactly what he'd wanted; the surly old devil was acting just as he'd expected him to. It was as if the trial had already begun, and he was polishing his questions, his mode of proof—it was an exam.

Grens was unhappy with the pause, swore just loud enough to be heard.

"What the hell are you up to? Looking for arguments in your book? It's murder. But it's murder with extenuating circumstances.

Request a long sentence if you think you need to, but content your-self with eight, or maybe ten years tops. You and I are society. Do you understand that? The society that couldn't protect Steffansson's daughter or anyone else."

Like a closing statement. He'd already written down the key words, which is what he'd learned to do, to summarize, to articulate the big picture to see it for himself, and then break it down one question at a time. Now, he raised his voice, he knew it was weak, but there wasn't much he could do about that—loudness only lent false authority.

"I hear what you're saying, Grens. However, society's failure does not give him the right to execute an alleged rapist and killer. What if Lund is innocent? You don't know for sure. Above all, Steffansson didn't know for sure. What is it you want? Shall we say that he had the right to execute Lund because he'd seen him near the crime scene? Is that the society you'd like to police? People going around this town taking the law into their own hands? Sen-tencing other people to death? I don't know, the law book I have doesn't say anything about the death penalty. We have a responsi-bility, Grens. We have to show every single citizen that if you act as Steffansson did, you'll be locked up for life. Even if you are a grieving father."

Grens had a ceiling fan. The kind you found in hotels on the Med-iterranean. Ågestam hadn't noticed it before, not until it stopped and the room fell silent. He looked at it, then at the old man in front of him, searching his face, wondering where all this fear came from. He was convinced that's what this was about, fear that had turned into inaccessibility and aggression. What was it he was so afraid of? Why was it so difficult for him to be present, to speak without swear words and accusations? After all the stories he'd heard, even at university, here he was, Grens, the cop who took his own path, who was better than the others. And now? He couldn't see what it was they'd been talking about. He saw a pathetic bastard who'd painted himself into a corner and sat there, alone and past his prime and unable to change.

The CD was in Grens's hand. *The Classics of Siw*, twenty-seven tracks. The detective opened the box and took out the thin piece of plastic. Put his fingers on the shiny surface, marking it with grease, he turned and twisted it, then put it back in its case.

"Are you done?"

"I suppose so."

"Then you can take this back. I don't have one of those machines."

He handed it to Ågestam, who shook his head.

"It's yours. If you don't want to play it, you can throw it away."

. The older man put the bit of plastic aside. It was Wednesday, two weeks since Lund had overpowered two guards and escaped. A little girl was dead. Her killer was dead. The girl's father sat in a building not far from here, behind a closed door, waiting to be arrested and tried. A prosecutor twat would soon be seeking life in prison for him.

Some days he didn't want to do this anymore. Sometimes he looked forward to the day this would all be over.

DEAD BODIES WERE somehow worse when it was hot outside. They reminded him of those nature films he'd come to detest, pretentious voiceovers guiding the viewer under the harsh sun of the African savannah, the flies buzzing insistently in the microphone, a predator on the hunt who is stalking her prey, about to throw herself over it, tear it to pieces, eat what can be eaten, and leave the rest—a piece of bloody meat to be attacked again, this time by the flies who are part of the process of decay, which smelled and hurried and annihilated.

That was what he saw, the image he always carried inside him when he went through those locked doors and down those narrow stairs on his way to the autopsy rooms of Forensic Medicine.

They'd been here a week ago, and he'd turned away when the fabric was lifted. The girl's serene face on a body that had been torn apart. Ewert had nodded to him, told him that he could look away, that he didn't need to rub more hopelessness into his chest, seek out any more meaninglessness.

She had been so unreal. Too young, too much on her way, she'd just begun. He remembered her feet. They'd been so small, as a five-year-old's feet are. There'd been saliva on them. Lund had licked them. After her death.

"Sven?"

"Yes?"

"How are you?"

Ewert was being neither superior nor sarcastic. He was asking because he wanted to know.

"I hate this place. I don't understand it. And Errfors seems so normal. How could you choose to work in this place? This is the end. Who needs that, who can stand it? How does a person who's just sawed a dead body apart function?"

They passed a large archive. Sven had visited it once. Binders, drawers, folders, shelf after shelf behind sliding doors, a catalog of dead people. He'd been searching randomly that time, along with a young coroner, looking for images they never found. The dead had been gathered in paper, typed notes in alphabetical order. He hoped he never had to open that door again. It had felt like tramping on graves, pawing at the only thing that was left.

Ludvig Errfors greeted them cordially. No sterile clothing this time either, nor did he offer any to the two police officers. They went into the autopsy room, the same hall that Marie Steffansson had been in. The coroner gestured toward the table.

"I autopsied both of the basement murder victims. I autopsied the Steffansson girl. Now, I've autopsied their murderer."

Ewert struck the man that lay before him lightly on the leg.

"This motherfucker? He was bound to end up here. But you know? You know for certain that this was our perp, this time, too?"

"I told you that last week. It was exactly the same procedure. Same assault. I've worked here longer than they recommend, and I've never seen such violence visited upon a child before."

He pointed to the body under the fabric.

"We'll prove it soon. In black and white. For the trial, you'll have a DNA sample. We already had his sperm. I'm quite sure, and the prosecutors and judges and judicial system will get it in writing."

"That prosecutor twat is going to push for a life sentence for Steffansson."

Sven looked at Ewert in surprise.

"Yep. That's how it goes. He's trying to fill his suit."

Errfors moved the body slightly, directly under the lamp, then turned to Sven and smiled kindly.

"It doesn't look too good. I don't know . . . You had some difficulty last time. You might want to look away?"

Sven nodded, made brief eye contact with Ewert, then turned his back. Errfors lifted the fabric back.

"You see. Not much of a face left. Steffansson hit him in the fore-head. Like an explosion. We used his teeth to establish his identity."

The coroner pushed the table slightly, now directed the light toward the stomach.

"He was hit first here in the hip. The bullet went straight through, destroyed part of the skeleton. Two shots. One in the hip, one in the head. It's consistent with the evidence I've read. The statements from witnesses described two bangs."

Sven didn't need to look. He was listening. Could see it anyway.

"Are you done?"

Errfors laid the fabric back over the body.

"Now we are."

Sven turned back to the outline of a man's body, looked at Lund's face in front of him. What was the purpose of such a sick person's life? How much had he understood of what had happened, what he'd done? To destroy your own kind like that, were you still human then? He'd asked those questions before, they always came to him more clearly when in front of the lifeless.

They got ready to leave, jackets on, and slowly finished their conversation.

"Before you go . . . I think there's something else you'll want to see."

Errfors moved from the table and opened the glass cabinet that stood along the wall.

"This. This was his. I found it when I undressed him."

A gun. A knife. Two photographs and a handwritten note.

"This, a gun, as you probably know better than I do, was attached to his leg. This, a type of knife I've never seen before, extremely sharp, kept in a holster on his forearm."

Bernt Lund had been armed. He'd been prepared to defend himself.

"And that idiot wants life. For a disturbed devil with a weapon who was hunting little girls outside a nursery school."

Sven picked up the photos and the handwritten note, lifted them up to the light, and studied the amateurish photography.

"These girls have been photographed outside the school where he was shot. They have summer clothing on. These are fresh images. We'll examine it."

Ewert handed back the two weapons, examined the photos and the note, and chuckled, as he'd chuckled at Ågestam this morning.

"Lund even had their names. This is exactly what we needed. He was planning to kill two more."

The detective held up the photographs again, two girls, the same age as the Steffansson girl, light sun-bleached hair, smiling in the pictures, sitting on the edge of the sandbox, smiling at something only they know.

"Do you know what this means? By murdering Bernt Lund, Fredrik Steffansson has almost certainly saved their lives. Two girls under the age of six can smile again tomorrow thanks to Steffansson."

Then Grens did as he usually did—Sven had seen it several times—he grabbed the corpse in front of him, knocked lightly on it a few times at the shoulder and hip, then pinched the foot, the toes under the fabric, he pinched and twisted and said something with his mouth facing in the other direction. It was difficult to hear.

IT WAS THE fifth consecutive year that Bengt Söderlund spent his vacation at home. They'd rented a cottage on Gotland one year, a few kilometers outside Visby, and it turned out to be too expensive, and the weather was rainy. It was his first visit to the island everyone raved about, but after an endless week, he'd decided to never go there again. They'd gone to Ystad the year after that, another summer cottage, windy and not much countryside. They'd seen Österlen, so now they didn't have to see it again. Two summers with a caravan, heavy traffic, and kids that wouldn't go to sleep. Once, they'd gone to Rhodes, ninety-degree weather for two weeks, and they only left their hotel room in the evening for dinner. A couple of bus trips to Stockholm, city slickers everywhere, the kind who *walked* up escalators. Bengt and his wife didn't need much more. The company did best when they stayed at home, and they did best, too. There was swimming in Tallbacka, two places if you counted the smaller lake, so the kids had something to do, and they had time, could take walks in the village, could have sex undisturbed now and then when the kids were out of the house, drink coffee in the garden, invite people over for dinner occasionally.

Right now, Bengt and Elisabeth were sitting at the kitchen table, just as Ove and Helena walked past their open windows. They waved them in to share in their usual fika snack: coffee and cinnamon buns. It was easy to get along with Ove and Helena. There'd been a brief period, almost ten years ago, when things had been strained between them, when they'd avoided each other as much as possible for a few months. Ove and Elisabeth had carried on too long with each other at a midsummer party, so the couples' friendship temporarily cooled until they all realized this village was too small to hide from each other. Eventually, they all ended up screaming loudly at each other late one night outside the kiosk, screaming until everything had been said and everyone understood that Ove and Elisabeth had no intention of breaking up any existing relationships—it had been just drunken curiosity stemming from their school years, and when someone turned on the overhead light in the kitchen, they knew immediately in the strong glare that there was nothing between them. None of them had ever discussed it again after that night outside the kiosk. Everyone had said what they had to say.

Ove held a newspaper in his hand. Bengt had a copy on the kitchen table. There wasn't much news these days, now that the Russian plane crash had been investigated, except for the Stockholm pedophile who'd murdered a five-year-old girl and her father who shot him. For the second week in a row, the front page was dominated by the story, by the latest interviews, the most recent analyses. The story belonged to everyone, and everyone had the right to an opinion. The girl and her father belonged to every family.

They'd been talking about the Stockholm pedophile every time they met since this all started, since the escape and the murder, except Elisabeth, who refused to participate. She'd sat in silence, and when they'd asked her why, she told them they were being childish, that their hate and devotion to the topic were somehow wrong. They'd tried to explain, defend themselves, but finally let her be—it wasn't illegal to be childish, and if she didn't want to talk she didn't have to.

Bengt poured the coffee, dark roast with drops of cream in it. It smelled like coffee should, like home, warm and cozy. He served them one by one and offered some of yesterday's cinnamon buns—that's how they liked them too, better for dipping when they had a bit of crust. He pointed to the picture of Fredrik Steffansson. A passport photo, the same picture they'd been publishing for the last few days.

"I would have done the same thing. Without blinking."

Ove dipped his bun, pressing it against the bottom of his cup.

"Me too. If you have girls, that's how it is, that's just how you think."

Bengt picked up the newspaper, turned and twisted it.

"But I wouldn't have done it like him. I wouldn't be thinking about anyone else. I'd have done it for my own sake. Pure revenge."

He looked around, waiting for the others' reactions. Ove nodded. Helena nodded. Elisabeth stuck her tongue out.

"What are you doing?"

"I'm so tired of all of you. Tired of hearing you harp on about this, morning, noon, and night. Every time we meet. Flasher-Göran, pedophiles, hatred!"

"You don't have to listen."

"Revenge? That's bullshit. He hasn't done anything. Hasn't touched anyone. He stood naked by a flagpole. You're pathetic."

She sobbed, cleared her throat trying to steady her voice, her eyes wet.

"I don't recognize any of you anymore. You sit in my kitchen, pretending you're involved. I'm not going to put up with this anymore."

Helena put her cup on the table, put her hand on Elisabeth's.

"Elisabeth, please calm down."

Elisabeth defiantly pushed her hand away. Bengt raised his voice.

"Fuck her. She likes the fucking bastards. Pedophiles!"

He turned to his wife.

"You think this is why I've worked my whole life? Worked like a fucking dog? So our society would lock up a man who saved the lives of small children?"

He turned toward the open window, demonstrated his anger by spitting through it. He watched it land on the lawn.

He also heard the door. Next door. He knew exactly which door it was.

"Fuck. There's that bastard."

He went to the window, looked out.

"The pervert's going out."

Flasher-Göran locked the door behind him. Bengt turned to the others, looked at Elisabeth.

"Pathetic, you say?"

He leaned forward, leaned out the window, roaring.

"Are you deaf, you fucking pervert? I don't want to see you! Stay indoors, goddammit!"

Flasher-Göran looked up, toward a voice he knew well. He then proceeded to walk along the gravel path to the gate. Bengt snapped his fingers. Twice. The Rottweiler came running immediately from the hall.

"Here."

The dog ran to the window, past the kitchen table. Bengt grabbed his collar, held tight, gave the next command.

"Baxter! Get 'im!"

He let go of the dog, which immediately jumped out the window and through the garden, over the fence. Flasher-Göran could hear the loud barking getting closer. He started running for the shed where he kept a mower and tools and some scraps of wood, his heart pounding and his stomach reacting. He shit himself and kept running, his own feces streaming down his legs. He reached it, opened the door, and pulled it shut. The dog threw himself violently against the door, barking even more loudly. Bengt stood in the window, Ove and Helena on either side, and he applauded hysterically.

"Good boy, Baxter! You can stay there the rest of the day, you fucking pervert! Stay, Baxter."

The dog stopped barking and sat outside the toolshed door, staring at the handle.

Bengt clapped, laughed, and turned to Elisabeth, who was still sitting at the table, saw her shake her head and could feel how she despised him.

IT FELT LIKE it had been a long time since the rain. One short day of coolness passed before the heat settled in again. It was more noticeable in a prison. The high wall, the open courtyard, the gravel area—the air was restricted, locked in, controlled. Hilding was walking by himself out onto the football field, wearing shorts, his chest bare. He was worried. Tinyboy was going to figure it out soon, find out who did it, and he wouldn't give a shit that it was his closest friend. Hilding was going to get a beating, and he knew it. He was even expecting it.

He'd run off Axelsson. The perv had gone to the guards and they'd snatched him away. Within a few minutes of his request, he was moved to voluntary isolation. Tinyboy had gone insane, suspected that somebody had warned him, but wasn't sure and, most important, didn't know who. He screamed like a madman and kicked the walls for a while, then he calmed down, even played Casino in the TV corner later that evening and managed to get two ten of diamonds in the same hand.

Hilding dug deep into the wound on his nose. He walked from one football goal to the other. Counted the circuits. Sixty-seven laps. Thirty-three left. He shouldn't have taken from their stash. But fuck it, the Axelsson situation had completely finished him. He considered it more of a reward. He deserved it, and he went in there to just take a little. He'd been alone in the shower room, lifted the ceiling tile and took down the Turkish Glass. He'd smoked a little, it was just as sweet as last time, and his body had felt calm again. Then he'd smoked a little more, inhaled the rest, and it had tickled like hell. Then he went to his cell and fell asleep and woke up in the middle of the night realizing what had happened, sat up in his bed, and waited for the morning and for his beating. Tinyboy never showed up. He hadn't discovered it. It had been a couple of days. He'd find out soon and attack. The hours went by. Hilding just waited, tore deeper into his wound, went around the netless goal one more time.

He walked a hundred laps. Sweat poured from his hairline down his neck, chest, stomach. He considered taking another hundred laps. For him walking was almost like getting high, the sun flooding over him, his thoughts floating away. He decided to keep going until someone else came out. One hundred and fifty-seven laps. Then the Russian appeared with a ball under his arm, and Hilding left the field.

He took a cold shower. Water on his face, on his aching wound, washed away the sweat. He got dressed—clean underwear, socks, shorts. He went out into the corridor, back and forth, pursued by his worries. He started counting again. Three hundred times through the corridor and past the cells toward the pool table corner and back. The television was on, it was always on, but otherwise the unit was quiet—the murder of the little girl, and then a mention of Lund forced him to listen for a while, cajoling him away from what concerned him.

He was scared. It had been a long time since he'd felt fear. When he was around Tinyboy he had protection, but now he'd fucked it up. Anxiety tore away at him. No weed left. He had to numb it. He had to numb it.

He knocked on Jochum's cell. No answer.

He knocked again. Jochum was sleeping.

"What the fuck do you want?"

"It's Hilding."

"Go away."

"I was just wondering if you were thirsty."

He'd already decided. He had to steal again. He had to get rid of the pain in his chest. With Jochum, it would be easier. Tinyboy wouldn't go after Jochum.

Jochum Lang opened the cell door.

"Where is it?"

"You'll see."

Jochum went in again, put on a pair of slippers, and closed the door behind him. He never left it open. Hilding had never been inside. They walked past the kitchen, past the shower room, past the pool table corner where Hilding had just done three hundred laps.

He walked over to a fire extinguisher hanging on the wall—a red metal tube with a black hose and detailed instructions on the side, more words than anyone would have time to read during a fire. He looked around, no guards, unscrewed the black hose, and laid it to the side. He took a small toothbrush mug out of the pocket of his shorts.

"Regular fucking water, a fat fucking loaf of bread, and some apples."

He grabbed hold of the fire extinguisher, turned it upside down, filled up his mug.

"Fucking hell, that tastes like shit!"

The mash smelled so strongly it nauseated him.

"But who cares?"

The cup to his mouth, he swallowed the cloudy liquid.

"You're supposed to feel it, not taste it, for fuck's sake!"

He filled the cup again, handed it to Jochum.

"Three and a half weeks. Almost ready. At least ten percent."

Jochum gagged, took it all in one gulp.

"One more."

They poured down five more each and started to feel the warmth and peace of the alcohol making its way through their bodies. They used to keep it in a broom cupboard, in a bucket at the back, but this was better, an empty fire extinguisher—the bread for the alcohol, the fruit for the taste, and the fermentation process inside a closed container that was readily available. They drank until they heard a hoarse voice in the corridor. It sounded like Skåne.

"Guards on the floor!"

It wasn't often that the guards went into the unit and a warning system had always been in place, someone shouted and everyone knew. Hilding pointed to the rubber pipe, Jochum threw it to him, and he screwed it back on quickly. They walked away and ran into a guard, who looked at them without saying anything. They continued to the couch and sat down.

They were tipsy, drinking buddies for the moment. No one says no to a pitcher of mash, and so, for the time being, Hilding and Jochum were united, familiar.

The TV was on in front of them, the same news. The whole unit had followed the hunt for Lund closely, but they'd had enough now—it was over, the father had blown that bastard's head off and now every damn perv knew how things worked. They leaned back and watched pictures of the father and Lund flow past without listening—a feeling of tranquility reigned.

"Where's the Gypsy? I haven't seen him for a couple of days."

"Tinyboy?"

"Yeah. The clown."

Jochum grinned, Hilding grinned. Clown.

"He's in his cell. He doesn't like this stuff. The shit on TV."

"What are you talking about?"

"I don't know."

"You don't know?"

"Tinyboy's got fucking ghosts. Damned if I know. He can't stand to hear about the little girl and the perv. He knows he could have finished him off before."

"What does that matter now?"

"Then this never would have happened."

"But it happened."

Hilding looked around. The guard was on his way back, on his way out again. He lowered his voice.

"He has a daughter, too. That's why."

"And?"

"Well . . . that's why. Surely, that could make you think."

"There's a hell of a lot who do. Don't you?"

"This one lives there. Where the girl was murdered. Strängnäs somewhere. Or he thinks so."

"Thinks so?"

"He's never met her."

Jochum's eyes left the television screen for a moment. He put his hand on his shaved head, looked at Hilding.

"I don't understand."

"This is important for Tinyboy."

"But it surely wasn't her?"

"No. But it could have been."

"Bullshit."

"He thinks so. He has a picture of her. He had it enlarged himself. It fills up his whole damn wall."

Jochum threw his head back against the sofa and laughed out loud, like you do when you're tipsy.

"Fucking Gypsy! Is he going around obsessing about something that didn't happen and absolutely can't happen, because the pervert has already been shot? He's in worse shape than I thought. He's hallucinating. That guy needs that mash more than anyone."

Hilding froze, afraid again.

"Don't say that, for fuck's sake!"

"Say what?"

"About the mash."

"Are you afraid of Gypsyboy?"

"Just that. Don't say anything."

Jochum laughed again and held his finger in the air, turned back to the TV. There were more reports about the execution of the pedo: an interview with the prosecutor, pushed up against a wall in a stairwell in the courthouse, a proper-looking asshole in a suit with blond bangs and a microphone in front of his face. He looked just like they usually did—too young, too eager, somebody who deserves to get shaken up a bit.

IT WAS ONLY after Fredrik Steffansson was arrested that Lars Ågestam finally understood what this was about.

What this whole story was about.

He'd laughed silently when he was first handed the pedophile case, when it was about a sick serial killer and his murder of a little girl. Later, he vomited in the bathroom at the Prosecution Authority when it turned into a grieving father and his murder of his daughter's rapist and killer.

So, when Steffansson was arrested, Ågestam felt like he'd lost his opportunity for a professional breakthrough in the Swedish courts.

It had turned into so much more.

His own fear, not being able to walk across the street without looking around, life, death.

He'd insisted that Steffansson be held *on suspicion of murder* in custody until his trial.

Steffansson's lawyer, Kristina Björnsson, whom he'd just informally lost to in the Axelsson trial, had claimed *self-defense* as a description of Steffansson's action and, therefore, disputed the arrest.

She'd argued that another person's life had clearly been in danger, and pointed out that there was only a slight risk that Steffansson would obstruct the investigation or flee from any upcoming trial, so it should be sufficient for him to report daily to the Eskilstuna police.

The presiding judge, van Balvas, ruled after just a few minutes that Fredrik Steffansson would remain in custody until his trial for suspected murder, the date of which would be determined later.

With the gavel still echoing, all hell broke loose. First, among those standing outside.

Those with microphones, who pushed him up against the stone wall of the stairwell.

Steffansson's become a hero.
Really?
He saved the lives of two little girls.
We can't say that for sure.
Bernt Lund had their photos on him.
Steffansson murdered someone.
Lund had their names. He was watching their nursery school.
Steffansson murdered someone, those are his actions. And that's what I'm concerned with.
So you think someone who has prevented the death of many innocents should be rewarded with a long prison sentence?
I have no comment on that statement.
Don't you think that he acted correctly?
No.
Why?
It was premeditated murder.
Yes?
Premeditated murder should be judged for what it is.
With life imprisonment?
With the law's most severe punishment.
You mean that it would have been better if the two girls had been murdered?
I mean that there's no special rebate for bereaved fathers when it comes to premeditated murder.
Do you have children of your own?

Then, the others: the public, those who were watching, listening, reading. Those who screamed and made threats—his phone never stopped ringing.

Fucking tool of society!
I'm just doing my job.

Tool!
I have no choice.
Little bureaucrat soldier!
If a person breaks the law, it is my duty to prosecute them.
If you do, you'll end up dead!
What you just said is called an unlawful threat.
Die!
It's called an unlawful threat, and it is punishable by law.
Your whole family will die!

He was scared. What was happening was real. There were crazy people out there—but also the greater public. They all hated him, and they meant what they said. He knew that and took it seriously.

He sought out Ewert Grens, who reluctantly let him in.

He thought their last conversation had opened something up, perhaps a kind of intimacy when he revealed his uncertainty about the indictment, but he was still what he was, just as prejudiced, just as predictable. Grens smiled mockingly when Ågestam talked about being threatened, about his family being threatened, that he was afraid and wanted police protection. He had been close to tears—they came suddenly and he cursed the fact that he was here, in this room—but Grens pretended not to see, explained that everyone got threats. You had to expect that if you wanted to be a tough-guy prosecutor.

He asked him to come back when he'd seen his ghost for real, not just heard voices.

Lars Ågestam slammed the door behind him. It was muggy outside. He walked slowly back.

He bought a newspaper and a bottle of mineral water at a newsstand; the humidity made him sweat profusely, and it took a lot more water than usual to keep hydrated in this heat. His picture was on the paper above the headline "Prosecutor Wants Hero to Get Life in Prison." Everyone was staring at him, he was sure of it and walked faster, sweating again, but kept up the pace all the way to Kungsholmen, to the Prosecution Authority.

He went into his office. His phone started ringing immediately.

He looked at the phone, didn't answer. It rang again, he didn't answer. It rang eight times, and he sat with the preliminary investigation material, read it over and over again until the ringing stopped.

BENGT SÖDERLUND HAD just finished telling the story of how Baxter had guarded the toolshed all night and into late morning, at which point his master commanded him to stop, and Flasher-Göran finally opened the toolshed door. It was the third time now. They'd all heard it: Elisabeth, who didn't want to, Ove and Helena, who'd seen it happen, and Ola Gunnarsson and Klas Rilke, who laughed more loudly each time they heard it. Just like when they were at school talking about a teacher, someone they'd given a nickname to and decided to laugh at all through high school, or like when they'd sit in the Tallbacka Football Club's locker room, liniment and cleats and crotch kicks aimed at the opposing team's fat butterfingers of a goalkeeper, a community built on remote humiliation. They'd stood for a bit in front of poker machines in Tallbacka's only restaurant, feeding them ten-kronor coins and losing a few hundred in the process, then they went to their table, the same table where they always sat. They all ordered a beer, toasted the heat, which forced them to drink more, and Baxter, who made them laugh.

They drank to the halfway mark, three or four every evening; the first filled the chest and quenched the thirst, and that was when the discussions really got going, as they do when alcohol loosens the tongue.

Bengt drank more slowly than usual. He knew what he wanted from this evening. He'd decided during this week, weighed the pros and cons, looked at the legal books, read the wooden legal statutes.

He lifted his glass, nodded to the others.

"Let's drink up. Then, I have something to say."

They toasted, emptied their glasses, one by one. Bengt raised his hand and made eye contact with the waitress behind the bar, made a sign to bring a new round. Then he spoke.

"I've been thinking. I know now what we should do. How to clean up this village."

The others moved closer to the table, held their glasses still. Elisabeth turned her face. She clenched her jaw and stared down at the table. Bengt continued.

"You remember the last time we were here? You remember Helena?"

He smiled at her.

"She stood up at the end, just before we went home. They were showing the pedophile murder on the TV, and Helena told us to be quiet. They were talking about the father who'd killed that pervert and that was when Helena said it. She said he was a hero. A modern-day hero. He wouldn't let any fucking pedophile get the better of him. He didn't sit around waiting. If the police weren't willing to do what they should, he'd do it himself."

Helena was pleased with Bengt's description.

"That's just what I said. He is a hero. He's good-looking, too."

She smiled lovingly toward Ove, pushed him gently. Bengt nodded to her. He was impatient, wanted to say more.

"The trial starts soon. It's gonna go on for five days. Then comes the verdict. The verdict will come not too long after the trial ends. That's when we have to be at it."

He looked around triumphantly.

"The defense is claiming self-defense. All of Sweden is claiming self-defense. If they lock him up all hell will break loose. I bet you they wouldn't dare. It'll be just like it usually is, only the judge knows the law, the rest of the lay judges won't have any legal education. You understand, right? The district court might free him, and that's when we act."

The others at the table still didn't understand, but they were listening. Bengt usually knew what was up.

"The moment that verdict is read, if he's freed, we strike. We'll get rid of that pervert. I don't want any pedophiles around here, not as my neighbor, not in my village. We'll get rid of him and claim self-defense."

The bar owner, a portly man who used to own one of the now defunct grocery stores, brought out new glasses of beer, three in each hand. They drank a few mouthfuls each, until Elisabeth turned her face up, looked at her husband.

"Bengt, you're starting to lose control."

"If you don't like this, Elisabeth, you can go home."

"Killing a person should never be the solution to a problem. This father is not a hero. He's a very bad example."

Bengt slammed his beer glass on the table.

"So what the hell do you think he should have done?"

"Talked to the man."

"What?"

"You can always talk to someone."

"Give me a fucking break!"

Helena looked at Elisabeth, and her eyes were filled with disgust.

"I don't understand what you're up to, Elisabeth. I don't get why you can't see things as they are. Can you tell me how you plan to talk to an armed rapist and serial killer who tortured and killed your own child? Can you? Discuss his tragic childhood? Broken toys and difficult potty training?"

Ove put his hand on his wife's shoulder as he stood up.

"For fuck's sake, there was no fucking Freud seminar going on at that day care center! No more of this fucking *poor him* talk."

Helena put her hand on her husband's, continued speaking when he fell silent.

"It wasn't right that the father shot the pedophile. But it would have been more wrong if he hadn't. Surely that's obvious? Life is sacred—until you come to a situation where your personal morals and your ethical judgments have to be set aside. If I could have taken a shot with that rifle, I would have done the same thing as the father. Don't you understand that, Elisabeth?"

She made up her mind when she left the restaurant. She'd just lost her husband. She hurried home, asked her daughter to grab whatever she could carry, their only child still living at home. She packed both of their bags with clothes. She took the car—that's all she needed. The summer evening was turning into night as she left Tallbacka, never to return again.

THE KRONOBERG JAIL cell was one hundred and seventy centimeters wide and two hundred and fifty centimeters long. A narrow bed, a small table beside it, a sink he could wash himself in every evening and piss in at night. Fredrik wore a blue-gray uniform that hung on his body, KVV in capital letters on the sleeves and legs. Completely restricted—no newspapers, no radio, no television. No visits apart from the interrogating officer, prosecutor, his defense lawyer, the chaplain, and the prison staff. Fresh air for an hour each day, a prescribed break in a steel cage on the roof of the building. The heat stood still there, and, so far, he'd always asked to end his fresh air after less than half an hour and go back down again.

Now, he lay in bed, thinking of nothing. He had tried to eat. The tray with his plate and juice cup was on the floor. Everything tasted like shit, and he'd put it down after just a few bites. He hadn't really eaten since Enköping. Whatever he got down came back up again, as if his stomach were in search of peace.

The walls around him were empty and gray. There was nothing to look at, nothing to focus on. He closed his eyes, and the fluorescent light shone through his eyelids.

Suddenly, there was a creak from the door. Someone was looking at him through the hatch.

"Steffansson! You wanted to see a priest?"

Fredrik looked at the hatch, two pairs of eyes staring in.

"My name is Fredrik. I'm not a last name."

The hatch was closed, but reopened again soon.

"Whatever you want, Fredrik. You wanted to see a priest?"

"I wanted to see anyone who isn't wearing a uniform or locking my door."

The guard sighed.

"Well, what do you want? She's standing here beside me."

"Well, there you go! Otherwise, I'd think the point of you keeping me here was to isolate me completely from the outside world. For some damn reason you seem to think I'm a danger to society if I'm free, right? And now that I'm sitting here, you think everyone else is a danger to me. Do you even know who you're looking at?"

He sat up in bed, kicked the tray. The cup of orange juice fell over, yellowish liquid spreading all over the floor. The guard stayed silent. He could see that the prisoner was close to collapsing. He'd seen it before. They often became aggressive, loud, threatening, just before they collapsed in a heap and pissed themselves.

Fredrik splashed his foot in the liquid.

"You have no idea. You're looking at a man whose crime is that he willfully executed a child killer. A child killer who would have fucked and butchered another five-year-old if he'd had the chance. Now it's your job to guard the man who may have saved the life of your child. Do you like that job? Do you feel like you're really making a contribution to society?"

He picked up the tray and threw it against the door. The guard shouted, closed the hatch just before the tray clattered against it.

It took a minute. Then they were there again, those staring eyes.

"I should call for reinforcements. What you just did qualifies you for the restraints. But I'll answer your question."

Fredrik waited. The guard swallowed, hesitated.

"No. My answer is no. I don't think what I'm doing at the moment is making a contribution to society. I don't think you should be sitting here at all. You were right to kill him. But now you are sitting here. It's that simple. So I'll ask my question again. Do you want to see the priest or not?"

He was on one side, and the others were out there. Hurried images. That closed door, he hated it. Instead of a hatch, this one had three small windows with thick, blurry glass like you'd find in a bathroom, and what he could see through those windows wasn't quite clear—his father and Frans in the living room, the TV on, Pappa screaming at Frans to take his clothes off, hitting him, Fredrik could just make out the hand and Frans's naked body through the distorted glass. Frans didn't make a sound. Their mother had reported him and said that Frans deserved a beating for something minor, for coming home late, or spilling a glass of milk, or leaving the light on, and then she'd disappeared. She sat in the kitchen drinking tea and smoking Camels, while their father hit and hit and hit until Frans screamed defiantly that he wasn't hitting hard enough, that he could take more, he could hardly feel it. Then, their father stopped.

The closed door. A guard with staring eyes.

"One more time. Then we'll leave. What do you want?"

Fredrik closed his eyes.

"Let the priest in."

The door opened. He didn't understand.

"Rebecka?"

"Fredrik."

"Why you?"

"I've ministered here before. Now I offered my services. I thought you might want to see me, since you don't get to meet any outsiders. Is that okay?"

"Come in."

He was ashamed. Because he was sitting in a four-square-meter cell with a gray prison uniform hanging off him, because he'd just pissed in a sink, because there was juice spilled all over the floor, because of his tantrum at the guard. And because he started to weep with joy as soon as she sat down on his bed.

She hugged him. Stroked his hair, his cheek.

"I understand. No need to apologize. I've seen people react worse than this to locked rooms."

He looked at her, trying to smile.

"Do you think what I did was wrong?"

She sat in silence for a long time, considering her answer.

"Yes. I think so. It's not your right to decide between life and death."

Fredrik nodded. He'd expected that answer.

"You know what I did? Saved the lives of other children? If I hadn't killed Lund, they'd be dead by now. You know that. Would that have been better?"

She took her time again. She'd known the man next to her since he was a child. She'd buried his daughter just over a week ago. Her words meant more than others, her responsibility was greater.

"It's a difficult question, Fredrik. I don't know . . ."

She broke off.

Suddenly, Fredrik started to hyperventilate. She put her hand on his chest.

He was shaking all over.

"I'm so sorry. I can't help it. It's so meaningless."

The funeral. The cemetery. The cold floor. The sound of the organ bouncing between the walls. The coffin, such a tiny coffin, so short and so narrow. With flowers on it. Rebecka had been standing there. Right next to it, saying something. Marie had been inside. He hadn't seen her, the casket had been closed, but they'd made her look nice, combed her hair and put her in a dress.

He took a couple of deep breaths.

"Marie no longer exists. She can't feel. She can't see. She can't smell. She can't hear. Not now. Not since. She doesn't exist, not in any way. Don't you understand? Do you understand what I'm talking about?"

"You know I don't agree with you. But I understand why you see it that way."

The hatch on the closed door opened again. The staring eyes.

"It's noisy in there. Is everything all right?"

Rebecka raised her hand to the door.

"Everything is fine."

"Well then, shout if you need something."

Fredrik was still lying down. His breathing was heavy, but he wasn't shaking anymore.

"When I realized that Bernt Lund was planning more murders, I decided then. I was going to shoot him. Kill him. Stop him before he could do it again."

He was searching for the words.

"You all think this was about revenge. But this had nothing to do with revenge. I died with Marie. When I decided to kill him, I was alive again."

He stood up, hit the table with his hand, then bent forward, slamming his head repeatedly against the tabletop.

He was bleeding heavily from his forehead.

"I killed him. What should I live for now?"

The door opened. The guard stepped into the cell along with his colleague—same uniform, same facial expressions. They passed Rebecka, approached Fredrik, took each of his arms and forced him away from the table. They pressed him down hard against the bed and held him there until he stopped throwing his head forward into the empty air.

IT RAINED ON the day the trial began. It was only the second day of precipitation, a gentle rain in an unusually hot summer, the kind of rain that waits as the day dawns and then patiently lingers, and continues to linger, until evening, until darkness.

The line had been long since early in the morning. It was the most high-profile Swedish trial in the last few years, and it would be held at the Stockholm Court House, in the old courtroom there. Long before nine o'clock journalists and the public started crowding into the old stairwell of the stone foyer. The number of spaces was limited to four rows and, with the exception of a few large media companies that had reserved seats, the spaces were first come, first served when the doors opened.

The coverage was extensive. Uniformed and plainclothes police officers stood next to the security companies' hired staff. There was the sense of a threat, the faceless citizen. In the weeks that had passed since Lund's escape and murder, frustration, anger, and a shared hate of pedophiles had given rise to a collective purpose among those who usually did no more than observe or comment. All of this was present, waiting, preparing, bubbling.

Micaela stood at the front. She'd arrived just after seven o'clock. It had rained a bit more by then, was almost cold. She hadn't seen Fredrik in almost two weeks, since Marie's funeral.

He had disappeared to what she now knew had been his pursuit of Lund. Then to the Kronoberg jail with full restrictions.

She was scared.

It was her first time in a courtroom, and the man she loved would be sitting a few meters in front of her, charged with murder, interrogated by a prosecutor who was asking for life imprisonment.

She'd had a family. Fredrik, who'd slept next to her at night, whom she'd learned to hold on to. Marie, who'd almost felt like her own, whom she fed and dressed and cared for. More her family than anything else she'd ever had.

Just a few weeks and it had all ended.

She smiled the best she could to the officer who searched the contents of her bag. He didn't smile back. She then had to go back and forth through the metal detector three times to get it to stop beeping. She'd had a key in her jacket pocket, one of Marie's bicycle keys. She got a good seat, third row, just behind the news agency and two TV stations. She recognized a few of the reporters, the ones who were usually reporting from some exotic locale. Now they sat taking notes on small pads with short sentences. She tried to decipher what they were writing, but it was illegible—she could see that both had written the time at the top, and that they continued to put the time next to each new note they took. A little farther away sat two sketch artists. Their pencils flew over the white sheets of paper, the contours of walls, floors, chairs. They were sketching the background, and soon they'd fill it with people.

She saw Agnes behind her and to the side, in the last row. She turned around for a moment too long and was discovered. Agnes nodded, and she nodded back politely. It was strange that they'd never spoken to each other. She had answered the phone a few times when Agnes asked for Marie, just a short *Can I speak to Marie?* and a short *Here she comes,* that was all, three years of communication. Farther away sat the two police officers who'd questioned her, the children, their parents, and anyone else who'd been in the vicinity of the Dove on that day. The older one, the one who was in charge, who limped; the younger one, who was more patient and seemed calm, a little religious. They saw her too, and both nodded. She nodded back.

It was packed. More people were waiting outside, she could hear protests from some of the people who hadn't made it in. Someone booed at the guards, one person was calling them fascist pigs.

There was a door behind the podium. She didn't see it until it opened, and they walked in one by one, in single file. First the judge, a woman, van Balvas. Then the lay judges, she'd never seen them before but had read about them in the newspaper, all of them older, local politicians moving away from their everyday occupations. The prosecutor, Lars Ågestam, whom she'd seen on TV, a small, pompous ass, the precocious type just a few years older than her, who made her feel very young. The defense lawyer, Kristina Björnsson, looked as confident and as calm as she had when they'd met in her office near Humlegården.

Fredrik came last. Two prison guards beside him.

They'd dressed him in a suit—she'd never seen him in a tie before. He looked pale. As scared as she was.

He kept his eyes on the floor, avoided looking out over the courtroom.

VAN BALVAS (VB): Your full name.
FREDRIK STEFFANSSON (FS): Nils Fredrik Steffansson.
VB: Address?
FS: 28 Hamn Street. Strängnäs.
VB: Do you know why we're here today?
FS: What a fucking question.
VB: I'll repeat the question. Do you know why we're here today?
FS: Yes.

She smoked three cigarettes during the break. One of the journalists had placed himself beside her in the depressing waiting room with dark heavy oak paneling on the walls and hard, worn wooden benches, somehow authoritative, placed in the middle of the room. He'd asked her how Fredrik was doing, and Micaela replied that she didn't know, that they weren't allowed to talk to each other, that she lived with Fredrik, but wasn't considered close enough to be a visitor, and then when he opened up his pack of southern European cigarettes with no filters, he'd offered her one and she'd accepted. She knew that Fredrik hated it when she smoked. It had been several months since the last time, but now she smoked them rapidly, one after another, and felt dizzy from how strong they were. Agnes was standing by herself a bit farther away drinking from a bottle of mineral water. They avoided looking at each other. There was no reason to seek each other out. What would be the point? They had no common reference points. A young, thin-haired journalist sat on one of the wooden benches, headphones on, taking notes from a recording. Beside him was his elder, one of the journalists she recognized. He was looking at sketches made of a moment in the courtroom: Fredrik gesturing with his hand and the prosecutor showing a picture of a nursery school in Enköping, taken from the very spot where Fredrik had taken his shot.

LARS ÅGESTAM (LÅ): Fredrik Steffansson, I don't understand. I don't understand why you didn't alert the police officers who were less than a few hundred meters in front of you.

FS: I didn't have time.

LÅ: Didn't have time?

FS: If two specially trained prison guards couldn't take down Bernt Lund when he was in body chains, how would two half-asleep police officers be able to capture an armed Bernt Lund?

LÅ: You didn't even try to contact them?

FS: I couldn't risk him getting away with another little girl.

LÅ: I still don't understand.

FS: No?

LÅ: I don't understand why you had to kill Bernt Lund.

FS: What is it that's so damn hard to understand?

VB: Mr. Steffansson, please sit down.

FS: Didn't you hear what I said? You had already proved that you were unable to keep him locked up. That you were unable to treat him for his problem. That you couldn't even capture him after he murdered Marie. What more do I need to explain?

VB: I repeat, Mr. Steffansson, would you please sit down? Ms. Björnsson, can you please assist me?

KRISTINA BJÖRNSSON (KB): Fredrik, calm down. If you want to make yourself understood, you have to stay here.

FS: Can you get rid of them?

KB: When you calm down, the guards will sit down again.

Their eyes met only once, after an hour of opening arguments, during the prosecutor's first examination. He'd been forced down into his chair after a fit of rage, and once he was sitting he turned around, looked at her and Agnes, a faint smile. She was positive that he tried to smile. She'd brought her hand to her mouth, blowing him a kiss. She could feel it in her gut again, how much she missed him, how he sat there dressed in a suit and tie, his face pale. He was on his way away from her.

LÅ: May I remind you, Fredrik, that Sweden is one of many countries that does not have the death penalty.

FS: If he had been arrested, if the police managed it, he would have been sentenced to psychiatric care. It's even easier to escape from that.

LÅ: Really?

FS: If Bernt Lund had been arrested, we would only have postponed the inevitable. He was going to kill more children.

LÅ: And so you chose to act as the police, prosecutor, judge, and executioner?

FS: You choose to misunderstand.

LÅ: Not at all.

FS: I'll say it again. I didn't kill him because I wanted to punish him. I killed him because he was very dangerous as long as he was alive, what you would do with a mad dog.

LÅ: Mad dog?

FS: You put it down so it won't keep putting people in danger. Bernt Lund was a mad dog. I put him down.

She lingered long after each hearing. She hoped he'd be moved past her, so she could see him, meet him. She sat outside different exits, waiting outside various entrance doors, but she never saw the prison guards and never saw him.

He'd stopped shaving after the first day of the trial. He no longer wore a tie. It was as if he didn't care anymore, as if he were giving up. Their eyes met sometimes during each session. He turned around, and she tried to look calm, like she knew everything would turn out well.

Agnes no longer came, the occasional journalist had disappeared, and the two detectives took turns sitting there. Micaela talked a bit to the younger one, Sundkvist, he was nice, softer than police officers usually are.

After the trial ended each day, she went back to Strängnäs, to the home she shared with Fredrik.

She had difficulty sleeping at night.

HE STEPPED OFF at the Åkeshov metro station and walked slowly through the neighborhood. He'd been singing quietly to himself, it was that kind of evening, the air warm, the day long gone. It was only when Lars Ågestam turned on his own street that he saw it.

The car was most visible. They'd spray-painted the words. Black letters on red paint. The letters bounced against him, attacked him.

Pedophile-lover
Kid-fucker
Shithole
Who's the real psychopath?

On both doors. On the roof. On the hood. Someone had spray-painted his hatred and then smashed whatever could be broken. The windows were crushed, the headlights kicked in, the mirrors gone.

———

He'd vomited in the sink at the Prosecution Authority, when he'd been told that the father had gone through with his execution.

He'd understood, even then.

———

It was a small 1940s house with yellow plaster that his whole family had helped to repaint just before summer started.

Now those words screamed all over its walls, from the kitchen window on the left side, to the front door, to the living room window on the right side.

The same black spray paint. The same handwriting. One sentence on two lines, from the foundation of the house to the gutter.

you're going to die
cunt bastard

Marina, his wife, sat in the garden just a few meters from the angular writing. She had her eyes closed and she was rocking back and forth in the porch swing they'd bought at an auction a week ago.

She coughed as if strained, said nothing as he approached, or when he held her.

———

After three days of trial, what was bound to happen had happened.

The father who'd killed his daughter's murderer, risking life imprisonment, was there, everywhere.

The threat, the faceless citizen, was taking action.

LARS ÅGESTAM COULDN'T stay in the house with words spray-painted all over its walls.

He woke up to go to the bathroom and couldn't go back to sleep again. He'd been lying in bed, naked—the blanket was wrapped around Marina—and he'd stared at the ceiling.

Out there, beyond the kitchen window, his car stood destroyed and spray-painted.

He was a pedophile-lover. A kid-fucker. A shithole and psychopath.

Marina's eyes were still swollen. She couldn't look at him, had looked to the side instead, away from him. He'd asked her if she was scared, and she had shaken her head, and he'd asked her if she felt violated, and she'd shaken her head, and he'd kept asking her, and she turned her face to the wall. He lay there alone with the psychopath spray paint and the destroyed car and, after a while, he'd started breathing heavily. She noticed it but kept her eyes on the wall, and he'd whispered her name again and again until she'd turned to him. She said she was sorry, they'd held each other in their nakedness, skin against skin, and they'd made love for longer than they usually did, and then they'd lain next to each other a long time before she turned back to the wall again.

He got out of bed, walked around his house naked. He looked at the clock. Three thirty.

He went into the kitchen, boiled water and put in instant coffee, made a couple of cheese sandwiches, a glass of yogurt in one hand and orange juice in the other. He read yesterday's papers, *Dagens Nyheter* and *Svenska Dagbladet*, and was surprised by the amount of text, images, and space being dedicated to what they were calling the Pedophile Trial.

It wasn't working. The worry, restlessness, anger lashed at him, and he abandoned his early breakfast after half a cup of coffee, got dressed, and grabbed his briefcase. He went into the bedroom and kissed Marina on the shoulder and explained that he was going to take a walk, think a bit before the city woke up. She said something he couldn't hear, and he walked out.

Seven steps along the concrete slabs in the lawn. Then he turned around.

you're going to die
cunt bastard

The letters seemed even larger in the dawn light, even blacker. The handwriting was childish and ugly—stiff, angular, unpracticed. As if it hadn't been written for real. As if it would soon wash off, down into messy piles among the flowerbeds of roses.

He walked past the car. One year old. Fully financed. A wreck, vandalized, looted, like the ones he'd seen in the outskirts of large South American cities.

It would have to stay there until someone took it away, until the words pierced through.

He walked into town. Two hours through the western suburbs, briefcase in hand, his jacket over his shoulder, his black shoes chafing a bit. He had time to think. Time to try to understand. What was this all about? He'd wanted to become a prosecutor. He became a prosecutor. He had wanted the big case. He got the big case. That's where it had ended. He wasn't ready. He was too young. He wasn't good enough. A big trial meant attention. With attention came both praise and threats. He knew that, of course. He'd seen it happen to his older colleagues. So why did a few letters on his house and car scare him? Why had he known when they made love in the middle of Marina's silence that he was on his way somewhere else, that he'd just lost his dreams, become older? He would finish this trial, push

PEN 33   237

for as long a sentence as possible. Then, he didn't know. He no longer had any clarity. He felt alone.

He arrived in Kungsholmen and Scheele Street just after six o'clock. The courthouse, so still, an occasional seagull searching for food in two trash bins outside, otherwise empty. He walked up to the large entrance, took a key out of his briefcase, and opened the door. He'd spent many a night and morning here alone in a courtroom. A roving guard used to let him in, until finally the district court made the unusual decision to give a copy of the keys to the young prosecutor who seemed to live in the old stone building.

He walked up the unwieldy stairs, all the way to the courtroom. He stepped in, sat down in the place he'd occupy in three hours, opened his folders, and took out the documents he'd be using today. Those that didn't fit he put on the floor in the order that he'd need them.

He worked for forty-five minutes. Then the door opened.

"Ågestam."

Lars Ågestam heard the hoarse voice. He hated it. He didn't look up from his papers.

"Your wife told me you were here. I think I woke her."

Ewert Grens didn't ask if he could come in. His limping steps echoed through the big hall every time he put his right foot down. He passed behind the prosecutor, a cursory glance at the stack of papers as he walked up to the podium and settled into the judge's seat.

"I also tend to start early. It's so quiet then. No idiots nagging for anything."

Ågestam continued working, searching through documents, memorizing questions, observations, answers.

"Can you please stop what you're doing? I'm talking to you."

Ågestam turned toward him. His face like thunder.

"Why would I do that? I don't give a shit about you. Just like you don't give a shit about me, Grens."

"That's why I came."

Grens cleared his throat, fingering the wooden gavel that lay before him.

"I made a bad call."

Ågestam stopped in mid-motion, looked at the old man who was searching for the words.

"When I'm wrong, I say I'm wrong."

"Well, that's good."

"And I was wrong. I should have taken that threat garbage seriously."

It was as quiet in the courtroom as it was outside those big, ugly windows. The early morning of a warm summer day.

"You should have had police protection. Now you're getting it. We already have a car outside your home and a car waiting downstairs. He's coming up soon."

Ågestam went to the window. A lone policeman had just opened the door of a car. He closed it, went to the little staircase in front of the entrance.

He sighed, suddenly felt tired, as if the night's missing sleep was coming to call him back.

"It's a little late for that."

"This is how it is now."

"You said it."

Grens held the judge's gavel, swung it, one bang that bounced around. He'd said what he came to say but still made no move to go. Ågestam waited for him to continue talking, but there was nothing. The lame fucker just sat there, as if waiting for something.

"Are you done? I'm here to work."

The detective superintendent smacked his mouth. An annoying sound.

"I'll take that as a yes."

"One more thing."

"Yeah?"

"I bought one of those CD players. I have it in my office. On the shelf next to the tape deck. I can play your disc now."

————

Grens remained there a long time. In the judge's chair. He said nothing, and after a while Lars Ågestam started working again. He sought the best arguments to explain to the lay judges, who were under intense media pressure to judge a premeditated murder as just that, regardless of the circumstances. He wrote, crossed out, wrote again. Grens smacked his mouth from time to time, the annoying sound in the distance, as if to show that he was still there. He sat leaning back, his face to the ceiling, almost half asleep.

It was half past eight when they heard voices outside. Through the thick glass panes, heard people shouting.

They both went over to the wall with the windows, opened one of them. Gentle air washed over them, and they leaned out in order to see the empty space four floors below.

It wasn't empty anymore. They both started counting, estimating that about two hundred people stood down there near the entrance door—a crowd in motion, as if it were electric, a wave, a pulse, as they took a few steps forward and the policemen with plastic shields pushed them back with equal force. They chanted, carrying signs, demonstrating loudly against the judicial process that would continue in thirty minutes. They taunted the society that would choose to prosecute and punish the person who'd been able to protect them when the system couldn't.

Grens shook his head.

"That's not smart. What do they think they're going to achieve by screaming? Do they think our police officers would let in idiots making threats?"

A stone flew through the air and landed next to the police officer standing at the end of the chain of shields. Ågestam winced, thinking of the car and the house and Marina, who might be awake now. There was a police car there. That was surely enough. He met Grens's gaze and felt compelled to explain out loud.

"They're just scared. They're afraid of pedophiles, so afraid that it turns to hate. So when a wounded father takes the life of one, it's natural that they'd turn him into a hero. He did what they themselves would like to do, but don't dare to."

Grens snorted.

"Look, I don't like scum. I've hunted scum my whole life. But there is a difference between scum and *scum*. They didn't *make* him into a hero. He *is* a hero. He did what we couldn't. He protected them."

The twelve policemen in front of the courthouse were getting reinforcements. Two more vans, with six shield-bearing police officers in each, drove quickly through the crowd.

They stopped abruptly when two of the demonstrators broke ranks and marched straight toward them. The twelve policemen rushed out of their vehicles, joined the others, making the human wall wider.

Slowly, those who were attacking calmed down, their cries were muffled, and the state of things shifted from acute to wait-and-see.

Ågestam closed the window and the sound from outside disappeared completely. He stifled the impulse to shove Grens away. There was something about Grens's tone of voice, as if he was finding fault with everything all the time. Instead Ågestam continued his argument, the same ground he would cover in this very hall in just a few moments.

"I don't know what you mean. Hero? Protecting the citizens?"

"He made them feel safer."

"He's a murderer. His actions are no different from Lund's. He took a life. What the people down there think is heroic wouldn't even be considered mitigating circumstances in a normal trial."

"You at least have to agree that we couldn't protect them. But he did."

There were people down there, outside the closed window. The kind you would describe as ordinary people. They'd made up their minds. The father had done the right thing. And what Ågestam was doing now, prosecuting him, was wrong.

"That doesn't give Fredrik Steffansson or any other grieving father the right to decide life and death. You don't know me, Grens. You don't know if deep down inside I think he did the right thing, that he was right to blow the head off a pedophile and a serial killer. You have no clue. And I'm not going to help you, because anything but a long prison sentence would be wrong. He has to pay. We can't give the people out there any other message."

Ågestam left the window and walked toward the pile of papers on the floor. He gathered together the documents, put them in the right order in two binders.

Ewert Grens lingered, one last glance out the window as the crowd began to disperse. He walked over to the witness bench at the back of the hall and sat down in the same place he'd sat during the first three days of the trial.

The door opened. An usher came in, and after him came the long line of media representatives and spectators who had managed to pass through the heightened security checks.

The trial of Fredrik Steffansson had entered its fifth and final day.

BENGT SÖDERLUND WOKE up early. Two weeks left of his vacation. He had to make the most of his days. He'd only slept a few hours every night for the last week. Only when he was in motion, when he was doing something, could he stop thinking about Elisabeth and the kid, who had gone to God knows where. He'd called obsessively that first day, to her parents and friends and former colleagues, but no one had seen her. He didn't tell them why he'd called. No way in hell anyone was going to laugh at his expense.

They were supposed to meet at half past nine. Just a few minutes left. He looked out of the living room window. They were already there: Ove and Helena. Ola Gunnarsson and Klas Rilke. He snapped his fingers, Baxter came running from the kitchen, and they went out together.

His toolshed was big and stood right next to Flasher-Göran's boundary—he would see them go in and wonder what they were doing there.

They greeted each other, took each other by the hand as they'd done since they were little. He didn't know why, that's what you did in Tallbacka.

Bengt owned two sawhorses. He lifted one, set it beside the other, and placed a long broad plank on top. Ove and Klas Rilke each carried a large plastic sack with empty bottles in their arms. Forty of them. Half of them wine bottles and the other half soda bottles. All glass. They both helped to place them side by side on the long sawhorse table. Meanwhile, Ola Gunnarsson opened the lid of the large oil drum behind the mower in one corner of the shed. It was filled to the brim with gasoline. He lowered an oilcan underneath the surface, large bubbles rose as it filled. He lifted it up. Gas ran down its sides. Helena waited until he was finished, then she went over to the first wine bottle and put a plastic funnel on top of it. Ola Gunnarsson poured the gas through it and into the bottle, filled it halfway, then moved the oilcan and funnel to the next bottle, filled it to half. They continued like that through all forty bottles, using almost twenty liters of gasoline. Bengt, meanwhile, had unfurled the dirty sheets he'd brought with him from the laundry basket and laid them on top of a pile of firewood. He pulled a knife through the fabric, cutting it into equal-size pieces, thirty centimeters by thirty centimeters. He then rolled them up and put a piece of cloth into each bottle and left a small piece of fabric sticking out of the mouth, like the head of a pin. Then they moved the bottles into a box on the ground, each bottle tightly packed so as to stand steady. In a smaller box next to it lay ten cigarette lighters, two for each of them, in case one broke.

It didn't take very long. The morning wasn't even over yet.

FREDRIK SAT IN the middle of the courtroom with his eyes closed, wanting to see what was around him, but

LARS ÅGESTAM (LÅ): Steffansson committed murder without a trace of compassion or concern for Bernt Lund's life. I see no mitigating circumstances regarding Steffansson's action and, therefore, urge that he be convicted of murder in the first degree and sentenced to life in prison.

didn't have the energy. It was the fifth and final day. He wanted to go back to his cell and

KRISTINA BJÖRNSSON (KB): Fredrik Steffansson found himself outside that nursery school. His act is considered self-defense, because if he had not shot Bernt Lund, then this pedophile and serial killer would have murdered two more five-year-old girls—whom we have been able to identify.

piss in the sink, it was nothing more than that.

The whole room was full, all these people around him. It made him feel so damn lonely.

Like the Christmas he spent after Agnes left him, a few weeks before he'd met Micaela. It was Christmas Eve and he had tried his best to push that knowledge away but couldn't quite manage to, so at five in the evening, when the darkness seemed densest, he'd gone to one of the few pubs in Stockholm that was open. He would never forget the people there, the communal loneliness. It had become unbearable when the show *Karl-Bertil Jonsson's Christmas* started on the TV at the end of the bar, became the center of their attention for half an hour. It was as if the story, which had played every year at this time for decades, was about them, Christmastime for the down-and-out. They'd all laughed and the evening felt warm for a moment and then it was over. Another beer and a cigarette, and they all returned home to a stuffy-smelling apartment that needed to be cleaned.

He looked around. He was sitting now as he had then, surrounded by strangers in a system he didn't understand, cheated out of his own future. The prosecutor

LÅ: According to the third chapter of the penal code first paragraph *the one who deprives another of life shall be sentenced to murder and imprisonment for ten years to life.*

was demanding life in prison and his lawyer

KB: According to chapter twenty-four of the penal code, first section of the first paragraph, *an act committed in self-defense is a crime only if it, in regard to the nature of the act, the significance of what is acted upon and general circumstance, is indisputably indefensible.*

was claiming self-defense, and the lay judges didn't seem to be listening, and the journalists behind him were writing and taking notes that he wouldn't be allowed to read. He didn't know who they were or what reality they represented. Behind them, the audience, the curious, who he'd come to hate, who pounded their knees in delight to be close enough to stare unrestrainedly at the father who killed his daughter's murderer.

LÅ: Fredrik Steffansson spent four days planning the murder of Bernt Lund. Steffansson, therefore, had plenty of time to consider his actions. Steffansson committed murder to, in his own words, rid society of a mad dog.

He avoided looking behind him. Just a few times to see Micaela. He wanted to say something, show something,

> **KB:** An emergency exists when the danger threatens life, health, property, or anything else protected by law. We believe that the apparent danger to two girls' lives existed, and that Fredrik Steffansson's actions saved two young lives.

but he had been afraid of those curious eyes and sniffing noses and so he'd given up trying. He'd sat there, hour after hour, staring straight ahead, refusing to watch or listen, and seeing Marie in a body bag on a table at the Forensic Medicine building, her face beautiful and her chest taped together and her abdomen cut to pieces by something metallic and her feet too clean with traces of saliva—he could hear the one speaking for and the one speaking against and answered their questions, but it was as if it wasn't happening, and a girl in a body bag on a table was all he had the strength to care about.

SUMMER WAS SLOWLY dying out.

The heat that reigned, week after week, had dissolved, cooler air had replaced it, and when the downpours became persistent, damp crept in under the tanned skin, and shorts and tank tops turned to long pants and jackets. But Charlotte van Balvas breathed easily. She'd been waiting to be able to walk quietly along the streets of Stockholm without squinting in the sun—soon it would be perfectly acceptable to be pale again, her fair complexion turned an angry red when exposed to the sun. Every day she'd lingered in the courtroom longer than she needed to, then hid out in restaurants and libraries, waiting to take to the streets again, just like everyone else. They all looked so happy.

She was forty-six years old, and she was scared.

She'd seen what happened to the prosecutor, Ågestam, how he'd been threatened, his home vandalized, simply because he represented society and was doing what had to be done: insisting on life imprisonment for a premeditated murder. She was the judge in this case and probably just as scrutinized and hated. In addition, she was joined by three lay judges, who lacked any legal background and who had been appointed after long and faithful political service. It was the lay judges she'd be facing in a moment in a meeting room behind the courtroom. She was going to try to convince them that the father, according to the laws they'd all agreed to follow, was guilty of murder and, therefore, should be punished with a long prison term.

She had no choice.

She was society, and society had no place for lynch mobs administering their own justice.

She crossed Kungsholm Square, nearing the courthouse. She observed them, crouching under their umbrellas, and wondered what they were thinking. What if they had fired the shots, if it had been their choice? Did they think one person had more right to live than another one? She wondered if they recognized her. All of their pictures had appeared widely in the news, both hers and the lay judge's.

They Determine the Outcome in the Pedophile Trial
Is Killing Right? They Decide
The Court That Might Make the Death Penalty Part of Swedish Law

She'd bought the papers, seen the headlines, but never read beyond that.

She'd been studying the father's face for five days, so fragile, so damaged. He'd tried to avoid the hyenas on the witness benches and so constantly kept his eyes focused straight ahead. She'd liked what she saw. She'd even read one of the father's books in the evening and realized he was exactly as he claimed. He had almost certainly prevented Lund from desecrating two girls. She also understood that this could be why he'd shot him. Dear Lord, she could caress that fragile face, he didn't scare her, and she believed him when he said he had shot his daughter's killer not in revenge, but so that other parents wouldn't have to experience the same thing.

One of the lay judges had asked her how she would have reasoned if it had been her own child he'd saved, if she'd been the one living near that nursery school in Enköping.

She had no children.

But she wasn't so stupid that she didn't understand how she might have felt differently, so she'd avoided answering him.

The courthouse, she could see it. She was close now.

At that very moment the rain started falling harder. Large drops rapidly formed into large puddles. A thunderstorm.

Her clothes were getting soaking wet. She stood still.

The water ran down her cheeks, along her neck, and it calmed her, gave her courage. She was going to be able to make it through these deliberations where, very soon, she'd try to influence the other judges to sentence a grieving father to life imprisonment.

IT WAS RAINING outside. Fredrik stood by the grating of the window, trying to find whatever was making that annoying clattering sound. A piece of the windowsill hanging loose? He could see the copper-colored metal, tried to count the drops of rain beating against it. He lay down on the bed—the dirty ceiling, the bare walls, the locked door and closed hatch. He tried to close his eyes, escape, but had slept so much in recent days that he was unable to disappear into that trance anymore. It was impossible to sleep away the hours.

He'd been locked up here for almost three weeks.

The guards laughed when he complained. They said Sweden had some of the world's longest detention times, but he was already having his case tried. Some spent months, almost a year, in here before their trials began.

He'd been lucky, they said, because he shot a famous pedophile and all that media attention moved things along faster. He had no fucking clue how that endless waiting with no end in sight was able to make people commit suicide in the night.

Somebody was here, despite the fact that there was still an hour left until lunch. He looked toward the door. Someone was standing out there.

Eyes in the hatch.

"Fredrik?"

"Yes?"

"You have a visitor."

He sat up, fiddling with his hair a bit. It was the first time in several days he'd thought about how he looked. The cell door opened.

A priest and a lawyer. Rebecka and Kristina Björnsson. They entered at the same time. And it was as if they were beaming.

"Hello."

He didn't have it in him to answer. They were people he liked and he should greet them, but he no longer had the energy. They meant well, but this space was his. Even the fluorescent lamp that made it even uglier was his.

"What is it?"

"It's a good day."

"I'm just tired. The damn rattling."

He pointed toward the window.

"Do you hear it?"

They listened for a moment, nodded affirmatively. Rebecka fidgeted with her clerical collar for a moment, then put her hand on his shoulder.

"Fredrik, I want you to listen to me now. Kristina has good news."

Kristina Björnsson sat down on the bed beside him. Her round body, her calm voice.

"This is how it is, Fredrik, you're a free man."

He heard her. He said nothing.

"Do you understand? Free! You were acquitted just a moment ago. A divided district court ruled that you acted in self-defense, nothing else. So you can leave this room, take off that uniform. Tonight, you only lock the door if you want to."

He stood up again, went to the window, where the windowsill was clattering even louder than before. The rain was falling harder. There was going to be thunder.

"I don't know."

"What did you say?"

"I'm not sure that it matters."

"What doesn't matter?"

"I'd just as well stay here."

For some reason, he thought of his military service. How he'd hated every minute of it, then one day it was over, and he'd walked out empty and silent from the open gate, all joy and longing, the anticipation gone. It had helped him to survive, and then it was gone.

Just like that all over again.

"I don't think you understand."

Rebecka and Kristina looked at each other.

"No. We probably don't."

He didn't want to explain, but they were worth the effort.

"I had a child. She doesn't exist anymore. Her genitals were slashed apart by someone who'd done exactly the same thing before. I had a certain view of humanity. It doesn't exist anymore. I thought life was sacred—then I killed a man. I don't know. I just don't fucking know. If you lose your life—what else is there?"

They'd stayed there on his bed waiting while he changed his clothes, changed his world.

He didn't belong here anymore.

He nodded to the guard with the staring eyes, stopped in the corridor on his way out, bought a coffee in a plastic cup from a vending machine that whined softly, continued in the entrance straight past twenty waiting journalists. It was just like in the courtroom—they wanted his face, and he said nothing, showed nothing. He hugged Rebecka and Kristina on the pavement and sat down in the waiting taxi.

BENGT SÖDERLUND RAN as fast as he could through Tallbacka. He dashed from his home, hip aching, the taste of blood in his mouth, just like when he won his school championship, not because he'd been the strongest or the most fit, but because he was the most determined to win. Now he was running again. It was as if he couldn't get there fast enough, as if every second had to be utilized, saved. He could see Ove and Helena's house in the distance. They were home, their car in the driveway, the lights on in the kitchen. He hurried up the stairs, didn't ring the doorbell, just stepped into the hall instead, waved the paper in his hand, and shouted toward the living room.

"Now, dammit, now!"

Helena was sitting naked in a chair. She was reading a book and looked in fright at the man shouting from her hallway. He'd never seen her naked before, and if he'd really looked, he would have seen that she was beautiful. But he didn't, because he couldn't stop, couldn't stand still. He went into the living room and walked around, waving the paper and trying to see through the window if Ove was in the garden, if he was home at all.

"Where is he?"

"What is it?"

"Where is he?"

"In the basement. He's taking a shower."

"I'll go and get him."

"He's coming up soon."

"I'll go and get him."

He opened the door to the basement, took a clumsy and noisy step down the steep stairway. He knew where the shower was. He'd borrowed it several times some years ago when they redid their bathroom—Elisabeth had wanted a bigger one, he'd knocked down a closet, and she got her hardwood floor. He opened the next door, went over to the shower curtain, large birds on a blue background, and pulled it to the side. Ove stumbled and cringed until he saw who it was.

"Here. Here, we have it! Now, dammit!"

Ove turned off the shower, dried himself haphazardly, and walked up the stairs with the towel wrapped carelessly around his waist, behind Bengt, who held the paper in the air: a first prize for the public that needed to be celebrated. They moved quickly through the hall and into the living room. Helena was still sitting there, quiet, but with her dressing gown on now.

"Can you believe it? Can you believe it?!"

He put the paper on the table, unfolded it while Ove and Helena moved closer.

"I printed it out from the internet. A news agency website. It was announced twenty minutes ago. Or nineteen, actually. Look, eleven o'clock precisely."

Ove and Helena were reading. Two pages, large text. Bengt waited impatiently, walked back and forth across the room.

"Are you done? Can you believe it? They acquitted him! Self-defense! He shot that fucking pedophile and saved the lives of those little girls and the district court ruled it was self-defense! He went home. He's sitting at home right now having a drink. Three against one, only the judge had any reservations, the others didn't hesitate."

Ove read again, Helena leaned back in her chair, Bengt hugged her and pounded Ove on the back.

"Now, dammit! Now he's gonna go away! It's our fucking right! He's going, it's self-defense, now, goddammit, it's self-defense!"

———

They waited until it was dark. They'd been sitting at Bengt's all afternoon, not saying much, just passing the time together. They knew what they were going to do. One more cup of coffee, each with a bun to dip, then it was half past nine—darkness had fallen, not black, but enough to obscure faces.

They converged in the garden—Bengt, Ove, Helena, Ola, Klas—let their eyes get used to the lack of contours. It was quiet. Days began and ended early here. Bengt asked the others to wait while he went back to the house, into the kitchen, snapped his fingers, and felt Baxter's tongue against his hand. They approached the garden shed in a line, opened the padlock, and lifted out the two boxes. First twenty tightly packed wine bottles and twenty soda bottles, all filled halfway with gasoline, a piece of fabric pressed into the glass necks, then the smaller box with ten cigarette lighters inside. Ove and Klas helped to balance the box of bottles, Ola took care of the lighters, he kept two for himself, gave the others two each.

A few more meters. The house next door, fully illuminated. They stayed hidden and could see him walking around inside, from kitchen to living room, from the living room into the bathroom. When the light in the bathroom turned on, Bengt made a sign to Baxter to stay put, took several steps forward, started to climb up the pole in front of him. He was agile and fast, reached the top quickly and hung there, grabbed a pair of pliers out of the side pocket of his work pants and used them to cut the telephone lines. The bathroom light was bright. The house's owner stood by the sink. Bengt slid down, stinging his hands. He moved to the next pole and used a square key to open an electrical box a few meters up, identical to his own, the master switch.

The house went completely dark. They waited.

It took longer than they'd anticipated. First, a pair of candles was lit, one placed in each room. Then, the flashlight. Its light flickered along the walls.

A few more seconds.

The flashlight neared the hall, the entrance door.

Bengt held Baxter by the collar. The dog knew it was time to attack. That his master would soon give him the command.

"Baxter! Get 'im!"

The flashlight shone on a door being opened.

Bengt released Baxter at the precise moment Flasher-Göran went down the front steps. The dog ran across the lawn, barking loudly, and Flasher-Göran turned, tore open the door again as the dog reached the steps, and slammed it as the animal took a run at it.

"Stay, Baxter."

The dog stopped barking and sat at the front door, ready.

Bengt tried to follow the shadow running through the house, glimpsed it several times through the windows. He was fairly sure that Flasher-Göran had stayed in the kitchen.

He screamed in that direction.

"Are you scared, Göran? Now when it's dark and cold? We're going to help you, Göran. We're gonna give you some light and heat again."

He pointed to Ove, Ola, and Klas, who quickly moved over to the open garden shed and retrieved the oil drum of gasoline. It was heavy. They lifted together and carried it over the lawn, turned it on its side, and rolled it up to Flasher-Göran's house. Ove hit it with a screwdriver, removing the lid, and lifted up the barrel again, just enough for the gas to pour out. They carried the container around the house, emptying it of its contents, gas in the flowerbeds and on the gravel path.

Helena, meanwhile, lifted up the glass bottles and put them in five equal piles. They lit the fabric pieces and waited quietly for the Molotov cocktails to light, then a signal from Bengt, and they threw five flaming bottles.

They hit various parts of the house. But the explosion was one and the same.

They threw again, at the same time, hitting new places. One by one, eight bottles each. The house was on fire already, the fire devouring it from several directions at once.

Bengt took a piece of paper from the same pocket as the pliers, and while the house burned fiercely in front of them, he started reading out loud. He read from the district court's judgment against Fredrik Steffansson. If a father murdered his daughter's murderer, preventing a pedophile from violating more children, and was acquitted because his act was a service to society, it was to be regarded as self-defense.

When he was finished, he opened the kitchen window. Flasher-Göran screamed and threw himself out.

He landed heavily and lay there. Bengt was convinced that Elisabeth would have understood if only she'd seen. She should have been here next to him.

Flasher-Göran started to move, and Bengt shouted to Baxter, who was still guarding the front door. The dog ran down the stairs, toward the man who was on his way up from the ground, threw himself onto him, and tore apart the arm Flasher-Göran was trying to use to protect himself.

IV
(one summer)

TALLBACKA BURNED THE day the verdict was announced. The attack on a forty-six-year-old man, who twenty years earlier had stripped naked in a schoolyard and was later sentenced to a fine, was the first of nine acts of violence in Sweden stemming from accusations of pedophilia and framed as self-defense. Three of the ones who were attacked and assaulted by local lynch mobs were also killed.

INTERROGATOR (I): I'm beginning the interrogation.

BENGT SÖDERLUND (BS): You do that.

I: This interrogation concerns the events that took place after you threw Molotov cocktails.

BS: Sure thing.

I: I don't like your attitude.

BS: What do you mean?

I: Your sarcasm.

BS: If you don't want my answers, that's fine with me.

I: We can do this for as long as you like. If you answer my questions this will go quickly.

BS: You said it.

I: What happened after you threw the last bottle?

BS: It burned.

I: What did you do?

BS: I read.

I: What did you read?

BS: A verdict.

I: Stop that now, dammit!

BS: I read a verdict.

I: What fucking verdict?

BS: The Strängnäs father. The one who killed the pedophile who murdered his daughter. It was his verdict.

I: Why?

BS: Because society approved of what he did. Don't you get that? Those bastards should be removed.

I: What did you do then? After you read it?

BS: I saw Flasher-Göran jump.

I: Where?

BS: From the window. From the kitchen window.

I: What did you do then?

BS: I set Baxter on him.

I: You set Baxter on him?

BS: Yes.

I: Why?

BS: He was getting away. He started to get up.

I: And then you set your dog on him?

BS: Yes.

I: What did the dog do?

BS: He bit the bastard.

I: Where?

BS: The arms. The thighs. A couple of nasty ones in the face.

I: In the throat?

BS: There, too.

I: How long did he bite him?

BS: Till I called him back.

I: How long?

BS: Two, three minutes.

I: Two, three minutes?

BS: Let's say three. It was probably three.

I: And then?

BS: We left.

I: You left?

BS: Yes.

I: Where'd you go?

BS: Home. We called the fire department. It was burning so bad, I didn't want it to spread. I live nearby.

In addition to Flasher-Göran in Tallbacka, who died from complications related to a dog bite to the neck, a man in Umeå with two previous sex offense convictions was beaten to death with an iron pipe by four teenagers when he passed a playground just outside town.

INTERROGATOR (I): I'm recording again now.

ILRIAN RAISTROVIC (IR): That's fine.

I: Do you feel better now?

IR: I needed a fucking break.

I: We're continuing.

IR: Sure. What the hell.

I: You did the majority of the beating?

IR: I don't know.

I: That's what the others said.

IR: Then it must be true.

I: Why did you hit him?

IR: He was a fucking pedo.

I: Pedo?

IR: He groped two little girls' boobs. His kid's friends. Dammit, you get that.

I: How did you hit him?

IR: I hit. At him.

I: How many times?

IR: I don't know.

I: Guess.

IR: Like twenty. Or thirty.

I: Until he died.

IR: I guess so.

And in Stockholm two days later, perhaps the worst of them all: an alcoholic man surrounded by a group of screaming young men with baseball bats in the middle of the day.

INTERROGATOR (I): Where were you sitting?

ROGER KARLSSON (RK): On the other bench.

I: What were you doing there?

RK: I was checking him out. I know who he is. He's been up to that shit for a long time.

I: That shit?

RK: To chicks. Small ones.

I: What did he do?

RK: He shouted at them. Three of them. He said they were sluts.

I: He screamed sluts?

RK: Then he tried to grab their asses when they walked by.

I: Did he?

RK: He's so fucking slow. But he tried.

I: What did you do?

RK: They ran away. He scared them. He always scares them.

I: What did you do then?

RK: Hit him.

I: How?

RK: With a bat. In his gut. Then in the head.

I: Just you?

RK: The others did, too.

I: The others?

RK: There was a group of us. Waiting.

I: Everyone had weapons?

RK: Everyone had a bat.

I: And when you hit him?

RK: He shouted something. What the fuck, I think.

I: What did you do then?

RK: I screamed, too. Screamed he was a pervert.

I: Then?

RK: Then we hit him. All at the same time. It didn't take long.

I: When did he die?

RK: I had a hammer, too. I used it.

I: When did you use it?

RK: Later. Just to be sure.

I: That he was dead?

RK: Yes. Mad dogs have to be put down. That's the law now.

It was difficult to identify him afterward. Two local police officers guessed, with the help of his clothes, his name was Gurra B., a local celebrity who'd sat drinking on that bench in Vasa Park for thirty years, shouting sexual epithets at anyone who passed by.

THEY'D STRIPPED NAKED as soon as they closed the front door. They'd made love for a long time, held each other until heat made them slippery and sticky, and they didn't let go for twenty-four hours. It was as if someone might step in at any moment and take this closeness from them, as if skin against skin was more than security, it was a requirement for survival. Fredrik had never touched a woman that way before, needed her. He smelled her, caressed her, put his penis in her, but it was as if it weren't enough. She wasn't close enough for him, and he wanted her even closer. He'd even bitten into her a few times, her bottom, her thigh, her shoulder, and she'd laughed, but he'd been serious, had wanted to have *her* inside *him*.

He hadn't left the apartment for the whole week. The journalists had been waiting down there, with their questions and cameras and smiles. He wanted to stay indoors until the day they disappeared. Micaela had gone out to buy food on two occasions. The reporters hadn't left her side, followed her from the fence along Stor Street down to the grocery, walked behind her in the store. They repeated their questions about how he was feeling, and she'd stayed quiet just as she and Fredrik had agreed. They'd shouted after her when she closed the front door again.

He had avoided Marie's room. She existed, but she wasn't there, not for real. Her room, which would remain imprinted on his mind, demanded every part of him, and he simply wasn't ready. He knew that sooner or later they'd have to move if life were going to go on, it wouldn't be here, inside what remained of the other life.

He was a free man, but still locked up. He didn't read the papers, he couldn't, and didn't watch TV. A girl had been murdered and her father had killed her killer, and for him, that was it. He couldn't understand how several weeks later they were still writing about it, that the public was still interested. He'd had a life, and now he had nothing, and even the life he didn't have had been taken from him, made public.

He'd held on to Micaela for the second day, too. They had made love again and again. All their energy and sorrow and solace and guilt and fear and those last times, they transformed into intercourse, mechanically pushing the buttons they knew how to push in order to reach orgasm as soon as possible. They hadn't been able to look at each other, or really feel each other, and knew that the stifling anxiety remained and would bloom again once they emptied themselves.

He got drunk on the third day. That was how he'd long planned to die, when his time ran out, when his body got so weak that he knew the day had come. He'd been convinced that it would be easier that way, to die. He tried it now and sure enough, the alcohol had paralyzed, pushed the day away for a while, but the fear still stood there, insisting upon the terrible loneliness.

Since then he'd mostly stayed in bed. Three days without sleep, he'd held her body tightly the whole time but couldn't make love. He'd almost gone to get the bottle, but he didn't have the energy to drink or eat. Micaela had said, again and again, they should contact a doctor. Fredrik had already been offered help but had declined it then, and turned it down again now.

That's probably why he didn't react very much when Kristina Björnsson called that evening. It was half past eleven. He and Micaela looked at each other and thought it was a journalist but answered the call anyway. Micaela began—once she understood—hysterically asking questions during the call. Kristina seemed to be trying to comfort her in a legal way, but he couldn't share their feelings, not at all, there was just nothing, not here.

The prosecutor had appealed the district court's verdict. It had been decided that he'd be taken into custody the next day. It was almost liberating.

They would take his daily life from him again.

They'd turn his hours into a process, something that took place outside him, which wasn't reality, but still forced him to participate, and in that way he could avoid seeing the other reality, the reality inside him, both now and then.

He ended the call and lay down in bed. He kissed her for a long time. He would try to make love to her.

IT WAS A black car, they were always black, with extra mirrors and windows you couldn't see through. They'd picked him up early the next morning, three police officers—the two he recognized from before, the lame one and the proper one and a third one at the wheel, a tall, young one. They'd all met him at the door, dressed in civilian clothes, didn't say much. They let him hold Micaela until he was done. They'd driven through Strängnäs in silence. Fredrik sat in the back seat with the old, lame officer beside him. A few minutes from the E20 highway and at a much higher speed, another black car had driven up behind them, and a motorcycle police officer in front.

Grens had asked them right away to lower the sound of the police radio a little, and to put the CD he held in his hand into the car's stereo. The proper one, Sundkvist, had asked if it was really necessary on the way back, too. Grens had muttered something, clearly irritated, until the tall young man said *fuck it, put in the CD* and pushed play.

Siw Malmkvist. Fredrik was sure of it.

you make promises and talk nonsense about cars and minks
and think I should blindly be at your beck and call

Grens closed his eyes, rocking his body slowly back and forth. Fredrik shuddered. The lyrics were unbearable. Her perky voice came straight from the late '50s and early '60s, from a naive Sweden, unspoiled and expectant, a dawning myth. It hadn't really been like that. He'd been a child then, but he remembered his father and the beating and his mother and her Camel cigarettes and when she looked away. There was no Siw Malmkvist then or now. It was a lie, an escape, and he almost asked the policeman, whose eyes were closed, what it was he was running from—why he refused to let go of something that never even existed in the first place.

She sang all the way. Fifty minutes to get to the Kronoberg jail and Grens didn't open his eyes once, while the two in the front stared straight ahead, their thoughts seemingly elsewhere.

They saw the protesters when they turned onto Bergs Street. Even more than last time—two hundred had turned to more than five hundred protesters.

They stood facing the jail, shouting in unison, shaking their placards, spitting, jeering, throwing the occasional large stone at the entrance. A few seconds, then one of them noticed the motorcycle and the two black cars approaching. They ran toward them, holding hands, and made a ring around the three vehicles. They lay down on the ground, formed a human chain, the cars and the motorcycle could go neither forward nor backward. The tall young man looked around the car for support as he grabbed the police radio receiver.

"Officer in need of assistance! I repeat, officer in need of assistance! A mob throwing stones!"

Almost immediately, a voice from the speaker.

`"How many?"`

"Several hundred demonstrators outside Kronoberg!"

`"Reinforcements are on the way."`

"There's a chance he'll be sprung!"

`"Drive on. Drive on!"`

Fredrik could see people outside the car, hear them screaming, could read their signs, but didn't understand them. What were they doing here? He didn't know them. Why were they using his name? What had happened had nothing to do with them. It was his fight, his hell. They were risking their lives. For what? Did they know? He hadn't asked for this. There was no difference between them and the journalists standing outside his fence. They were living through someone else. Right now it was him. Why? Had they lost daughters? Had they shot and killed another human being? He wished he had the courage to roll down the window and ask, force them to look him in the eyes.

They sat quietly in the car, surrounded, paralyzed. The young one looked stressed, was breathing heavily, waving his arms as he alternated between releasing the handbrake and changing gears. Sundkvist and Grens were both calm, didn't seem to care, didn't move, waited patiently.

Again, the voice over the police radio in the dashboard of the car.

```
"To all cars. Officer in need of assistance at Krono-
berg, Bergs Street entrance. Approximately five hun-
dred protesters armed with rocks. Please disperse the
demonstration, nothing else. Leave your own views at
home."
```

Grens looked at him, trying to read his reaction. He didn't get it. Fredrik had heard the message, was astonished by the contents but revealed nothing, said nothing.

The young man put the car in reverse, revved the engine, and drove a few centimeters just to test the demonstrators' courage.

They still lay there.

They screamed.

He put it in first gear and drove forward a couple of meters, revved the engine. They remained, mocking them now, singing about pigs.

Suddenly, a few of them got up and walked over to the car.

One lifted a stone and threw it at the rear window. The glass smashed and the stone bounced off the seat between Fredrik and Grens and hit the backrest of the driver's seat before landing on the floor. Fredrik felt shattered glass on his neck, it hurt, and he looked at Grens, who was bleeding from his cheek. The young officer shouted *dammit, dammit to hell,* rolled down the side window and drew his weapon, aimed it toward the sky and let off a warning shot.

The demonstrators threw themselves down on the ground.

Suddenly, someone hit the young officer's arm, another blow, and the gun fell from his grasp. A protestor in his twenties picked it up and held it with both hands, took aim at the young police officer's face.

Ewert Grens roared.

"Drive! For fuck's sake, drive!"

The young man had a gun to his head. In front of him, people lay on the ground. Behind him people lay on the ground.

He hesitated.

The shot went off next to his left ear, passed out through the front window.

He couldn't hear anything after that, fixed his eyes on a tree farther away, pressed down on the accelerator. The people outside screamed as he drove over them. Their bodies hit the underside of the car unevenly. The car drove back out onto Bergs Street, just as the first of two SWAT team vans arrived. The demonstrators stood up now, ran as a group toward the new vehicles bearing combat-ready police officers and surrounded them, threw themselves against the sides of the vans, rocking them a few times, lifting them, overturning them both. Then they took a step back and waited for the riot police to crawl out, formed a line in front of them, some with their pants pulled down, and proceeded to pee on them.

HE DIDN'T GET the same cell as last time. Another floor, more in the middle. But it looked the same: four square meters, a bed, a table, a sink to wash in and piss in. The same uniform hanging off him. No newspapers, no radio, no television, no visitors.

He had nothing against that.

They couldn't break him. It was what it was. He didn't want to read, didn't want to meet anyone, had no wants.

He passed another prisoner as they took him down the corridor to his cell. Fredrik had seen his picture several times before, one of Sweden's best-loved criminals, who time and again charmed and gained people's trust. The well-known prisoner started when he saw Fredrik. He turned and approached Fredrik, pounded him hard on the back and shoulder, told him he was a hero, that he should stand up for himself, and if the guards didn't treat him well, just say something, and he'd make sure they behaved themselves.

The guards behaved themselves. Whether they did so voluntarily or because they'd had help, the results were they didn't stare so damn much through the hatch in the door, and he got more coffee, and when he went outside in the cage on the roof, they gave him more than an hour. He knew it, and the guards knew it, and there were a few days when he got twice his rations, two hours behind the chicken wire and barbed wire, with the sky above.

Kristina Björnsson visited him every other day. She referred to documents and strategies, but there wasn't much more now than there was before, their appeal wasn't going to be so different from what they'd argued in the district court. She was there mostly to keep his spirits up, bring him greetings from Micaela, convince him to believe in his prospects, his future.

He appreciated her efforts. She was just as capable as rumor had led him to believe. But this time, no, it wouldn't work—in district court the judge, the only lawyer, had expressed her reservations. This time, in the court of appeal, there were more lawyers than laymen, and lawyers based their reality on the written word, on clauses and precedent. He had given up. He said that to her, and she got upset, explained that if you gave up, you were already doomed. They can feel that in the courtroom, and it was like pleading guilty. She gave him example after example. Several of the verdicts he knew from before. She had defended people who'd committed the most idiotic crimes, and they'd been acquitted because they were confident they would be, and they carried that feeling with them into the courtroom.

The guard knocked on the door. A tray with some juice and a piece of meat and some potatoes. He shook his head. He wasn't interested. It probably tasted good. But he wasn't hungry. It was as if eating meant acting like nothing had happened. If he didn't eat, he wasn't participating. This wasn't his life. He hadn't chosen this.

Once the trial began, he was transported every morning to a courtroom, a newer one, on Bergs Street—the hearing had to be moved after they received threats. The appeals hearing was shorter, some witness statements had been replaced by tape recordings, and some questions had been tightened. It took three days. He sat in the same chair as before and answered the same questions. A play, a repeat of the last time, now they were having their premiere, and the show would be reviewed. He tried to keep his back straight, appear calm and confident of a new acquittal, but it was tough. He didn't really care, wasn't even sure he wanted to go home. They could probably sense that, see it on him.

———

He no longer wanted anything. That was over. He lay on his bed in the evenings after the day's trial, staring at the ceiling, trying to find something of his old life in that piss yellow.

One hour.

He didn't have many friends, never did, and those he did have lived far away, one in Gothenburg and one in Kristianstad, and they weren't really a part of his daily life, a prison sentence wouldn't really change their relationship.

One hour.

He had no siblings, no parents.

One hour.

He had Micaela and he felt like he loved her, but she was still young, she couldn't live with him inside his grief for his child, it wasn't right.

One hour.

She said that was what she wanted, and he believed her, but that was now. One day they would have to move on, and she shouldn't have to cope with having a little girl who was raped and murdered stuck in her every breath.

One hour.

The piss-yellow ceiling.

One hour.

It was strange.

One hour.

His whole life he'd been running, filling up every moment, afraid that it might suddenly be empty, might suddenly cease to exist.

One hour.

He'd held on tight to it, entrenched himself in each day, trying to conquer the restlessness and avoid the loneliness.

One hour.

Back then, he was surrounded by people he depended on, and he tried to be in the present in order to see them.

One hour.

Then, suddenly, they were no longer there, and when he really didn't need to be in the fucking moment, that was all he had, piss-yellow ceiling, time, thoughts, none of it mattered anymore. He couldn't change or alter anything, and that made him calm, calmer than he'd ever been before, calm as death.

It took them almost a week to decide the verdict. It was postponed twice. Every document was essential, every word loaded. It was a verdict that would be dissected by the media, printed in full in the big newspapers, legal experts would appear on television to analyze it on newscasts, the father who shot and killed his five-year-old daughter's murderer was followed

by the people who shared his grief for his vanished daughter

by the people who believed that a murder was a murder no matter the reason

by the people who celebrated his courage and the protection he'd given them by getting rid of something that society couldn't

by people who said the father's revenge was indefensible and demanded a long prison term to set an example

by people who abused and killed other sex offenders with the support of the district court's self-defense argument.

It came on a Saturday. At precisely ten o'clock in the morning. It could be collected in its entirety from an usher outside the Stockholm Court House. Journalists stood in line, mobile phones in hand, ready to reach their editors as quickly as possible with the new text, their photographers next to them, ready to document the bundles of paper from every direction, the prosecutor Ågestam was there, Kristina Björnsson, and a few curious onlookers. Fredrik Steffansson was told through the door he hated. The guard who'd given him extra coffee and extra break time mumbled behind the door. He said he was sorry, that it was terrible, that there'd be a hell of an uproar.

Ten years.

The court of appeal had sentenced him to ten years in prison.

TINYBOY REGRETTED IT. He shouldn't have done it. He shouldn't have beaten poor Hilding to a pulp. Goddammit, Hilding! Fucking idiot! Why the hell did he have to steal all that Turkish Glass? Why the hell did he have to sit with that fucking hitman and empty out their fire extinguisher? Mash up his fucking ass! He'd been forced to fuck him up. How the hell would it have looked if he'd let Hilding pull that kind of shit without any consequences? There was no way. No way! But he shouldn't have been quite so hard on him. He looked awful. They'll sew him up, they do that, but he won't be coming back. Not here. They'll send him to Tidaholm. Or Hall. That's how they do it. Never coming back.

Not many left now.

Hilding in the infirmary. The fucking pedophile, Axelsson, got his warning and ran off to hide in isolation. Bekir had been released.

Skåne. And Dragan. Damn. Not many to get high with. Then there was that fucking hitman. And the Russian. And those other fools.

He regretted it. He shouldn't have beaten him for so long. He should have stopped when he passed out.

It was still raining outside. Had been a few weeks now. Fucking weird. First, heat, week after week, so hot your cock refused to stand. Then, so wet no bastard could even go out for air. Make up your damn mind. Fucking idiots.

He looked out the window. The rain ran down the wall. The football goals were about to blow apart. Two people were out walking the track. He couldn't see who it was. They were both wearing raincoats, hoods pulled down over their foreheads.

He turned. Four guys stood around the pool table. The Russian circled it, grunting, chalking his cue, he sank a few balls, gave the stick to Janoz, who grunted too, louder when he sank the black and lost. Tinyboy had never liked pool, a bitch game, long sticks on a green table. He played cards. Casino, sometimes poker. But not today. Not for a while. He had no desire to. Now Jochum sat there, with Skåne and Dragan, dealing and bluffing. It wasn't the same without Hilding Wilding there.

He was on his way outside anyway. Needed some air, fuck the rain. He walked toward the exit, approached the door, and peered out at the guard station. Three guards. What the hell did they do in there all day? Sit on their asses getting paid? For fuck's sake!

He stopped just in front of their window. He couldn't see them. But he heard them. They were talking loudly, seemed upset. He couldn't quite follow what they were saying, words flying around, impossible to know without context.

He recognized one phrase. *Sex offender.* He heard it several times. *Long sentence.* He heard that: *long sentence.* He heard another half a phrase: *with Oscarsson and perverts.*

What the hell were they talking about? Not another pedo. Not here. Hadn't they understood anything? Didn't they see how Axelsson had to hightail it out of here? They'd gotten hold of his social security number, found out what he was convicted of, and they would have killed him if he hadn't been warned.

The ones who never made a sound. Who walked around in their units with their fucking keys and kept their mouths shut. Now they were upset. All three were complaining. He heard *hero*. He heard *murdered*. He heard *sex offender* again.

A fucking pedophile coming here! Another one! For fuck's sake!

Tinyboy had a hard time standing still. He was filled with fury, his cheeks turning red, the anger clawing its way up his throat.

A few chairs scraped against the floor. They stood up and he took a hasty step backward. They came out of the guard station still talking—one of them was waving his hands around. He heard the last sentences, they were standing outside, and he heard them clearly now. The first asked what would happen if the hero came here. The second said he didn't know, but they didn't get those long sentences here. The first one again, he said there wasn't any danger anymore, he wouldn't attack again, that was over. They went into the unit, the Russian looked up from the pool table and shouted guards on the floor! Tinyboy kept walking, past the guard station, looking through the raincoats and finding one that fit. He grabbed a pair of boots, too, that were a little too big. He went out into the rain, it was pouring down, and he headed for the track, lengthening his stride. The anger that had a stranglehold was now on its way out. He was shaking, screaming, now motherfuckers, now motherfuckers! He'd made up his mind—he was gonna take down that bastard, never again would they try to squeeze a perv into this unit again. No way in hell. If that pedophile bastard came here, he'd never leave here again.

HE PISSED IN the sink. He had no desire to call for the guard to be taken to the toilet, or to answer any curious questions about the verdict.

Ten years.

He didn't even know what that was. Kristina Björnsson had visited him the day before. She'd arrived in the afternoon and gone over the verdict with him, explaining the wording. She had wanted to appeal to the supreme court. She wanted a precedent to prove the strength of the self-defense argument. He'd said he didn't want to continue. That this was enough. He wasn't interested. What had happened had happened. He'd shot the man who'd taken his daughter away from him. That was enough for him. Prison or no, it didn't matter.

Ten years.

He'd be almost fifty by then.

He rinsed his hands and stood in the middle of his cell.

An already convicted rapist and serial killer had escaped, stuck sharp metal objects into Marie's genitals, masturbated on her, torn her apart. And Marie's father had stopped him from doing it again. Therefore, he should sit in a cell, separated from real life, for ten years, from the age of forty until he turned fifty. He had to laugh. He kicked at the sink and laughed until it hurt in his chest.

The guard who gave him extra favors knocked anxiously, opened the door.

"What are you doing?"

"What do you mean?"

"There's quite a bit of noise in here."

"Am I not allowed to laugh?"

"Yes."

"Then let me be."

"I just don't want you to do anything stupid."

"I won't do anything stupid."

"That kind of verdict can make people do the wrong thing."

"I'm laughing, okay?"

"Good. I'm coming back in a few minutes. You should pack."

"Pack?"

"You've been placed now."

He sank down onto the bed. The piss-yellow ceiling, the white walls, the dirty floor. He was going away. He should pack. What? A plastic bag with toothbrush, toothpaste, soap? He stood up, opened the plastic bag, stuffed his toiletries in it. He'd packed.

The guard knocked. He opened the door. He was young, hardly more than twenty-five. His hair stood straight up. A ring through one nostril. He was a musician. Or wanted to be a musician. He often talked about it. As if he thought Fredrik would want to know. As if he wanted to prove he was more than just a prison guard, a man with dreams. This was just a job, while he was waiting for a record deal. He'd waited a few years and was ready to wait a few more. Until he got too old. Thirty or so. Now he went into the cell and put his hand on Fredrik's shoulder.

"You know what I think."

"Sorry, I'm not interested in what you think."

"It's insane. Locking you up is probably the weirdest thing I've heard so far."

"Not interested."

"We all think that, everyone in here. Guards and prisoners, there's no difference, everyone thinks alike. I don't think we've ever agreed on anything else."

Fredrik held out the plastic bag.

"I've packed."

"I understand that it's not very comforting to hear that."

"I'm ready to go now."

"You should have been acquitted."

"Ready."

"There are a lot of people out on the streets. Who know where you're going."

"I don't even know that."

"A lot of us do know. We've made sure they'll be heard. The protesters."

"You're right. That's no comfort."

He was alone again. Waiting. He'd been given his normal clothes. He was supposed to wear them for a few hours. Then he'd undress, lock them up in a cabinet until the day he was free to go again. He'd wear something else instead, something that hung off his body. The prison uniform.

They didn't knock the next time. They just opened the door and stepped inside. Two guards and two uniformed police officers. Grens waited outside the door with Sundkvist beside him.

Fredrik had known they were coming. Still, he was surprised. He turned away from the four who'd entered the cell and made eye contact with Grens through the doorway.

"Why?"

Grens pretended not to understand.

"Why so many? Why the uniformed police officers?"

Sven couldn't pretend. He answered.

"We've made an assessment."

"I see that. I'm wondering why?"

"We've received information that we might encounter problems while we transfer you to Aspsås prison."

Fredrik winced.

"Aspsås? Is that where I'm headed?"

"Yes."

"That's where he came from."

"You're going to another unit. A normal unit. Lund was in a special unit for sex offenders."

Fredrik took a step closer to the door, closer to Sven. The uniformed officer immediately moved in between, holding him. He shook himself, irritated, until they released him, and he went back into the cell again.

"You said problems?"

"Your transport is going to have a police escort."

"Does it look like I'm going to escape?"

"That's all I can say."

It was still early morning. It was raining outside, beating down on the metal windowsill outside the bars, just as hard, just as persistent as it had done for several days.

It was almost as if he was going to miss it.

HE WAS BEING transported in a minibus. It was still raining heavily, and he got soaked during his very short walk between the Kronoberg jail's entrance and the vehicle, which stood idling on the street outside. His steps were short, his ankle restraints chafed if he tried to lengthen them.

He was hardly considered an escape risk.

He was considered at little risk of repeating his crime—he'd shot the only man he intended to shoot.

Nevertheless, he was transported using the most extreme security measures. Two police cars with rotating blue lights a few meters in front of the minibus. Two motorcycles driven by uniformed officers behind it. The demonstration a few weeks earlier outside Kronoberg had left its mark. The people who'd put themselves on the ground, who'd been run over and injured when the car fled the scene, the gun leveled at the police officer's temple, the SWAT team vans that had been overturned, the demonstrators who urinated on them as they crawled out. Not again. Never again.

He sat in the back seat, between Ewert Grens and Sven Sundkvist. It was almost as if they knew one another. After Marie disappeared, they'd interviewed everyone outside the Dove, one after another. They'd been waiting at Forensic Medicine by her table. They'd come to her funeral dressed in black. They'd picked him up in Strängnäs before the court of appeal—an hour of Siw Malmkvist. This trip, too. Then, they were done with him.

He should talk to them. Say something. He couldn't.

He didn't need to.

The proper one, Sundkvist, started.

"I'm forty years old."

Sundkvist looked at him.

"I turned forty the day your daughter was murdered. I had wine and cake in the car. I haven't celebrated yet."

Fredrik Steffansson didn't understand. Was he making some kind of joke? Or did he think Fredrik should feel sorry for him? Fredrik didn't answer. He didn't need to. Sundkvist wasn't looking for a conversation.

"I've been a cop for twenty years. That's my entire adult life. It's a fucked-up job. But it's the job I have. That's what I'm able to do."

They were going to drive for fifty kilometers. Thirty-five or forty minutes. Fredrik didn't want to hear any more. He wanted to close his eyes. Start counting the hours. Ten years.

"I always thought that I was doing some kind of service. Been good. Done right. And maybe I have."

Sundkvist was sitting close to him, Fredrik could feel his breath.

"But this. Do you understand? Of course you do. Do you understand how ashamed I feel to have to sit here and guard you, take you to a prison and lock you up? For fuck's sake! I almost never swear, but now, Steffansson, for fuck's sake!"

It was surely sympathy. Fredrik didn't care at all about sympathy. Sundkvist leaned forward and pulled on Steffansson's wet shirt.

"This is just how Lund sat just a few months ago. Now you're sitting here. Like some ordinary murderer. And I'm making sure that you do. And for that, Steffansson, I sincerely apologize."

Grens had been quiet on the other side. Now he cleared his throat.

"Sven. That's enough."

"Enough?"

"That's enough."

They rode in silence. Took the road north of Stockholm. It was still raining outside. The wipers beat from side to side, forcing aside the water whipping against the windshield.

The bus left the main road, went through a roundabout, passed by two gas stations, then turned onto a smaller road with houses on either side. That was where the first demonstrators started to line up.

Kilometer after kilometer. A long chain of people singing, shouting in chorus, waving large signs.

Fredrik felt the same stomach cramps he'd felt during the demonstration outside Kronoberg. Other people singing his name, people who didn't know him, who had nothing to do with him. What gave them the right? They weren't there for his sake. They were there for their own. This was their manifestation, not his. This was their fear, their hatred.

They stood closer together for the last bit, a gravel road that led to the Aspsås prison's big gate. Fredrik looked down, staring at his thighs. It was quieter this time, not as threatening, not as aggressive, but he couldn't look at them, the feeling was intense, almost like disgust.

The minibus stopped some distance from the main gate. It couldn't go any farther. Grens made a quick calculation, counted a few thousand demonstrators.

"Just sit. Wait it out."

Grens spoke to his younger colleagues in the front seat, to Steffansson, to Sven.

"It won't be like last time. They're just trying to draw attention. Don't provoke them. They'll be moved soon."

Fredrik continued to look down. He was tired, wanted to sleep. He wanted to leave this bus and the people outside it, wanted to put on a shapeless prison uniform and lie down in his cell. He wanted to look at the ceiling, at the lamp there, one hour at a time.

They waited for twenty minutes. The demonstrators didn't sing, didn't shout, just stood there together, a silent human wall, until reinforcements arrived. Sixty police officers. They approached the crowd with shields and weapons and moved them one person at a time. No fights, no threats. They methodically carried immobile people away from the gate, who hung like heavy lumps in their arms. When the gap was sufficiently large, the bus drove slowly forward. Those they carried away did not run back. They didn't move at all. There were only a few centimeters between those who stood closest and the minibus. Their backs were straight as they watched it pass, nearing the gate, driving through it when it opened, and into the prison yard.

Grens and Sundkvist each held one of Fredrik's arms those last steps toward the central guard station. They looked at him, nodded, turned, and walked away. Fredrik Steffansson was no longer their responsibility. They'd caught him, he'd been convicted, and then sent to prison. Now he would be the prison's responsibility. For ten years. So he wouldn't commit the same crime again.

Fredrik saw the two policemen returning to the other society, the one on the outside. He was taken by two guards into the building to an open room immediately to the left. He had to sign in.

They watched him undress. They had rubber gloves on when they examined him in his mouth, parted his buttocks, and felt inside his anus. They took his clothes and put them in a cabinet. He was given some fabric that hung on him, put it on. Now he was a prisoner among prisoners. The guards moved him to the next room: a bed, a chair, a grille on the window, and the wall outside. They asked him to wait there, locked the door, and explained that soon he'd be moved up to his unit.

HE'D SAT ON the chair and waited for an hour.

The rain outside had made puddles on the lawn between the gray concrete wall and barred windows.

He tried to think of Marie but couldn't.

She didn't want to stay in his thoughts. He couldn't grab hold of her. Her face was blurred, her voice, he couldn't hear it, didn't know how it sounded.

There was a knock on the door.

Keys in the lock. A man in a guard's uniform stepped in. Fredrik recognized him vaguely, had seen him before, but didn't know where.

"I'm sorry, I was looking for someone else."

The guard looked hastily around, already on his way out. Fredrik searched his memory. Familiar. But not quite.

"Excuse me."

The guard turned around.

"Yes?"

"What do you want?"

"Nothing. I'm in the wrong place."

"I recognize you. Who are you?"

The guard hesitated. For months he'd tried to keep his feelings of guilt in check, and now they overwhelmed him.

"My name is Lennart Oscarsson. I'm head of one of the units here. The one they call the pervert unit. One of two units for sex offenders."

On TV. In interviews. Fredrik had seen him there.

"It was your fault."

"I was responsible for him. I was the one who approved the transport he escaped from."

"It was your fault."

Oscarsson looked at the man a meter or so in front of him. And it was as if the guilt he'd carried was no longer sufficient.

"I have talked a lot about you with a colleague. A colleague I trust. And we agree. Lund served his time here, and we gave him all the care we could. We tried every form of therapy that exists."

Oscarsson was still standing in the doorway. They were the same age. He had beads of sweat on his forehead, his hair moist.

"I'm sorry for what happened. Now I have to go."

"It was your fault."

Oscarsson held out his hand.

"Good luck."

Fredrik looked at it, but didn't take it.

"You can put that down. I'm not going to shake hands with you."

Hand still in the air. It trembled. Fredrik looked away. Oscarsson waited, then gave up, put his hand on Fredrik's shoulder for a moment, then closed and locked the door behind him.

It stopped raining just after lunch; the only sound he'd heard, the patter against the glass, disappeared almost abruptly. Several days of persistent rain, and it was suddenly over, almost empty. He went to the window, searched the sky. It would clear up by evening.

He waited on that chair for another six hours. It had been morning when they passed the demonstrators in front of the gate, and it was late afternoon when two guards unlocked the door and entered—two hefty men with batons and authoritative steps. They'd brought in new guys before. That was when you showed who was in charge—respect and order. One of them, the one with blue glasses, held a couple of pieces of paper in his hand, flipping through them, reading them.

"Steffansson. Is that your name?"

"Yes."

"Well, then. You're going up to your unit now."

Fredrik remained seated.

"I've been sitting here for seven hours."

"And?"

"Why?"

"That's how it works."

"Are you trying to tell me something?"

"What are you talking about?"

"Is that why I've waited so long?"

"There's no particular reason. That's just how it is."

Fredrik sighed, got up, got ready to go.

"Where am I headed?"

"To your unit."

"Which unit?"

"A regular unit."

"What kind of people are serving there?"

The guard had decided to stay calm. He looked around the sterile room—the bare walls, the bed without bedding, the chair, which was now empty.

"You sure have a lot of questions."

"I want to know."

"What do you want me to say? A normal unit. The people serving there have committed every kind of crime that can be committed. Except sex offenders. We have a special unit for them."

He stopped, threw out his arms.

"You probably haven't understood yet, Steffansson, this is your home now. The other inmates, well, they're your friends."

———

They walked slowly along a corridor. Fredrik saw the painted walls, the results of prisoners' art therapy, as they passed through three locked doors and at each one the same ritual: the guard looked up toward the camera, a popping sound as the door was opened by a guard somewhere else, the guard's nod toward the camera afterward, a kind of thanks. He counted the steps—the subterranean hallway was at least four hundred meters long. They met other prisoners being escorted by other guards. They nodded to him, and he nodded back. They swung into the last part of the corridor, white arrows with Unit H on the wall. So that was the name of it, his unit.

Up two flights of stairs. A new locked door. The sign with Sec H on the door.

It smelled strongly of food. Something fried. Herring? The guard who opened the door noticed him breathing in.

"They've just eaten. You'll get food later."

An ugly corridor. First, a TV room, a few inmates reclining on the sofa and playing cards around the table. Then a narrow hall with cells on either side, most of the doors half open. At the other end, a smaller room with a table tennis table standing at an angle.

"You're a bit farther down. Almost all the way. Cell number fourteen."

The gang playing cards looked up as he passed. A dark, pock-marked man with a gold chain, talking the loudest, stared at him, never took his eyes off him. Beside him sat a large ponytailed, body-builder type. Opposite, a short, dark man with a mustache, Turkish, maybe Greek. In the corner was a skinny guy whose appearance just screamed junkie, probably Finnish.

He went into the open, empty cell, a little larger than the one at the jail, but otherwise identical. Grille on the window, a view toward the wall. Pale green walls, same piss-yellow ceiling. He sat down on the unmade bed. A blanket and a sheet at the foot of the bed, a pillow with no pillowcase.

He did what he'd done in his jail cell this very morning, released the pain, hit his palm against the wall, started laughing out loud.

"What is it?"

"Nothing."

The guard fiddled with his blue-framed glasses.

"You were laughing."

"Am I not allowed to?"

"I thought you were having a breakdown."

Fredrik grabbed the blanket and sheet, made the bed. He wanted to rest. He wanted to close the door and stare at the ceiling.

"You were kind of right before."

Fredrik looked at the guard who was speaking.

"You were down in the reception for a long time. You might want to shower now. If you want, I can get you a towel."

He dropped the pillow.

"Maybe."

"Then I'll get one."

Fredrik stopped him.

"Is it safe?"

"What do you mean?"

"To shower."

"Take a shower?"

"You know, the risk of rape."

The guard smiled.

"No need to worry, Steffansson. At Swedish prisons they don't tolerate rape. Nobody fucks in the shower."

Fredrik sat down on the half-made bed and waited. He should finish making the bed, should unpack his bag of toiletries. He counted lines instead. Someone had made tally marks with a red pen along the baseboard. He counted to one hundred and sixteen before the guard came back with towel in hand.

He walked in his flip-flops through the corridor. Two men, probably his closest neighbors, greeted him with strong handshakes. He passed the TV corner and those playing cards. The junkie was whining about how there was one king too many in the game and the dark one with the gold chain told him to shut up—and then he saw Fredrik, stared at him like before, with crazy eyes. He hated Fredrik, and Fredrik had no idea why.

A large room. Four showers. He was alone. He closed the door to the hallway, wanted to escape the voices while the water ran over his body, helped him to forget for just a moment.

————

Tinyboy saw the new guy and remembered the guards' agitated conversation the day before. He remembered what they said. When that bastard came back with a towel over his shoulder, he put his cards down in the middle of the game.

"Damn. Gotta go to the john. Skåne?"

"Yeah?"

"You have to finish playing, just make sure to build in the Big Ten and sweep it."

He handed over his cards and headed for the bathroom, turned around, making sure the others continued to play, walked past the bathroom, and opened the door to the shower room instead. He was inside no more than a few minutes.

It sounded like someone was beating on the door. At least, that's how the guard who was first on the scene described it later. As if someone were banging on the door trying to get out. When he then saw Fredrik open the door and almost fall out, he first noticed the hand pressed to the belly, at the point where the blood flowed out the fastest, where the tip of the blade had gone the deepest. The guard set off the alarm and ran to the man who'd fallen to the floor, who lay there trying to say something while blood pumped rhythmically out of his mouth. Without a word, he'd sought out Tinyboy Lindgren with his eyes, which looked scared—those were the guard's words, his eyes looked scared. Two colleagues had now arrived and were trying to stop the bleeding and find a pulse, until finally they both realized they were holding a dead man.

The cards lay in piles on the table. They'd stopped playing immediately when the new guy opened the door and fell onto the floor, bleeding. They knew the damage a knife could do to your internal organs, and they realized he was a goner. Jochum Lang was watching it all from a distance in the corridor. His shiny head was sweating—just a few minutes earlier he'd visited Steffansson, welcomed him and told him they were in neighboring cells, told him that he'd been following his fate on the news. He'd said to let him know if he needed any help. Now the father lay there, dead. Jochum quickly passed by guards, who were trying to stop the bleeding, over to the table with the card game. He put his face a centimeter from Tinyboy's and hissed as he spoke.

"What the hell was the point of that?"

Tinyboy smacked his mouth.

"None of your fucking business."

Jochum raised his voice.

"You fucking . . . you know who the hell you just shivved?"

Tinyboy smiled now, looking pleased with himself, whispered something to the face in front of him.

"I sure as hell do. Sure as hell. A fucking pedo. He won't be fucking any more kids."

The door to the unit was torn open.

There were fifteen of them. Helmets, visors, shields. The task force formed a semicircle around the inmates.

"You know the drill!"

Jochum pushed Tinyboy away from him, looked at the guard who was screaming and slamming his baton on the table.

"No fucking around now! You know the drill! Go to your cells, one at a time!"

Those at the far end of the corridor went first. One by one, with two guards walking behind them, locking the door once they were in their cells. Then the two in the kitchen. The guard in command pointed to the sofa, to the card players.

"Your turn."

Skåne stood up, staring at the guards he hated, gave them the finger before leaving the table.

"And you."

The guard pointed at Tinyboy.

"Go to your cell."

"Forget it."

"Now!"

Tinyboy stood up—instead of going toward the corridor and his cell he leaned forward, grabbed the table, and flipped it over toward the black-clad guards. The cards flew across the room and landed in front of a semicircle of feet. He climbed up on the couch and jumped nimbly over a large aquarium standing along the wall.

"Fucking fascists! Can't a man finish playing Casino around here? Get ready for a fucking ride!"

He continued screaming while he pushed both of his hands against the glass panes of the aquarium. Four hundred liters of water rushed out toward the guards as the rectangular container fell to the floor. Before the first guard could get near him, he rushed to the pool table, grabbed a cue hanging on the wall, and started swinging it around like mad and hit the first guard who got near him hard on the throat. He ran toward the guard station, went in and locked the door, started smashing everything in sight with the cue: the television, the two-way radio, a refrigerator, lamps, flowerpots, mirrors. In the meantime, five guards pried open the door and attacked with shields raised to protect themselves from Tinyboy's long weapon. They surrounded him, and his escape routes were cut off.

The leader of the task force stood in the corridor next to the shattered aquarium shouting commands.

"Hold him there! He's headed down to isolation!"

In the corridor the four prisoners who hadn't been locked up in their cells waited. They'd watched Tinyboy's insane outburst, his flight, and the chase. Jochum looked at him, irritated, through the unbreakable glass of the guard station, at the guards surrounding him. He turned to Dragan, whispered a few words in his ear. Dragan nodded, he understood, and ran at full speed up to one of the guards waiting outside the station and kicked him hard between the legs. The guard fell and his colleagues turned to him. A moment of confusion. That was just what Jochum wanted. He struck a sharp blow to the temple of the guard closest to him, took a few quick steps toward the station, broke through the wall that had formed around Tinyboy.

Tinyboy smiled, screamed.

"Holy shit, Jochum! Fucking now, *tjavon!* Now the pigs have to work!"

Tinyboy turned toward the guards, waving his pool cue. He felt strong again with a fellow prisoner at his side. He never saw Jochum's arm, but he felt the fist in his face, into his midriff. He leaned over, whimpering.

"Fuck, what the hell was that for?"

Jochum Lang threw himself over the bent body, clutched his head, and ran with it into the wall. Tinyboy was unconscious when he let go of him, by the time the guards made it to his side.

GRENS CLOSED THE car door, looked at his colleague, and shook his head.

"It never ends. The whole damn summer. And they're still at it."

Sundkvist stared down at the ground. A stone he wanted to kick.

"I told Jonas this was over. I told him the father was locked up. That he'd be there a while, until they let him out again. Jonas said that was super cool. That's exactly what he said. It was super cool that the father got punished, that it was fair, also fair that he would get out again, because it was his little girl who'd been murdered first. I don't know what to say now. He knows already, of course. There's too much news on TV."

They walked toward the wall. The small door in the big gate. Grens pressed the intercom.

"Yes?"

"Grens. And Sundkvist. City Police."

"I remember. You can enter."

They walked across the internal parking lot at Aspsås prison toward the central guard station, where they were waved past.

They stopped in the large entrance hall. They weren't going much farther—they'd reserved one of the visitor's rooms. The door was open, and they went in. There wasn't much to it. Grens pointed to the plastic on the bed, to the roll of paper towels on the table, disgusted by the knowledge they were going to be meeting in the room for conjugal visits, where prisoners met their women once a month and fucked away the worst of their anxiety. They moved the table to the center of the room, put the two chairs on either side, and returned to the entrance hall to find one more chair. Put the tape recorder on the table, a microphone on either side.

———————

He arrived flanked by two guards. Grens greeted him, then pointed to his companions.

"You two can wait outside."

"We'll wait in here."

"You'll wait outside. If we need you, we'll let you know. This interrogation is closed."

> **EWERT GRENS (EG):** I'm turning this on now.
> **JOCHUM LANG (JL):** Fine.
> **EG:** Your full name.
> **JL:** Jochum Hans Lang.
> **EG:** Very well. Do you know why we're here today?
> **JL:** No.

Ewert glanced at Sven. He was tired. He was going to need some help. This bastard couldn't be budged. Lang knew why he was there, not that that would help them.

> **EG:** You need to answer our questions. You need to tell us why Fredrik Steffansson fell out of that shower and ended up a corpse shortly afterward.

There was silence in the room for a minute. Ewert stared at Jochum, who stared out the barred window.

> **EG:** Enjoying the view?
> **JL:** Yep.
> **EG:** Goddammit, Jochum! We know Tinyboy stabbed Fredrik Steffansson!
> **JL:** Great.
> **EG:** We know that!

JL: Great, I said. Then why the hell are you questioning me?

EG: Because you, for some damn reason, knocked out Tinyboy. I want to know why.

Ewert Grens waited for Jochum Lang to respond. He looked at him, realized that this bastard would be very dangerous as a free man. Large, broad-shouldered, shaved head, steady eyes, he'd definitely slaughtered a few.

JL: He owed me money.

EG: Come on!

JL: Quite a bit.

EG: Bullshit! Dragan shoved aside the task force and you took down Tinyboy. You were mad at him for putting his knife into Steffansson.

Grens stood up. Red in the face. He leaned over the table toward Lang, lowered his voice.

EG: Stop this now, goddammit. We're on the same side for once. If you just tell us Tinyboy was the one who did it, I promise no one will ever know you talked. Do you understand that if no one in your unit talks, then Fredrik Steffansson's murderer will go free?

JL: I didn't see anything.

EG: Help me!

JL: Not a goddamn thing.

EG: Hello?

JL: Turn off the tape recorder.

Grens searched for a while until he found the button that stopped the tape from rolling.

"Satisfied?"

Jochum Lang leaned over to the tape recorder, making sure that it really was off. He looked up, his face tense.

"Grens, goddammit! You know the rules here. No matter what crime's committed inside these walls, whoever leaks is dead. Let's just say this. And listen very carefully to me. Yes, Grens, we know who took down Steffansson. And that fucker is on his way out of here forever. Feet first. That's all. Now I want to go back to my cell."

IT WAS A quarter past eight. The interview with Jochum Lang hadn't even taken half an hour, and Grens sighed. This was exactly what he'd expected. Had he ever gotten anyone in prison to talk? These damn rules of honor. You could stab someone to death—that was fine. But if you talked, you were in trouble. Honor, my ass.

He slapped his hand hard on the table.

"What do you think, Sven? What the hell do we do?"

"We don't have much of a choice."

"No. That's true."

Ewert turned on the tape recorder, rewound the tape a bit, then let it roll. He wanted to make sure everything was working. First, Jochum Lang's voice, leisurely, uninterested. Then his own, angry, strained, he knew that's how he sounded, but it still surprised him when he heard it—his voice was always higher, more aggressive than he remembered it. Sven also listened to the tape, now he looked up from the floor.

"I don't think we should interrogate Tinyboy Lindgren tonight. We'll just hear more of this if we do. He's not gonna say anything more than Lang. Let's just check in with him, talk for a moment informally. It can't get any worse."

———

The governor of Aspsås prison, Arne Bertolsson, decided to isolate Unit H that evening. They'd all been sitting for a while now, locked in their own cells without the right to go out into their unit. They ate, peed, and counted the hours in silence. Ewert Grens and Sven Sundkvist could, therefore, walk freely down an empty corridor. A man had just died here. A man who they'd come to like and respect. They walked into the battered guard station where Jochum Lang had broken through the guards and reached Tinyboy, then rammed his head into a wall. Grens touched the still visible mark, traces of blood and wallpaper torn to pieces. They walked over the remains of a mirror and a two-way radio as they went out, sharp remnants against their shoes. There, outside, in the TV corner, lay an overturned table and a card game on the floor. A short distance away a shattered aquarium, pieces of glass, sand, and shiny fish. The linoleum they walked on was still wet, so they both slipped, the soles of their shoes leaving tracks as they continued toward the cells.

They approached the shower room, stopped at the large pools of blood. He'd been lying there not long ago. Grens looked at Sundkvist, who shook his head. They followed the stains into the shower room. He'd been cut several times before he even reached the shower, somewhere close to the sink: the white porcelain shone a bright red.

Tinyboy was in bed. Wearing tracksuit bottoms and bare-chested. Smoking a hand-rolled cigarette.

They said hello. Tinyboy took the two policemen by the hand and smiled broadly—his face scratched, one eye hidden by swelling, the gold chain glistening on his bare chest.

"Grens and his lackey. Well, I'll be damned. To what do I owe the honor?"

They both looked searchingly at the cell. It was homey. Someone who'd been here a long time. Someone who regarded it as a home. A television, a coffee maker, flower pots, red-checked curtains, one wall covered with posters, the other covered with a huge photograph.

"My daughter. Same as here."

He pointed to a frame on the bedside table. The same girl, not very old, smiling, blonde, plaits with bows.

"Would you like something? Tea?"

Grens answered.

"No, thanks. We just drank some dishwater. When we met Jochum Lang."

Tinyboy pretended not to hear the last part. If he had any response to the fact that they'd already interrogated one of the other inmates, he certainly didn't show it.

"Just as well. No tea. Then I'll make some for myself."

He took the jug of water from the simple table and turned on the machine. A few heaped spoons of leaves from a plastic jar.

"Sit down, dammit."

Grens and Sundkvist sat down on the bed. It was clean, the room. Also smelled clean, he had a pomander hanging from the curtain rod, and Grens swept his hand through the air.

"You've fixed this place up."

"When you're in here for a while. Well, there's not much more of a home than that."

"Flowers and curtains."

"Don't you have a home, Grens?"

The detective superintendent clenched his jaw, ground his teeth. It occurred to Sven that he had no idea if Ewert had flowers and curtains. He'd never been to his home. How odd, he knew him well, they spoke to each other often, Ewert had visited him and Anita several times, but he'd never been to Grens's apartment.

Tinyboy poured his tea, drank it hot. Grens waited until he put down the cup.

"We've met a few times, Stig."

"That's true."

"I remember you as a teenager. We picked you up in Blekinge. You put an ice pick into your uncle's scrotum."

The images, Tinyboy fought against them again, he could see Per, bleeding, could feel how he wanted to castrate him, pull his scrotum apart and laugh.

"You understand that you are suspected of having stabbed someone again. Right? That we're here because we believe you killed Fredrik Steffansson a few hours ago?"

Tinyboy sighed, rolled his eyes, sighed again.

"I understand that I am a suspect. I understand that very well. Me—and the rest of the unit."

"It's you I'm talking to now."

Tinyboy turned serious now.

"Well, I'll tell you one thing for sure, he got what was coming to him. That's all I'll say. He was a fucking pedo who got what he deserved."

Grens heard what Tinyboy said but didn't understand.

"Stig. Are we talking about the same thing? There are many words you could use to describe Fredrik Steffansson. But *pedophile* is not one of them. Quite the contrary."

Tinyboy put down the cup he'd just lifted, looked in surprise at the two policemen, his voice frantic.

"What the fuck do you mean?"

They both saw his surprise, felt the shift in his mood. Tinyboy's reaction was genuine.

"What I mean is, have you ever watched the news?"

"I do now and then. What the hell does that have to do with anything?"

"Then you've been following the story of the father who shot and killed his five-year-old daughter's rapist and murderer?"

"Followed a bit. I saw the beginning. I don't like that sort of thing. This little girl here, I don't know, I can't take it."

Tinyboy pointed at the photograph again, the one on his bedside table, blond hair with braids.

"I didn't see much but understood well enough. I thought her father was a real fucking hero. They should die, those bastards. Die! What the hell does this have to do with the pedo?"

Grens glanced at Sundkvist. They had the same thought simultaneously. He turned back to Tinyboy but said nothing.

"What the hell is it, Grens? What the fuck does that perv have to do with it?"

"The father was Fredrik Steffansson."

Tinyboy stood up from his chair. His face started twitching.

"You shouldn't . . . say bullshit like that right now."

"I wish I was bullshitting."

He turned to Sven again, gestured to Sven's briefcase.

"Give those to me."

Sven opened the briefcase, unzipped the main compartment. He thumbed through sheets of paper and plastic folders, found what he was looking for. Two newspapers. He put them on the table and Grens handed them to Tinyboy.

"Here. Read."

Two tabloids. From the day after Fredrik Steffansson shot Bernt Lund. The headlines, just as bold in both editions, the contents the same: *he shot his daughter's murderer—saved the lives of two little girls.*

Two photos next to the headline from an autopsy of the dead Bernt Lund. His next victims, already selected, in the courtyard outside their nursery school in Enköping, both smiling, one with blond hair and braids.

Tinyboy stared at the faces in the newspaper for a long time.

At the text.

At the pictures of two five-year-old girls.

Then at the photograph he had in the frame on his bedside table and magnified on the wall.

As if it were her. As if that were his girl on the front page of the newspaper.

He was still standing up.

He started to scream.

about *pen* 33

WRITING THE NOVEL you just read was a strange journey. We knew where we wanted to go—to tell a story that begins from the perspective of the perpetrator and the child he destroys, just before a terrible sex crime, and ends with the actions taken by the child's parent—but the subject matter wasn't the straightest path to success for a debut.

We had no choice, though. It was the book we had to write.

We knew that children who are subjected to abuse experience terrible, lasting trauma. And we had firsthand experience of how such abuse impacts you, becomes part of your life without you being aware of it.

Conveying a sense of the lifelong curse every injured child carries and fights against became our first mandate, and we felt we had the right to express it through a work of dramatic tension, in the clothing of fiction.

In addition, we were both parents—at the time, I to two seven-year-old boys, Börge to a seven-year-old daughter. Parenthood provided us further license to tell this story. We could understand and imagine the sorrow of a father, the hate and anger he felt when his child—his love and life and reason for continuing to live—is violated, as the child in this story is violated.

We had so often had the thought, the one that most parents have: If anyone hurts my child, I will—just that one time—cross any boundary, strike back, do anything to make sure no other parent has to feel like this.

Most people stop right there, at that thought, even if the unthinkable happens. Most are controlled by limits, and maybe that's what makes us human. But the father in this story, Fredrik Steffansson, does not stop at the thought. He sees his child raped, destroyed, and then does what many of us have only thought about.

Fredrik knows that most sex offenders repeat their crimes. He knows how awful it is when your sorrow is so great it leaks from your stomach. He feels he has no choice, that he has to make sure that his child's murderer can never kill again.

So he takes up the hunt, finds the monster, and—as he says himself—puts him down like a mad dog. He does this, as he says, not for revenge, but to protect society from a threat the government will not or cannot defend against.

And right there, right in the middle of the book—what seems like a tidy finale to a crime novel, the father exacting revenge on his daughter's murderer—that's when our story really begins. Because before the writing we had three questions:

"How far would a parent go to protect his or her child's life?"

"If you knew you could save the life of your child by killing the person planning to take that life, would you be prepared to commit murder?"

And so: *"Whose life is most valuable?"*

That last question seems so simple. The life of a sex offender, a pervert, is of course worth less than that of an innocent five-year-old child. But you've just read Fredrik Steffansson's story, and he finds it's not that easy . . .

Much of *Pen 33* unfolds inside the walls of a prison, where in Sweden (as in North America and elsewhere around the world) there is one regulatory framework decided by the authorities and another one entirely that the prisoners themselves have created—a hierarchy of prisoners based on the crimes they've committed and the lengths of their sentences. A murderer with a life sentence is at the top of this hierarchy, and at the bottom are child molesters.

Pen 33 deals with people who are broken and who then strike back. That act of transformation was what moved us and, in telling it, turned Anders and Börge into Roslund & Hellström.

I had been working at SVT, the Swedish national public broadcasting service and by far Sweden's largest news network—equivalent to the BBC. It was during my eighth year of fourteen as a news reporter, documentary filmmaker, news manager, and editor that our paths converged.

For several years I had been reporting on Swedish crime and I was told that there was a newly formed organization called KRIS— Criminals Returning to Society—an organization founded by a former criminal and addict. Several of the members had been in and out of the country's prisons and knew that the crucial moment was the release itself, the moment of freedom, when the gates opened to the outside world. The moment when you decide whether to walk out of prison and seek out a new way of living or return to old friends and old behaviors.

KRIS would form a circle for newly released prisoners to exist in, a support network of people who understood your past but no longer participated in it. They would stand there at the gate, meet you upon release, and you would head out together from there.

I rang them up. It was the best damn thing I'd heard of for halting the cycle of crime. It happened to be Börge, one of the founders, who answered.

I asked if he would be willing to have a camera follow him, if I could come along, make a documentary—*Lock 'Em Up*—about the organization's first year. We continued to meet, when in the course of life our roads would normally have diverged after the completion of our project.

We had certain similarities: The violations we wanted to discuss, the experience of questioning our roles as fathers, the fact that we had both volunteered to help former prisoners reenter society, and of course our love for the crime novel. We discovered that we clicked as narrators.

But we had real differences, too, of course: My journalistic background and Börge's journey through twenty-four years of drug addiction to KRIS and counseling juvenile offenders. We decided to find a way to use these similarities and differences, to create an authorship that adhered to the basic rule of half-and-half—half fiction and half facts, some things that have happened and some that could happen. And all of it brought to life through storytelling.

Writing a novel can be strange work—from your keyboard you are able to control a world, pointing and showing how things should look.

We have done that. We have used prisons and forests and roads that nobody has seen; we have moved the nursery schools around in Strängnäs and Enköping and used rooms in the Stockholm police station that were never built.

But there are some things we wish we had imagined, that we wish were just our exaggerations created in order to tell a good story.

The destructive man who destroys himself is real. Bernt Lund, who licks feet and puts metal objects into the vaginas of young girls, who lacks the ability to identify emotionally with other human beings, is real. Tinyboy, who was molested as a child and then stuck ice picks into everything that reminded him of that fact, is real. Fredrik and Agnes Steffansson, who lost everything they had and had to try to find a new way to keep living, are real. Lennart Oscarsson, who despises the pedophiles who are his livelihood, is real. Hilding Oldéus, who can't stand to feel anymore, who turns himself off with heroin, who is afraid, who serves his time in prison by seeking out someone else for protection to feel less afraid if only for a moment, is real. Flasher-Göran, who made a mistake and was given a life sentence by his neighbors, is real. Bengt Söderlund, who has beautiful children in a beautiful garden and thinks that if the law won't protect them, he will, is real. They are all somewhere among us, too absurd to be made up.

The original Swedish title, *The Beast*, refers to the sick person who rapes and destroys small children. But later, perhaps, the beast is the man who decides that he has the right to choose who will die and who will live, who in his sorrow becomes judge, jury, and executioner—and perhaps it's he, the beast, who prevents more people from dying. Or maybe, maybe the beast is all the people of the community who come together through their hatred of sexual offenders, who protest outside the courtroom or who take the law in their own hands on the basis of convictions—perhaps it's precisely those people who have become the beast during the course of the story. In the end, it is for the reader to decide.

Pen 33 eventually had a fantastic ride—it was awarded the Glass Key for the best Nordic crime novel, translated into thirty languages, published in seventy-five countries, filmed, read for excitement and entertainment, and occasionally served as the basis for debate and discussion. And beginning with this book, we decided to donate 10 percent of the profits to organizations working on issues related to the plot of each book, making it a debut in more ways than one. For *Pen 33* we donated to Save the Children, an outstanding organization that combats child pornography in Sweden and internationally.

Börge lost a battle with cancer in 2017, but I know he would be as pleased as I am that the journey we began all those years ago has led to this moment, with the book available at long last to American readers.

Anders Roslund
October 9, 2017
Stockholm, Sweden

Award-winning journalist ANDERS ROSLUND and ex-con BÖRGE HELLSTRÖM are Sweden's most acclaimed crime-fiction duo. Their unique ability to combine inside knowledge of the brutal reality of criminal life with searing social criticism in complex, intelligent plots has put them at the forefront of modern Scandinavian crime writing. *Three Seconds* was awarded the Crime Writers' Association International Dagger Award and the Best Swedish Crime Novel Award, previously won by both Stieg Larsson and Henning Mankell, and it was a *New York Times* bestseller.

ELIZABETH CLARK WESSEL translates Swedish fiction and writes and edits poetry. She is an editor at Argos Books and *Circumference: Poetry in Translation*.

about the type

Typeset in Minion Pro Regular.

Minion Pro was designed for Adobe Systems by
Robert Slimbach in 1990. Inspired by typefaces of the
Renaissance, it is both easily readable and extremely
functional without compromising its inherent beauty.

Typeset by Scribe Inc., Philadelphia, Pennsylvania.